ON THE OTHER SIDE

By

Roland Twynam

ISBN 979 8 647425737

Cover design by Pro-eBook
Photograph of American flag by Ryan Gerrard (Unsplash)
Photo of Irish scene by author

Historical Notes

Today, Cobh is the port to Cork, in southern Ireland, and a port and tourist centre. Originally it was called Cove (its English name).

In 1849, after a visit by Queen Victoria, its name changed to Queenstown. It became Cobh in 1920 (still pronounced Cove). During the late 19th century this was the emigration port for the many Irish people who made their way to America.

Castle Garden, the Battery, in lower Manhattan

Before Ellis Island opened in 1892, Castle Garden was the immigration centre for new arrivals to America. It is situated at the tip of Manhattan and it opened in 1855 and closed in 1890.

It was built as a military fort and served many purposes over its life, mainly for entertainment. Today it is called Castle Clinton.

When it closed, a temporary immigration centre was opened at the US Barge Office, on the eastern edge of the Battery waterfront to accommodate the new arrivals until Ellis Island opened.

Molly Maguires

The Molly Maguires were a secret organisation of Irish coal miners who, in the latter half of the 19th century, set out to fight the oppression they saw in the anthracite coal region of Pennsylvania.

Routine discrimination based on both religion and heritage often saw signs displayed that read, 'Irish need not apply'.

Prologue
Lackawanna County, 1889

Brendon O'Neil pulled his camouflage covering over his head and settled his back as tightly as possible against the tree trunk to stop the rain running down his neck. A face, a human outline even in the dark, stood out. Under his leafy cover, Colonel Jeremiah Caswell's stewards, as they liked to be called, would never find him.

Through a slit in the front, O'Neil looked out onto a wet, miserable night, an August night that after torrid heat had given way to the inevitable storm that had raged for eighteen hours. He could barely make out the trees opposite against the sky, while any sounds were lost amidst the drip, drip, from the foliage.

O'Neil knew that the stewards would shoot on sight. This was the colonel's land, and anyone caught on it was deemed a poacher, even if the bag was only one rabbit. All this was fair game for the several men who worked and carried out their master's wishes and if this included death then so be it, after all the stewards had families to keep, and an extra dollar kept the wolf from the door. Furthermore, no-one would complain because any complaint went to the local magistrate, and who was the local magistrate? Why, the colonel himself. And who sponsored the private police force…?

O'Neil had time to think and reflect and, as he did so, his anger soared, but he reminded himself repeatedly that anger could be his undoing; he had to remain calm and carry out his mission with care and precision. He laughed quietly to himself and looked at the sky. There was just a glimmer of smoky-white breaking through, the moon would soon find a chance to escape, and when it did it would be time to move.

For many people – said to be up to no good – a moonlit

night would not find favour but for Brendan O'Neil the strong shadows gave cover. The secret was, not to break the shape of the light, and in this way, he could get close to the hill, the one where the rabbits came out to play, and the one where the stewards could be waiting. Most certainly the two snares he had set earlier in the day were partly visible, but the bad weather and the flooding in the village might just keep them away. His big worry was that a man called Watts was back after a week away at Scranton. He was the head steward and it was said he delighted in despatching poachers as easily as the rabbits.

The moon broke through flooding the tree-lined avenue with light, and with it came angled shadows that bore down on O'Neil. Quickly, he realised he was in a shaft of light – he sat still – if his bush form didn't move, he would be part of the backdrop. He waited until the moon hid for a second, then, with the landscape printed in his mind, he moved across the opening and crouched amidst an outcrop of bushes that brought him closer to rabbit hill.

He didn't have long to wait, the moon painted its own picture, silvery-blue barring the avenue in an abstract pattern of light and dark. It was then O'Neil saw the fox, it loped towards him, stopped, sniffed the air only a yard away, before moving away to his right. O'Neil swore inwardly, no rabbit would venture out with a fox around.

Again, O'Neil scanned the sky, it was clearing, the almost full moon would be with him for at least half an hour, possibly more, time enough to bag dinner and possibly a rabbit to barter. O'Neil moved carefully, keeping as low as possible until he was looking at the mound on the edge of the wood. It was here that the sandy soil erupted into a crisscross of paths and burrows. He could see the numerous rabbit droppings but, more importantly, his two snares were still in place. This was the dangerous moment; he waited, straining his ears to catch any sound.

On the far side a rabbit head popped out, then back in, and this was repeated from several of the burrows. Suddenly, to O'Neil's delight, a large rabbit skipped out, straight into his snare. Almost immediately a medium-sized rabbit met the same fate. O'Neil never liked to see animals suffer, he wanted to move in quickly but hesitated; were the stewards hiding behind the mound or behind the trees? If caught he could be shot on sight. Of course, the stewards would claim it was an accident, or he was deer hunting, though he had never seen a deer on this side of the valley. Now it was a case of waiting, however long, to outsmart the stewards and bag his catch.

It was at this moment that the fox decided to make his move, his slinky run sending the rabbits scattering down their holes, leaving only the two snared rabbits writhing on the sandy slope. O'Neil cursed; would the fox make off with his dinner?

The crash and flash of a rifle froze O'Neil. He saw the fox try to turn: he gave a barking cry and fell over onto his side, then tried a second time to get up, struggled for a few seconds, coughed, lowered his head, then slowly his legs stiffened, and he lay still. From behind the mound came a shout of joy and a man whom O'Neil recognised but could not name, grabbed the fox by the tail and called behind him. 'He's a big brute… make a good stole… should fetch a good price.' A small man called Vadim, whom Brendan did know by sight, joined the shooter, and both noisily examined their kill. Then, to O'Neil's surprise, Watts appeared, passing him only a yard away. He had been further down the track and O'Neil realised how close he had come to detection. The fox had been his saviour; more than likely his own movement had been mistaken for that of the fox.

O'Neil decided it was time to go, he would have to await another day. Anna, his wife, would be disappointed as they hadn't eaten meat for weeks, but the risk wasn't worth taking. However, he had to wait until Watts and his stewards moved to the far side of the forest. O'Neil knew Watts by his reputation. He was a big bulky man, a known fighting man, someone to steer clear of. He was a second-generation American, who showed complete contempt for new migrants. He now unleashed his anger on his two stewards. 'You stupid bloody shithouses… haven't you a brain in your heads? I ought to wrap this fucking fox around your necks… d' you see these?' He gestured at the snared rabbits. 'Whoever was coming will be back in The Parade by now.' He released the rabbits, put them out of their misery with a hand chop and placed them in the sack he was carrying. 'You might as well piss off back home, now you've awakened the whole fucking country.' He pointed at the shooter. 'This will come out of your wages, you prat.' Vadim, the Russian, tried to argue with the few words of English he knew.

'Boss, it no my fault.' Pointing at his accomplice, he continued, 'He shoots I no shoot. He is… ' He shrugged, pointed a finger at the shooter's head, shrugged again and moved away as if to absolve himself of all blame.

It was here O'Neil saw an unexpected chance. Suddenly, a cloud moved across the moon bathing the far side of the mound in light, throwing the part nearest to him into deep shadow. Watts was now showing an interest in the fox, and to see it better he pulled it into the light several feet away, leaving the sack with the rabbits lying close to a thorn bush within three yards of O'Neil. Quickly he moved in knowing that the human eye needs several seconds to adjust from light to dark; the bush was a good cover. He reached for the sack, found it, twisted its loose mouth around his wrist and cautiously began to make his way back to the footbridge known as Kroos.

He had almost reached the footbridge when he heard Watts' angry voice echoing through the trees. O'Neil climbed down and hid his camouflage under the bridge. Now, his only problem was how to get back to his cabin without being seen. Watts would turn the village upside down at the thought of being outwitted.

The bridge was made up of wooden sleepers that spanned the brook that took the same name, Kroos. At each end, rock spoil from the nearby anthracite mine supported the main limbs while the surface was a tacky mixture of coal dust and clay. The bank, on the forest side, was higher than the other and here bushes had grown around the opening. It was under this crude bridge that O'Neil, on an earlier reconnaissance, had found his hiding place. Where the timbers met the bank, he had formed a hollow and into this, he kept his leafy covering. It could also conceal a man if that man could stand the stench of the brook that ran through the local mining village called The Parade. Into this brook was deposited every effluent made by man. For O'Neil the smell meant safety, few would think of stepping into its foul infested water. Now, however, the heavy rain had washed it clean, but few would still venture down its insecure banks.

O'Neil sat back. He estimated it was close to two o'clock; he would have to wait for dawn. He was soaked through, but it was a warm damp – bearable. He could hear the angry shouts of the stewards and he knew they would be covering every exit from the forest, but because Kroos Bridge was such an obvious approach, it tended to get less attention.

The sound of a shot roused O'Neil from his slumber, he could only guess the time, he listened but the sound came from some distance away; he relaxed and waited until the first light crept in under the bridge. The stewards, as dawn broke, would hopefully give up and return to their better homes on a plot behind the general store, leaving the guardians, the colonel's private police force, to carry on the task of searching for anyone coming out of the forest carrying any type of bag, or acting suspiciously. This group of men, five in number, patrolled the mine area and the village both day and night. At one time the idea had had some appeal for the villagers, to be safe in a lawless area was to be welcomed, but quickly the families renamed the group "The Snoopers" and came to regard them as the enemy. The two who did the night shift were Americans born and bred, though their names told a different story. Rees Ackerman denied his German ancestry while his partner, Matt

McGovern, was ever ready to claim his Scottish roots. The three who did the day shift were a collection of misfits from Denmark, Austria, and Italy. Most hated of the three was Erik Pedersen from Denmark, head of police, who seemed to delight in his position of power, which he used freely but rarely wisely. Stefan Bauer and Mario Ricci were more sympathetic and understood the poverty and corruption they found. Both would often look the other way, especially if a pheasant, woodcock, or a rabbit found its way to their homes at the better end of The Parade.

The Parade was a collection of cabins built with timber from the forest, packed with clay to keep out rain and wind. They belonged to the colonel and were purpose-built for the mining families who dug out anthracite for shipment to the great cities. Families had used this basic structure to invent their own means of comfort, and O'Neil, remembering the home of his grandparents in Ireland, had covered their roof with a layer of soil and finished it off with turf. This kept the temperature down in summer; he had yet to experience winter.

O'Neil's cabin was last in a line of log cabins and stood on the only corner leading to the track that led to Kroos Bridge. The road, such as it was, was a combination of crushed anthracite and anything to hand that would even out the surface for transport.

He lay back and decided to wait until it was fully light. His mind travelled back to his home in Donegal, Ireland, how he had battled to make a living on the family farm until, by chance, he had found a new trade, that of stonemason. This had found him work in England.

His thoughts turned to Anna, his new wife. He laughed to himself, only twenty and as spirited as a young colt. It had been an impulsive decision to bring her with him to America, to marry her in Dublin; but he had no regrets. He had expected that they would face difficulties in America, but to be robbed on their first day in New York, and then having to flee because he had killed, or at least aided in killing a man who had attacked him with a knife, was hard to believe. Now, he was a coal miner, hiding in the Lackawanna Valley, on the run from Pinkerton agents; what more could go wrong?

He pushed such thoughts away and cautiously looked out. He judged it to be about 4 am and watched as the full flush of dawn picked out the trees across the track. He could almost see his cabin as he crossed into a copse of trees; again, he waited, checking for any sign of movement.

On this side of the track, it was beyond the jurisdiction of the stewards. Even the colonel recognised the boundary of his empire, though his police often failed to observe the rules. For this reason, O'Neil made a detour of over a mile through decimated woodland to the west, and as he did so the sky cleared, that heralded a beautiful August day. Everything looked so fresh after months of heat, and O'Neil paused to enjoy its freshness; he'd forgotten how much he missed the rain of home. Again, he checked himself, carelessness could still see his detention. Getting the rabbits home without arousing suspicion was still the problem. For O'Neil, the advantage lay in his end cabin and the hill behind, only two hundred yards from his backyard.

He came up behind the dead tree on the knoll above his cabin and lay down. From a hole he pulled out the crow's nest that he and Anna had constructed and placed it in the branches; he waited for Anna to come out. At last the door opened, and Anna moved into the yard, looked quickly in his direction, saw the nest, gave Brendan a quick wave, and moved back inside.

Brendan O'Neil lifted his sack inside the door, smiled with triumph, took Anna in his arms and showed her the rabbits, both with plenty of meat on them; today they would eat well. Anna drew back.

'Yer soaking, go and change, I heard the shot... thank God yer okay, I don't want yer ter die of pneumonia.' The tears came. 'Brendan O'Neil, d'yer realise what yer've put me through, we've gorra get out of here.'

CHAPTER 1

Brendan O'Neil was working in Derbyshire, England, in 1889, when the letter from his sister Mary arrived, telling him that Ma had died. He had a contract for two years as a stonemason but, with only two weeks to run, his employer George Moffat, a generous and kindly man, paid him his dues and gave him a testimonial; he immediately returned home.

Since the death of his father in 1886, aged fifty, Brendan felt guilty because he knew he was the only one who could keep the farm going but, he knew it was impossible to make a living. The soil was too hard to work while jobs outside the farm were few, with many unemployed moving to the towns in search of work. Recovery from the potato famine of '45 was still fresh in many minds and many farms had been abandoned. All the talk in the local bar centred on escaping to America, the land of plenty, the land of opportunity; it was impossible to fail.

The problem was that the stony land made any crop difficult to grow. In dry weather, the grass was sparse for grazing, and their two cows and one horse suffered. This meant renting a field in bad times from their neighbour, Oliver Murphy, who enjoyed green fields because of a watercourse from higher land. Fortunately, no cost was involved because Oliver made good use of the horse as well as helping himself to a good share of the milk.

At nineteen, with his da unable to work, Brendan set about the task of clearing one part of his field of stones, only to find a shelf of stone that ran diagonally across two of his fields that ended in a drop to lower ground at a place called Cromwell's Tongue, so named because of its rather rude outlying shape. Brendan's plan to bring in seaweed from the nearby cove at Killenbeg to fertilise a plot big enough to grow vegetables was abandoned. His intention to support Ma and Da, by selling at local markets, dwindled to nothing. This was, he thought, his last chance to make any sort of a living.

As his da's illness worsened he knew his only course was to find work away from Mollybeg, possibly England, where many local young men had ventured. All this was forgotten when an English landowner called George Moffat, who had married an Irish lady of substance, built a house in the style of a castle called Moynedale on a ridge a mile from Brendan's farmhouse. Stone was required, and the bank of soft workable stone that angled across Brendan's two fields came to the attention of Albert Merryweather.

Merryweather was an English stonemason from Lichfield, who quickly realised that there was a source of stone sitting on their doorstep; the initial cost of importing stone could be cut by two thirds. George Moffat was so pleased with this news that Brendan found himself not only being paid for the stone but also employed in its transportation; this involved strengthening an old cart track over the field to Moynedale. Ma and Da watched in horror as their field became a quarry but its income paid the bills, at least for a time.

Albert Merryweather took a liking to Brendan and under his wing Brendan began learning a new trade as a stonemason. He listened fascinated as Albert told him about his work on Lichfield Cathedral in England. In turn, Albert was delighted to have a young man so keen to learn, and the two passed many an hour as Albert drew diagrams and explained building techniques.

Brendan was bereft when his da died, more so when he had to leave his ma behind after an invitation to join another Moffat project. He was barely twenty-one when he moved to England to help build a mill in Derbyshire, and it was here almost two years later that the letter found him.

Brendan had regularly sent money home to his ma. Now,

with his employment at an end, he knew that the run-down farm could no longer sustain a living. The thought came that his new skills could find employment elsewhere, and, with money saved his thoughts turned to the so-called New World, America.

At twenty-three, Brendan was a strong young man. He stood six feet tall, his shoulders broad through hard work, and unlike many of the young men in his village he did not wear a moustache, while his rugged features, tanned through wind, rain, and sun, along with his long unruly brown hair gave him a dashing appearance that had not gone unnoticed by some of the local girls. The one girl whom he had been keen on had moved to Liverpool in England and quickly found herself a rich English boy.

He arrived home too late for the wake arranged by his sister Mary, who had travelled from Donegal town with her baby of six months. Her husband, a lawyer called Sean, could not attend. Brendan's two brothers Fergal and Ryan were still making their way from Galway where they worked on a fishing boat; they arrived just in time for the interment in the cemetery. Mary was the eldest at twenty-eight, Ryan twenty-six, Fergal twenty-five, leaving Brendan the youngest at twenty-three.

It was while Brendan was talking to Father Devlin, his ma in her last resting place, that he looked up to see a young woman, whom he barely recognised. She caught his eye and fluttered her hand in recognition. To his surprise, he suddenly realised it was his next-door neighbour Anna Ferguson. She had been a gawky girl of seventeen when he had last seen her. She had a ready laugh and a cheeky way about her that he had never felt comfortable with. Now, he saw a different young woman. She had filled out, her hair was shoulder-length, cascading from her bonnet either side of her face. O'Neil noted that her smile was still there, and though few would call her beautiful she was attractive in her own way. Possibly it was her hair, her good complexion, and her fine white teeth. He fluttered his hand back in recognition and gave her a smile.

After family and friends had paid their last tributes to Ma, villagers drifted away leaving close neighbours to gather in groups. Everyone wanted to know what the O'Neil boys had been up to, and what they had in mind for the future. Fergal and Ryan had no wish to stay overnight in the cold cottage and needed to get back to Galway to catch their next sailing, or they would lose pay.

It was Father Devlin who cornered Brendan and asked him if he was staying on to run the farm, to which Brendan gave a non-committal answer. To tell Devlin he was off to America would give him the scent of money, and Brendan needed every penny.

As Father Devlin moved away Brendan joined Brian Ferguson, while Anna, his daughter, was busily talking to Mary and making a fuss of baby Andrew. When the same question came up, he told him quietly, 'Between me and you, Mr Ferguson, I'm off ter the other side but keep it under yer hat or I'll have half the village here.'

Brendan liked Brian Ferguson, but he had never liked his wife, Sarah. She was an austere woman, who wore a haughty look as if life had failed to give her all the privileges she deserved. He knew she had moved out of the family home to live with her sister. Brendan said goodbye to Brian and moved to his brothers and wished them every success, and quietly told them he intended to try his luck in America.

Back in the cottage, with little Andrew safely asleep, Mary and Brendan shared their thoughts. Mary was happy with her life six miles away in Donegal town. Her concern was for Brendan.

'Bren, get out of here, there's nothin' worth selling or saving… just leave the lot and it'll soon disappear, and the land's worth bugger all, but you might earn a shilling selling the quarry you've begun.' At this, she laughed and pointed to the large trench on the far side of the field. Brendan shrugged, the digging he had begun had turned into the local quarry for anyone who wanted a road repaired or a ditch filled; that is until it filled with water.

'I've no intention of staying on here… by the time I establish me right of ownership and pay the legal fees, I'll be out of pocket.' He added, 'I might buy a ticket and join the others.' She knew what he meant.

'Well, there's no future here, that's fer sure, and if yer go yer'll find yerself a nice Irish girl on the other side, I'm told there's more out there than here.'

Brendan laughed – it was his very thought.

'Or, of course, next door yer've that sweet Ferguson girl. Ma loved her… d'yer know after yer left fer England, she came most days ter read ter her, and she cooked and cleaned.'

Brendan was taken back. 'Ah, she's just a kid. But when I see her, I'll give her me thanks.'

The next morning, he waved goodbye to Mary and baby Andrew. Bradley's trap came to take them home.

For a time, Brendan stood surveying his three fields and thought back over his years, and the stories his da had told him. They were lucky to own their own cottage. For miles around cottages stood derelict, many burnt out by the authorities during the early eighties. All were tenant farmers, their land and cottages owned by rich Englishmen who had ignored the bad harvests and put rents up. Some of his da's neighbours had ended up in the poorhouse. The tenants' riots of '81 had led the English parliament to sit up and take notice, and the Land League Reforms had helped but, for many, it was too late. For the O'Neils good fortune came when Mr Harold Milner, the owner of both land and cottages, decided to cut his losses and return to England. He wasn't making a penny, the land was too poor, and he gave out hastily made transfers of land to four local tenant farmers.

Now, as Brendan looked towards Moynedale, he could see two of the cottages stripped of stone, overgrown and little to show they had ever been lived in. Putting these thoughts aside, his mind made up, he moved to his bed and from under it, he took out an old battered map of America given to him by an uncle who had emigrated but returned after many misadventures.

CHAPTER 2

At fifteen, Anna Ferguson, like many of her friends, became boy conscious, and she listened to the tales whispered when adults weren't about and wondered what the big mystery would be like – when it happened! Her mother, aware of her age and developing figure, counselled her on the danger of boys and warned her what boys expected to get without giving much in return. Daily, Anna was told about fifteen-year-old Sadie Slevin who had had to go away... because she had sinned! In fact, everyone knew that Sadie had been sent to a convent with a special unit for "Lost Girls" where she had had her baby. 'Sin, sin, sin.' The word rarely left the lips of Anna's mother.

However, Anna was familiar with birth, she'd seen foals and calves born, so it was easy to interpret the human act, but the difference was, while everyone was delighted for their animals to give birth the same was not true for daughters; unless of course a ring was in place. All this Anna took in, and decided that contrary to the teachings of the local church, and observing that nearly every girl of her age was exploring some of the great mysteries in life – with boys – given the chance she would... might... give it a go, later on, if and when she found the right young man.

As regards her ma, Anna spent more and more time with her grandma after an incident she could never forgive or forget. It happened one Sunday morning. They were passing Albert Morrow's field on their way to church, when the stallion, in an amorous mood, climbed on the back of the white mare. Anna's ma pulled her roughly to one side and told her to ignore the spectacle.

Anna cried. 'D'yer see that, Ma... they're sinning again.'

Da killed himself laughing but Ma was not amused and

not for the first time she beat Anna round the shoulders and head with her handbag, causing a cut above Anna's right ear. From this moment Anna played the dutiful role of daughter, doing the jobs she had always done, but keeping a cold distance between herself and her ma, who told anyone who would listen, what an ungrateful brat she was.

Da, for his part, quietly confided to Anna that Ma wasn't the woman she once was, leaving Anna wondering as to when she had ever known her to be any different.

As for Anna's brother, Richard, four years her senior, she had never really known him, but she could guess as to why he had left home at seventeen to live and work on a farm nine miles away. He rarely visited but when he did, he spent most of his time with Da.

Near to sixteen, Anna was aware that her lovely dad was increasingly finding a reason to keep out of his wife Sarah's way, her tongue finding plenty to remind him of how he had failed in life, at how she should have known better and done better. All came to a head one day when Anna heard her da erupt in a fury she had never heard before. She sat on the wall awaiting a good moment to sidle into the kitchen. The door opened and her name was called. 'Anna, go get Bradley's trap... yer ma's leaving.' Da was red with rage.

Anna delivered the message and waited while Willy Bradley finished his tea. He then gave her a lift back home, and Anna waited to see what would happen. Her ma, carrying a case, and grim-faced, climbed into the trap as she jumped out. 'I'm sure the two of you will do very well without me – I know where I'm not wanted.' Anna said nothing.

'Mr Bradley, can you take me to Cushlie? My sister lives there.'

'You'll have to pay me an extra shilling... my old horse canna do twelve miles there and back... I'll have to stay over.'

'I'll pay yer now in full.' Da stepped forward and handed over the money.

Anna, not sure how to react, stood watching as her ma, sitting bolt upright, without a glance back, disappeared around the bend. Da's hand squeezed her shoulder. 'Don't fret... some things have ter be.' It was only later that Anna found out that her da was "*sinning*" with Widow Oakley.

Without Ma, Anna and her da settled down, trying to scrape together a living, doing any odd job that would bring in a shilling but often it was a case of living on a few vegetables and potatoes, though with the sea close by fishermen came weekly to the village and fish became almost the daily diet.

With time on their hands, Da reminded Anna how important education was, and to forget that she was a girl, all the time telling her that reading was the gateway to all knowledge; Anna needed no prompting. From the age of ten, she had taught herself to read and write, and there wasn't a book in her da's small library that she hadn't waded through. Above all, she loved to read about strange lands, far away, over the seas.

Anna was proud of her da because he was one of few men in the area who could read, and this had come about because his own father had worked in Dublin where it was considered compulsory, that is, if you wanted to get on in life; this he had passed on to his son Brian.

Anna was a quick learner and began to borrow books from Mrs Quinn, an educated lady who lived in the village. She was only too pleased to help, and one of her textbooks introduced Anna to basic arithmetic and how to solve sums.

Several attempts had been made to introduce a school in the area, but the problem was, the villages were scattered over a large area. Thus, where to build a school, to bring in all the children, remained a topic for discussion but, it saw little action. For the same reason, primary education had been limited to two days a week at the local church, with a teacher travelling the parish with the occasional assistance of two nuns. This didn't last very long because the few teachers available found the travelling daunting, especially in winter.

It was at this point Father Devlin decided he would become an educator, but it quickly became clear that there was only one important subject – religion!

With her ma gone Anna grew closer and closer to her Grandma Harriet – on her da's side. And Anna was fascinated to hear all about her life, hearing tales about when she worked in Scotland and later when she moved to England and worked in a great house in Cheshire.

On her eighteenth birthday, Anna walked the mile to her village. It didn't even have a name sign, but most knew it as Mollybeg, a line of whitewashed houses that could be passed in two hundred yards. In the middle house, Grandma Harriet was waiting. They hugged, and Grandma sat her down in her small front room that overlooked the street.

'Eighteen? My God, how the years fly, and just look at yer, a fine young woman, an' one ter capture a boy's heart. Have yer a boy? Yer can tell me?'

Anna shrugged. 'Gran, it's not a boy I want… Christ, the boys of me age are so infantile… what I need is a young man of twenty or more, but where are they?' She answered her own question. 'All buggered off ter Dublin, England or America and who's ter blame them; there's nothing here.'

Gran smiled. 'I've got yer a present, but it's ter be a secret between us, no telling yer pa. If he says I'm a mean old cow, so be it.' Grandma Harriet opened a small leather bag she held in her hand and tipped out a ring. 'I'm giving yer this but yer to keep it… and yer only ter sell it when yer absolutely down on yer luck an' I mean when yer truly desperate. Yer tell no-one, not even the man yer fall in love with. Yer'll know how much he loves yer when yer down to yer last farthing – now promise me.'

Anna promised, took the ring and held it to the light. 'Gran, is it diamonds? I've never seen a diamond in me life.'

'I'm told they're wonderful stones, and worth a king's ransom but who knows? All I do know is I want yer to have it, an' mind again what I tell yer, hide it away somewhere an' say nothin'.'

Anna got up, hugged her, and intrigued asked, 'D'yer mind me asking, Gran, how did yer…' She didn't finish.

'Where did I get the ring?' Gran chuckled. 'Well, I didn't steal it fer sure… it's a long story. I worked in a great house near Chester. I was about twenty-five at the time and I worked as a nanny. I had two children of me own then, yer da was me second. Yer granddad, Robert, who yer might remember, worked as a coachman, and we had a lovely cottage in the grounds. Mrs Gillespie, a wonderful lady, had four children, and all the children played together, there was no side ter her. Her husband Arthur was often away, he worked in the diplomatic service. One night there was a great fire, and I rescued the children. When they left ter go ter India she gave me this ring, and a letter ter prove I was the rightful owner – I think they call it provenance.' The old lady paused and smiled. 'Anna, yer'll have this problem because I have no idea where the letter is,' she laughed, 'if yer wear it on yer finger you'll lose both… so, keep it hidden. Now, I've another present fer yer, one that has no value, but it could be the most important thing in yer life… d'yer know what this is?' She unfolded an old silk scarf to reveal some very soft, almost white sponges. 'At eighteen I was given these by me ma… they come from the South Seas… I'm told the natives dive for them.'

Anna took one and marvelled at how soft it was, for once she was completely lost. 'Are they fer cleaning the ring, Gran?'

The old lady lay back in her chair laughing and wiped her eyes. 'I don't suppose that ma of yours has put yer in way of the facts. Very soon yer goin' ter meet a young man an' he'll want what every man wants… an', if yer get your passion up yer'll want the same, no matter if yer married or no. Do I have ter spell it our fer yer? An' he might promise yer that he has a fish tube or a bladder ter stop yer havin' a baby… even worse he might tell yer he's read the calendar. DON'T believe any man.' She pointed at the sponges and said, 'Soak them in white vinegar an' put them in… yer know where…

he'll never know an' yer won't have the worry... it worked fer me.' She added, 'Never trust a man till yer know he truly loves yer.'

Anna had heard talk about such things. She knew that the fishermen used fish innards as a sheath, while there was talk that in America the rich used a rubber cover.

Grandma Harriet paused to let her words sink in. 'If yer look around yer, how many children d'yer see? Mrs Couglan has thirteen, Elsie Cassidy has ten with another on the way. And how many did I have? Four but I lost two... I've only got yer da now... Frank? He went ter Canada years back, but I never hear from him.' The old lady paused; sadness clouded her face. More quietly she said, 'Anna, d'yer want ter spend half yer life flat on yer back? I don't want ter see yer bellied by some local useless bugger. My advice is, get out as soon as yer can, make somethin' of yerself. I hear yer a fine reader... go ter Dublin, find a good man an' be happy.'

Anna took the two presents home and hid them away; both could await the future. In the meantime, education was, as Da said, the most important thing in life – if you wanted to leave Mollybeg.

Anna was near to her nineteenth birthday when her thoughts returned to the great mystery her friends still whispered about. A young man from Donegal town arrived in the village. He delivered supplies twice a week to the local store and he stayed overnight. And it was while Anna was giving his horse a rub between his ears that he came out of Bells and introduced himself as Michael O'Dowd. For Anna, he was exciting, twenty-two and from the town, and he had so much to tell her. He asked if, when he came again, could they meet up somewhere.

Anna, aware of the gossips and word getting to her da, suggested that in the evening he crossed the field behind the pub – unseen – where there was an old isolated cottage left by the O'Brian brothers. Naively she wanted to know about the bigger world beyond Mollybeg.

However, the more experienced Michael, who had a few

girlfriends scattered around the villages saw the invitation as less about talking as having his way with Anna. He did talk, but his kisses soon reminded Anna what her grandma had told her about passion, and now she took to it nervously; except she remembered what to do with her South Sea sponges.

The romance went well until winter set in. The chill of the cottage cooled the ardour of both, and this led to more talking than lovemaking. This was when Michael announced it was all over, but he might see Anna the following summer. Anna was shocked and hurt. *I'm like a candle in the church being snuffed out,* she told herself. However, rumours soon reached her about Michael's shenanigans in Killenbeg. A sixteen-year-old was in the family way. Anna put it down as a life experience, a preparation for what lay ahead, and she told herself, *at least I haven't been bellied.*

CHAPTER 3

It was three days after the funeral, just after midday when the knock came. Brendan opened it to find Anna Ferguson smiling at him. Before he could say a word, she launched into a spate of words that both surprised and amused him.

'Brendan, I'm told yer leavin' – off ter America. I haven't a penny ter offer but I'd like ter come with yer, and I'll do anything ter help, anything yer want. Yer'll need someone ter look after yer.' She hesitated, then added, 'And I'm yer girl.'

Brendan was rarely lost for words but now all he could think of saying was, 'Anna Ferguson, I'll have enough problems lookin' out fer meself.'

'Well, if yer take me ter New York, and yer don't find me ter yer liking, sure yer can dump me.'

'Look, Anna, yer know I couldna do that.' However, O'Neil was intrigued by this feisty girl.

Anna pulled a face, thought for a second, then declared, 'Look, I know I haven't a face ter lure sailors on ter rocks… or ter lure farmers… such as yerself… but I've other parts of me which I know to be desirable.' At this, she raised her eyes in a knowing way. 'I can offer yer all the comforts a man needs when he sets his face ter the world.'

For a second O'Neil was shocked: it was obvious what the girl was offering.

'Anna Ferguson… an' what if yer get pregnant? I'm trying ter make a start in a new country and the last thing I need is a woman and bairn trippin' me up.'

Anna rolled her eyes. 'D'yer think I'm a turnip… I know how ter look after matters like that. Fer Christ's sake if yer look at the other girls around here they're all bellied by seventeen.' She paused, then added, 'With me yer won't need a fish bladder.'

O'Neil roared with laughter. 'An' what's a good Catholic girl like yerself telling me such things?'

Anna looked at him coolly, 'That's fer me to know and not ter tell – at least fer now. But, me granny had only four mouths ter feed and not the dozen yer often see, she passed on her little secret ter me when I was eighteen… and I'm now twenty, and I've no lines on me belly. And I might as well tell yer that the holy fathers might talk about sin, but I have no intention of spending half me life flat on me back but don't tell Father Devlin or yer'll finish him off. Take me with yer, and tonight I'll come over and cook yer a meal, and afterward feed yer desires, such that will make yer never want ter let me go.'

Brendan thought for a moment, then said, 'Ah… there's many a girl who's made such a promise, said ter be a trap fer the foolish fella.' Anna leaned against the door, mock dismay written on her face.

'And have yer no seen the girls in trouble around here… and where are the boyos? Headin' for Queenstown and New York in a cloud of dust.'

Brendan knew this to have some truth, you married the girl, not always of your dreams, but the one who was carrying your bairn; big brothers and the local priest made sure you did the right thing. However, for the first time in months Brendan felt that hot flush that reminded him he was a man, and now when he looked at this girl with her lovely smile, clear skin, a warm full mouth, good teeth and a wonderful mop of rich brown hair, suddenly, she became more attractive as the seconds passed. He remembered what Mary had told him, how Anna Ferguson had looked out for Ma, and now she wanted to look out for him. He found himself making a quick analysis of costs if he took her on.

'Am I ter stand on yer doorstep all day? Do we have somethin' ter discuss or no?'

O'Neil stood aside and made a gallant gesture; she quickly moved past him, pulled up a chair and sat down.

'An' do yer parents know yer thinkin' of leavin'?' Brendan

asked.

'Me da's moving in with Widow Oakley, and as yer know me ma has scarpered. Me brother Richard's taking over the farm, such as it is. He's now a wheelwright an' he needs premises ter start up, I think he could do well with the wheels that come off around here.' At this Anna laughed, shrugged and then asked, 'And where am I ter go?'

Brendan O'Neil had a reputation for being a sober young man who did not make rash decisions. He had worked in England from the age of twenty-one, and he had, as his English friends had told him, his head on the right way; he rarely acted on impulse. Now, however, he found a kaleidoscope of images spinning through his mind, not least at how well Anna filled her simple blouse, and how her careless posture showed more of her legs than the local priest would have approved.

For the first time, it was Anna Ferguson who looked shocked.

'We'll need ter be wed, as a couple we can save five per cent on the crossing. Dublin would be a fine place.' Brendan smiled brightly; he had made up his mind.

Anna Ferguson quickly crossed to Brendan, took his face in her hands and slowly kissed him. 'Brendan O'Neil, d'yer know that I've fancied yer since I was fourteen.'

Brendan slowly lifted from his chair, taking Anna with him, and as he did so he buried his face in her soft neck. 'And d'yer know, Anna Ferguson, that two days ago yer didn't exist? But from now on yer'll fill me thoughts.' Anna turned her head and Brendan kissed her.

CHAPTER 4

Anna left Brendan's farmhouse in a daze; she just couldn't believe what had happened. Bren was going to marry her and soon they would be off to Queenstown, the port to Cork, then off to America, everything she had hoped for, well, except for the marriage bit; she giggled to herself.

She crossed the field and turned her mind to the meal she would prepare; it had to be good. Suddenly, the thought of what she had offered hit her. *Oh God, what will he think of me... I offered him me body. What if he just takes me te'night and has no intention of taking me on? But Jesus, he kissed me lovely... I'm sure he likes me.*

Anna climbed over the last fallen stone wall to her cottage, thoughts cascading so fast through her mind that she couldn't hold on to one to give it any sort of reason. She sat down on the turf basket and leant back against the chimney wall, she had played a dangerous game, but it had paid off – or had it?

Anna Ferguson had found in life that people expected different things from her. Some saw her as a polite, caring young person, while others thought her to be flighty and too flippant, indeed, cheeky to her elders. All would describe her as a girl who didn't lack confidence. In fact, this was only partly true because Anna played to the gallery. If they wanted her to be funny she could please, and she had a ready wit that rarely lost in the exchange, and for this reason she was popular with some, while others, such as Father Devlin, cautioned at her headstrong ways. Under this chameleon skin she hid her insecurities and wished at times she could hide in the crowd, but something always seemed to draw her out.

Anna set about her fish pie, there were always fishermen

calling at the village from nearby Killenberg, and that very morning she had bartered potatoes for a nice cod. Her da had stored potatoes, carrots and parsnips from the previous summer, and these would make a fine meal for two; the secret was to cook it slowly. While this was in the oven, she made some soda bread on the griddle, and when cool placed it in a basket and added the jar of homemade gooseberry jam, given to her by Mrs Quinn. It was then Anna fidgeted with nerves; the waiting was terrible.

With Da living most of the time with Widow Oakley she had the place to herself. Again, her thoughts turned to the evening and what might happen. Time for a bath she told herself and fetched the tub from the yard. An hour later she combed her hair and felt pleased that it was now shoulder length. From her wardrobe, she chose her best and only Sunday dress; her shoes would have to do. She reached for her night shift. Again, her morning promise came back; she could hardly swallow. She tossed her head and took a deep breath, more worryingly she had intended to buy white vinegar, but Da only made the trip to Donegal town about three times a year; the store in Mollybeg had no need of it. She had explained how marvellous it was – for cleaning!

She asked herself if Brendan had something to stop her from getting bellied. This thought almost spoilt her anticipation of a lovely evening. If he did take her and she got pregnant then the chances were, he would just bugger off without her. She knew of at least two girls left in such a state. It was then the further thought came that she had never slept with a man, her dalliance with Michael O'Dowd had been a blanket on the floor. She shuddered at the memory; she wouldn't be able to claim maiden status with Brendan when the time came; what would he think – would he mind?

She stood looking out over the field, she could just see the roof of Brendan's place. Her thoughts turned to him, he had lived in England, and at twenty-three no doubt he was very familiar with events that took place in the bedroom.

After all, he was a handsome man, well, not exactly handsome, but attractive in his own way; and she had heard about English girls!

Putting these thoughts to one side, near to seven, she crossed the field to Brendon's farmhouse with her basket hooked onto one arm and her fish meal in a large soup urn. Hidden away at the bottom she had her night shift. The door was open. She entered, and again assuming her bright and cheerful manner, she called, 'Hello, Bren, I've yer dinner here.'

'It's about time, woman. I'm starving.'

Brendan was on his hands and knees surrounded by papers and maps; he didn't look up. Anna was pleased to enter the banter game; it was made for her. 'Now is that any way ter talk ter yer future wife?'

Brendan turned with a grim look about him. 'I mean ter start as I mean ter go on.'

'Well I've heard it said that the way ter a man's heart is through his stomach, so we'll see what me fish pie does.' Without further ado, she set about preparing dinner.

'It's ready, Bren.'

Brendan pushed his maps to one side and sat down at the table. He ate his fill without comment and downed the fresh buttermilk. It was when Anna gave him a large slice of soda bread with freshly made butter and gooseberry jam that Brendan, exclaimed, 'Jesus!' Anna watched as her soda bread and gooseberry jam disappeared. Finally, Brendan sat back, patted his stomach, smiled and said, 'Anna Ferguson, minute by minute, I believe that I may have made a very wise decision.'

Anna wondered if later he would hold the same opinion. For a second, she thought of finding some excuse to undo her veiled promise of feeding his male desires. However, any such thoughts were blown away when a very serious Brendan told her to clear the table; there were many things to discuss.

Anna listened carefully and for the first time realised just how much planning was needed for their journey to America. Brendan pointed out that once on the ship at Queenstown, the rest was the easy part. You sat back and waited until you reached New York. There, it would be a case of finding out as you went along, whereas how to get to Dublin and on to Queenstown was the big problem. Money was the main factor Brendan pointed out, and now his money had to be shared by two, it would be a case of keeping costs to a minimum.

For a second, panic swept over Anna. She thought of her promise to Grandma Harriet, wasn't this the desperate moment to declare the value of her ring? She felt she was trading on Brendan's generosity and was about to withdraw from their hastily made agreement when he said, 'Anna, yer might be sitting there feeling a little guilty that yer've not a penny ter throw in the hat, but I want yer to know that I am very happy to have yer beside me. Yer a strong girl with no fancy ways and I canna think of any other girl I would have with me. We'll be walking a hell of a lot. I've saved me money from me English work, and I've a tidy sum put by, but if we use transport ter get ter Dublin, then on ter Queenstown it will disappear very quickly. I wish ter save every penny fer the other side.'

Tears leapt to Anna's eyes, she brushed them away and tried to think of something to say. Now was not the time for any more of her blarney. Instead, she looked into Brendan's face; she could hardly see him through her tears. 'Brendan O'Neil, all I can tell yer is that I thank yer and I'll never let yer down.'

There was an uncomfortable silence. Brendan pretended to collect his papers, then he smiled and said, 'That's why yer coming with me.'

Anna sat with her head bowed until a finger lifted her chin. Brendan gently thumbed away the tears on her cheeks, and quietly he told her, 'I've made a list, an' I want yer ter see it. I call it me programme. I'm leaving Mary the farm; she can dispose of it as she wishes. If she can make a few pennies, then she'll share it with me two brothers. The quarry might still fetch a few shillings, but I have me doubts. Me brothers have moved on… fishing is now their life. I've given Oliver me old horse, and me two cows are going fer slaughter; that should pay fer the funeral.' Brendan took Anna's hands and smiled. 'Now fer the important bit… I hope yer can turn yer hand ter sewing because most of what we carry will go on me back. I've a turf cutter's frame here, and canvas, and I need yer ter make satchels ter fit the frame. We've miles ter walk an' I need the weight high on me shoulders and yer'll need ter make yerself a bag fer yer womanly things, I'm sure yer can do it.'

Anna nodded.

'Most of all,' he told her, 'yer'll need a good coat and stout footwear, but I canna fund yer. Perhaps yer da can help.' Again, Anna nodded as if it was of little concern. She sat impressed by Brendan's planning. She mused; *he's like a general before the battle.*

Up to this time Brendan had been forthright in airing his views, suddenly he seemed less comfortable, he paused for several seconds; Anna waited.

'Anna, it's the middle of April. We must leave here by the end of the month, it could take a fortnight ter get ter Dublin, and I need ter register me money with the bank and buy tickets fer the crossing. I'm told there's many waiting ter cross, and I have no idea how long we might have ter wait. We must be in New York by the end of May. We need ter settle in before winter, I'm told that the winters there can be very hard.' Brendan busily collected his maps and papers; he gave Anna a quick but nervous smile before adding, 'We'll be wed when we can, but I want yer, when we leave, ter wear this. I hope it fits.' He rose, reached in his pocket, took out a wedding ring and placed it on the table. 'It was me ma's, and as a married couple doors will open that will shut in our faces if 'tis known we're not wed. We'll surely have ter share a bed… erm, at some time… and… erm… what must be must be.' He shrugged and added, 'A shilling can find us a corner fer the night.' Brendan paused again. 'Anna, I'll not share a bed with yer tonight as it seems a little too early... erm, fer... yer can have me bed, no point crossing the field at this time of night, and it's a cold one. I'll put a warm stone in yer bed – if yer ready?'

Brendan showed Anna to her bedroom, his room; he would sleep in his late parents' bed. He placed the oil lamp on the small dresser and told her he would come to put it out when she was in bed.

Anna snuggled under the heavy sheet and felt the warmth of the hot stone, covered with a small blanket, creeping through. She felt pleased that she would not have to share a bed with Brendan, it had seemed a good idea in the morning but now, she chuckled to herself, the sins of the flesh, as Father Devlin called them, could await the right moment. She looked at the ring on her finger – a perfect fit – it would really be hers when they married in Dublin. Married! How many girls could say they were married in Dublin?

It was then the thought of their journey ahead, and the seriousness of their venture, filled her with both excitement and fear.

The door creaked open. Brendan picked up the lamp, came over to her and quietly said, 'Anna Ferguson, I think we're going ter be fine together, and I truly thank yer fer lookin' after me ma so well.' He lowered his face and gently kissed her on her eyes, forehead, nose, and lips.

Anna had never felt so happy.

CHAPTER 5

Brendan was pleased with Anna's work; the canvas satchels were well sewn and ready to take the items needed for their journey. He fastened the satchels to his turf cutter's frame and fastened Anna's smaller bag below. On his shoulders, he hoisted the frame high and fastened a strap around his middle that had once been part of the livery for a horse. He was satisfied. The weight was less across his broad shoulders and it also left his arms free, possibly to deal with any ruffian who got in their way.

Brendan hoped to find cheap accommodation at inns along their route; however, he painted the poorer picture so that Anna would be prepared for whatever situation they found themselves in. He showed her the blankets, with a waxed waterproof cover he had made, ready for a night under a hedge, or in a barn. He outlined time and time again to Anna his plans for the journey until, in the end, the dutiful Anna told him that the sooner they got going the better, it was impossible to plan for every eventuality, they had to improvise as the situation demanded. This pleased Brendan, it was clear to him that Anna Ferguson was the right woman for him, but he did not go to her room at night. The idea persisted that should she get pregnant, then all would be lost; he dared not risk anything at this stage.

At last, all was ready, and Brendan told Anna they would leave on the 30th of April. They had one more day to finalise every detail and he suggested it was goodbye time. This was the moment Anna dreaded, she knew it would be the last time she would see her da and grandma; Richard might, one day, be able to join them.

In the morning she left Brendan to his affairs and began the big clear out. From childhood, she still had dolls and more importantly books, and these she loaded into a wheelbarrow and trundled them down to the village, to the house of Mrs Quinn.

By now the rumour of her leaving had swept the village, but Anna was giving little away and told Mrs Quinn she was having a grand clear out in anticipation of leaving – soon!

Back home she wrote a letter for Richard, telling him that she was going to America with Brendan. Then she set about tidying the house and had a bonfire of items of little use.

Later, Anna returned to the village and knocked on Widow Oakley's door. She answered, smiled a welcome and stood back. Her da looked surprised because, while Anna had never commented on her ma walking out, he wasn't sure if she approved of the time he spent with Etta Oakley. For Anna, Etta was a kindly soul who would look after her da, and she liked to think that when she left, he had someone who would look after him.

He knew right away that something was in the wind; Widow Oakley moved to the parlour.

'Da, I'm leaving here te'morra. I'm off ter New York with Brendan O'Neil, and we're ter be married in Dublin.'

Brian Ferguson went to speak, swallowed hard, considered the news, and then held out his arms. Anna moved into them and he held her for seconds without speaking. Gently he pushed her away. 'It's a bit further than Dublin, but that's what we Irish do.' He tried to laugh but faltered. 'Brendan, er? Well, yer could do worse.'

Widow Oakley joined them and made tea. For half an hour the three tried to talk about everyday things but Anna was aching inside. Finally, she said it was time to move three doors down to see Grandma. She gave Da a hug and held Etta by both hands. 'Look after him.' Etta nodded in reply.

Anna pushed open the door that was always left ajar during the day, and shouted, 'Gran,' walked in, pulled up a chair, and took her hands.

'Yer off then?'

Anna was always surprised that Gran seemed to have an

instinct for such matters. 'I'm off ter America te'morra with Brendan O'Neil. We're ter be married.'

Grandma Harriet pursed her lips, and just said, 'Hmm!' She sat for a minute, then said, 'Help me up will yer.' Anna took the old lady's arm and guided her to her bedroom, to a large old wardrobe. Anna opened the door. Grandma leaned on her stick and reached in. 'Yer'll need a warm coat.' She handed a coat to Anna. 'Try this on, it was always ter big for me.' Anna took the coat; it was the most beautiful coat she had ever seen – green-grey, with a diagonal pattern of brown running vertically. It had a fur collar and a matching raised hem. Only a top button was missing. She tried it on, it was a perfect fit.

'Ah! It was meant fer yer.' The old lady explained that she had been given it by the daughter of a family she worked for in Scotland. 'It'll be difficult ter find a matching button. I don't know how or where I lost it,' she paused, 'and yer'll need boots.' She told Anna to look for a pair of high-laced boots. Anna pulled them on, she was thrilled; they had seen little wear and matched the quality of her coat. 'If yer boots are ter big no matter... if it's plenty of walking yer'll be doin' yer don't want yer toes pinching. Anna, me lovely girl, yer fit fer a prince. Now look up top and choose two bonnets, it'll make me a bit of space.' Anna chose a dark green and black to be kept for Sundays, and a smaller, tighter, brown and grey that pulled in around her jaw. In tears, she embraced Grandma Harriet, held her close for several seconds; both knew it would be their last.

'Now take me back ter me seat.'

Back in the parlour, Anna carefully folded her lovely coat and wrapped it in an old blanket. She decided to keep the boots on, to break them in. They were a little too big, but she could make insoles from the left-over canvas. She sat sipping another cup of tea she didn't want and looked at Grandma Harriet wondering what more she could say. The old lady pointed at the door. 'Anna, yer life's ahead of yer, now go and don't yer worry about me... I have yer da to look after me.' Anna went for a last embrace, but she was shooed away.

She returned home sad, yet at the same time elated, because now she wouldn't have to explain to Brendan why her coat and boots were so worn and unfit for so many miles. These went onto the bonfire in the backyard.

Anna held up her new coat. She knew it would be impossible to find a matching button. The three wooden buttons in place were a dark oak colour, square but rounded at the edges. In the wardrobe, she took out three old shawls. One immediately caught her eye, it had a single large square button with a carved motif of a harp, and it was similar in colour. She recalled that if you cannot match then go for a contrast. It was larger than the other buttons but, by easing the stitching around the buttonhole, the shawl button pressed through. Once stitched in place, it looked as if it was meant to be, a feature top button, possibly designed to add a scarf or a brooch. In the mirror, Anna was pleased with her work, and her new bonnet matched perfectly. It was then another idea came to mind; she looked at the hem. How safe was her precious ring if she wore it around her neck? Wouldn't it be better to hide it away from sight, even from Bren? She remembered her grandma's advice. Carefully, Anna unstitched the fur a few inches inside the right-hand side hem, pulled out the wadding, then placed the ring in a piece of linen and rolled it into a ball. Gently she pushed the ring inside the hem. Several stitches later Anna looked at her work; no-one would know it was there.

Anna had a last look around, the only home she had ever known, she locked the door, put the key under the water barrel, and climbed over the broken-down wall and crossed the field to Brendan's, her sadness tempered by excitement; he wasn't there. A note told her he would be back within the hour.

Anna placed her new coat, travel bonnet and boots by her bed and prepared their last meal in his cottage. She heard the foot scraper rattle; Brendan was back. He was carrying a large parcel. He opened it and said, 'Anna, I can guarantee some things but the weather I canna. I've been down ter see an old fisherman friend and he's given me these capes, they're soaked in linseed oil, they don't smell nice and they don't look nice, but they'll do the job.'

Anna tried one on without a word; it was the ugliest thing she had ever seen in her life and the smell! The thought came, *fine fer sea-goin', and it's ter big but, it'll keep me lovely new coat safe from the worst of the weather... Jesus, just look at the hat!*

Brendan, dismayed by Anna's lack of response, added, 'They'll come in handy if we have ter find a corner ter bed down.' Anna smiled, shrugged and made dinner. Little was said as they ate. Now that the moment to leave was near it weighed heavily.

Brendan packed his satchels and stored Anna's garments, those she wouldn't need until New York, except for her best Sunday dress – wedding dress – which he folded carefully and placed ready for Dublin.

The evening passed slowly, and as the last turf burnt down Brendan looked at his watch and said, 'I think it's time fer bed; we need ter leave at six in the morning, I only hope ter God the rain holds off.'

Anna tried to sleep but the excitement was too great.

Next door Brendan went over and over his planning until, as dawn broke, he gave up trying, got dressed and moved to the kitchen to rekindle the fire for breakfast. Anna, hearing the noise in the kitchen, washed and dressed. She put on her high-laced boots, pulled on her wonderful coat, then with her travel bonnet fastened under her chin, she looked in the mirror. She was pleased with the result. Brendan had his back to her when she entered the kitchen.

'I'm making some porridge, make the tea will yer?' he called over his shoulder. He turned and almost dropped the bowls.

'My God, Anna, yer look absolutely... er... beautiful... where on earth did yer get all this?' He waved his hands and then noted her high-laced boots ideal for the journey to come. 'Yer look truly regal and what do I look like? Surely a country...' He didn't finish. Instead, he lifted her chin and slowly kissed her. 'Anna Ferguson, yer make a good man's resolutions difficult ter keep.' Anna fluttered her eyelashes.

'And what may they be, Mr O'Neil?' Brendan laughed.

'Anna Ferguson – I mean O'Neil,' – he could see the ring in place, 'we'll wed in Dublin, but I must warn yer, we could end up in some doss house in Queenstown 'til we gerra crossing.'

They ate in silence, each full of their own thoughts.

Back in her bedroom Anna checked her personal bag and made sure her small bottle of white vinegar was well protected, along with her sponges.

CHAPTER 6

On the last dark morning of April, Brendan listened to the rain beating on the windows. Dressed like a fisherman he locked the door and put the key under a stone by the foot scraper. He turned to look at Anna, the rain was running off her hat like a broken drainpipe. He thought to say some words of encouragement but instead strode down the path, hitching his pack as high as he could on his shoulders. His intention to say, America here we come, suddenly seemed so unreal, and he wasn't sure he had the voice; indeed, he could hardly swallow.

Anna was pleased that no-one would see them. She looked down at her lovely boots, already filled with mud from the lanes. She followed a step behind Brendan, who had no idea how difficult it was for her to match his stride. However, she didn't want to complain; after five miles she felt her legs were on fire.

Thankfully, near to Donegal, they got a lift by a farmer in the back of his cart, who took them into town. They walked past the rows of silent white cottages, windows dark, yet the chimneys alive spiralling smoky twists into the rain misted air. Only the general store was lit, and as they passed, they could hear movement inside. Brendan assured Anna that no-one would know who was hidden under their fishermen's capes and hats.

At midday, the rain ceased, and a weak sun broke through. As the afternoon wore on Anna's legs were again burning with fatigue. She wanted to call for a halt, but pride wouldn't let her. Then, thankfully a timber waggon stopped, she climbed in the back, while Brendan sat with the driver, engaging him in his work, chatting about timber.

By the end of the day, Brendan estimated they had

covered twenty miles. They found a deserted cottage – of which there were many – to pass the night. Inside, Brendan lit a fire and Anna cooked the eggs, bought from a nearby farm, and fried soda bread in the only pan they carried.

Very tired, Brendan laid out the blankets that he had sewn into a large sack and told Anna to get in. He threw more timber on the fire that flared, throwing shadows around the small room. He then wriggled in beside her and pulled her onto his chest. 'Yer've done well, me darlin', it'll get easier once we're broken in.'

Anna was too tired to even speak, she gave him a squeeze, and felt the warmth of his body that gave her a feeling of comfort and security. Morning came too quickly for both.

The trip to Dundalk took four days: one day they came across a coach with a broken wheel and Brendan helped to fit the new one which so pleased the coachman that he allowed them to ride up top free of charge. Nearer the town and coast, they met more traffic and worked their passage or begged lifts from drivers, often a few shillings exchanging hands.

On one very wet night, Brendan delved into his savings, which he carried in a money belt around his middle. It was out of the question to sleep rough, they needed warmth, a good wash and a warm meal. Pleased to find his budget still in credit they looked for lodgings and found a small inn, where a kind lady showed them to a little bedroom over the kitchen.

Downstairs she made them a hot nourishing stew, and for an hour they sat in front of a blazing fire. Mrs Lyle, their host, then offered them hot water in their room at a small extra charge; Brendan accepted.

It had been a good day; Brendan lay back on the bed relaxed. Now their journey was underway his nervousness had gone. He had always found that physical effort helped him to relax, whenever he was worried about anything a good walk down to the coast, or a good dig seemed to work. For the first time since Mollybeg, they had a nice room, hot water, and for Brendan, a chance to look at his wife to be. She was a wonderful girl; not once had she complained, and her sunny nature seemed to captivate all they met. It was also their first chance to get out of their clothes that Anna had arranged around the room – after a good shake – and as she had said, 'Ter get the bugs out!'

Now he lay his eyes on Anna. Yes, she wore Ma's wedding ring on her finger, and she was Mrs O'Neil in the book downstairs, and soon it would be official, but was this the right moment? Anna's questioning eyes made him look away as she washed.

He felt the bed sheets move, and Anna in her night shift snuggled down and gave him one of her wondrous smiles.

Brendan noisily roused himself, went to the bowl, stripped and washed with the second jug of water. Finished, he put the bowl and jug outside the door and turned to find Anna's eyes on him; for once she didn't look fatigued. Her lovely face smiled at him and he could no longer ignore the desire he felt for her; he reached for the bed sheets.

'Anna, as we are ter be wed next week I don't think it will be a great sin if I take yer tonight, because the truth is, Anna Ferguson – I mean O'Neil – if I don't me breeches will go on fire and be of no further use. But don't yer worry because I have here a fish bladder ter prevent me seed from spilling out.' Anna laughed.

'Truly, Brendan O'Neil, yer the most romantic man I've ever met. What girl could refuse such ardour, but truth be known yer can spill yer seed for all yer worth because I have me secret in place.'

Brendan pulled the sheets away; Anna was naked. He didn't ask about her secret, he just looked at her lovely body, and as he reached for her, the manliness he had kept on a leash for so many weeks, found freedom at last and he entered the woman whom he now adored.

CHAPTER 7

Dublin turned out to be easier than O'Neil had thought. Seemingly every carriage and cart were heading that way, and the many hostelries along the route offered a bed and food that suited Brendan's pocket. The two, now very fit, strode on in good spirits with the nights spent in each other's arms. On one occasion they were offered free accommodation if the two of them would clean out the stables. This was music to Brendan's ears, while anything to do with horses delighted Anna. Most pleasing for Brendan was to keep their spending within the allowance he had set for their journey to Queenstown. This told Anna that it was very important to make sure "her secret" was in place. However, she was surprised that Brendan never questioned or asked about this, he seemed content not to know, only too pleased to find a warm bed where, as he said, 'He could please his woman.'

Anna's thoughts warmed at the thought: *he was the most gentle, romantic lover a girl could wish fer, he didn't just lie with her, he told her over and over how much he loved her, and how much he wanted ter marry her. However, there was one little worry: she sensed that Brendan wanted to ask her about her experiences with men before they met.*

Anna decided not to wait for the question to arrive. On the second day into their travel along the Dublin road, at a small inn, she looked at Brendan and said, 'Bren, yer always sayin' that I'm fillin' yer head with me foolishness, and yer may be right, but I want yer to know that the other night was the most wonderful time in me life. Ter make love with the man yer love and who loves yer back is truly, truly wonderful, but I know yer know that I lost me maidenhood before yer came along and judging by yer actions I think it wasn't yer first time.' Anna paused, and thought, *why's he*

39

smiling at me, but she pressed on. 'As yer know, Bren, I have about me a great curiosity, and I just want yer to know that it was just a biological adventure.'

Anna, in one of the few times that she felt lost in an exchange of words, watched as Brendan skimmed his bowler into the air, caught it, and laughed until he was almost sobbing. After a pause, he repeated, 'A biological adventure,' at which he collapsed laughing again.

Anna decided enough had been said and waited.

At length, Brendan picked up his pack, struggled into it, then lifted her bag onto her shoulders. He then gently kissed her eyes, nose, and mouth and said, 'Anna, yer truly an original, what would I do without yer? Let's say we've both had our biological adventures, and not mention them again.'

Anna, never one to end up at the wrong end of an argument, smiled brightly, rolled her eyes, and said, 'I've heard about yer English girls and I'm sure yer did well.'

Brendan tipped his bowler back, a mock-serious look on his face. 'Anna, why d'yer think I don't go ter confession? They'd be a queue a mile long and the priests would have a fit.' With this, he walked briskly back onto the Dublin road. Anna followed and tried to think of something to say but for once Brendan had had the last word.

It was their first visit to any large city, and they were astounded by Dublin. Both were captivated by the fine buildings, the wide avenues and the horse-drawn trams, and the sheer industry of the place.

Brendan explained that first, they had to find a church and a priest to marry them, and he wasn't sure exactly what the procedure would be as the law seemed to change from county to county, but he did know they would have to have their marriage registered to make it legal. Also, he had to open a bank account, pay in his savings and have a certificate of the transaction to allow him to draw on the other side in dollars. Anna was amazed that this could be done but Brendan explained it was the wonder of a telegraph service by an American company called Weston Union. He added that they had to find accommodation for at least three days, and his main worry was how much money was needed to cover their Dublin stay and get them to Queenstown, or nearby Cork, and of course, to buy their tickets.

It was late afternoon when Brendan and Anna walked along the banks of the river they had heard so much about. The Liffey was full of river traffic, the colours vibrant under the late sun. However, it was the smell, on a warm May evening, that appalled them, and they were about to take to a side street to escape this when Brendan noticed a group of men working on a stone jetty and, as ever, his interest in stone led him to walk over to observe the work. Part of the bank had collapsed, and repairs were underway to not only rebuild the jetty but also to construct a holding pier for barges. The dressed stones lay in a pile and four men were working within a stout wooden barrier; the support wall was almost up to street level.

'I've no work if that's what yer looking fer.' A man, Brendan thought to be in his forties, settled his wheelbarrow.

Brendan smiled and said, 'There's a pity, I could do with a few days' graft ter earn me a few shillings. We're off ter the other side very soon.'

The man, calling himself Flynn, and obviously the foreman, was intrigued. 'Ah, I have a brother out there – somewhere.' This led to Brendan explaining his interest in stone and telling Flynn that he had worked as a stonemason in England. Brendan shook hands and they were about to leave when Brendan thought to ask Flynn if he could recommend a cheap lodging. At this, Flynn thought for a second and told them to wait. He moved to speak to an elderly worker, and Brendan could see their faces turned to look at them.

Flynn came back. 'D'yer know I might be able to help yer after all.' He nodded at the stone and said, 'If I leave that lot lying about overnight it'll disappear.' He then pointed to a small barge moored below the nearby steps. 'Harold over there has been sleeping here every night ter keep an eye on things but he needs ter get home as his good lady isn't ter well. And as yer need somewhere ter lay yer heads I'm thinking that we might help each other. How about yer sleeping aboard and keeping an eye open? Mind yer, no pay, but yer'll have the days free ter do as yer wish. In three days, we'll be finished.'

Brendan looked at Anna, she was smiling and nodding her head for him to say yes. He held out his hand to shake on the deal. Flynn put up a warning finger. 'Mind yer, it needs yer start now as we're leaving. Yer must stay on the job till seven tomorrow. There's a small stove yer can use.'

On-board, the river smell was stifled by the new smell of tar and cooking. It was cramped, untidy, but it would do, the only problem was food, which was solved by Anna who had already noticed a small quayside food stall. Within minutes she was back with duck eggs, a roll of bread, cheese, carrots, and one onion; it was a strange meal, but there could not have been a happier couple.

Later, they sat on the deck in two chairs enjoying the beautiful late May evening, a sudden breeze allaying the smell from the river. The many barges and boats, the sounds, the changes in colour excited Anna. 'Bren, after Mollybeg...' She didn't finish and waved her arms in her excitement. Brendan took her hand.

'My God, Anna, this is some adventure. Who would have thought that we'd be sitting on a barge on the Liffey.'

Anna smiled and said, 'Ah, Brendan O' Neil, and here's me thinking yer had it all planned.'

CHAPTER 8

The night passed peacefully until the sound of men at work brought Brendan and Anna onto the deck. They got a friendly wave and a reminder to be back at six.

On the riverfront, they found a tea house and had a breakfast of potato cakes and eggs before exploring further. College Green was delightful and next to it stood the magnificent building of The Bank of Ireland.

Inside, a nervous Brendan explained his purpose and was taken to an office where he took off his money belt and counted out his pounds, shillings, and pence. The bank clerk was very helpful and explained how the transfer would be telegraphed to the Weston Union in New York. Brendan signed the transaction and another clerk added his signature as witness. He was then given the transaction certificate with a number and told that it was an important document and, if lost, so would be his money until such time he could prove his identity, and this could take weeks.

On Friday they climbed the hill to St Catherine's and asked to see the priest. At the grand house, a lady told them he would not be back until the evening, too late for the O'Neils to attend to their jetty duties. A meeting was arranged for the next morning at eleven o'clock.

The day dragged: suddenly Dublin, after revealing a few of its secrets, was holding them back; it was time to move on.

The next morning, Father Nolan greeted them and took them into his small office and explained that a marriage could not be arranged in a day. They would need two witnesses, and he only solemnised marriages on a Saturday.

In desperation, Brendan told him they were travelling to

Queenstown to cross the water and needed a wedding certificate for accommodation. Father Nolan pursed his lips as if in some great quandary. 'I can, I think, combine yer wedding with two others on Saturday evening, but there is the question of the fee because I'll have ter arrange for the witnesses and I have no proof of yer identity.'

Brendan showed him his Bank of Ireland transaction certificate with his name and address in Ireland clearly marked. And he added that on top of the registry fee he would be obliged, because of the Father's sympathetic guidance, to add a few shillings to the church maintenance fund. Father Nolan chuckled. 'I think 'tis a bribe yer offering but all the same I feel yer intentions are fer the good. And by the way, I did think yer were already married.' He pointed at the ring on Anna's finger.

Brendan closed his eyes in embarrassment, to hear Anna explain. 'Father, I was trying it on fer size but I canna get it off.' She gave one of her wondrous smiles.

Father Nolan stood up. 'I'll see yer both at six on Saturday evening and I'm sure by then the ring will be in yer pocket.' He smiled disarmingly.

Outside, they hugged and laughed, just one more day and they would be Mr and Mrs O'Neil and on their final journey to Queenstown.

Saturday morning, Brendan watched the men finish the jetty and explained that they would be moving on Sunday morning. Flynn was delighted, it fitted in well with his plans and he explained that they could store their tools under the hatch and move the barge downriver on Sunday afternoon, to a new site, ready to start work on Monday.

From his satchel, Brendan unfolded Anna's special dress, her wedding dress, a cream coloured creation with orange-brown frills; the creases would fall out. He then set about cleaning their footwear that had taken a beating since leaving Mollybeg. At midday, he took out his frock coat and a waistcoat that was far too warm for the lovely May day. However, he loved the fancy brocade, given to him as a present on his eighteenth birthday.

Late afternoon Anna dressed for her big day. She pinned her hair up and from her personal bag she took out a little hat that was no more than the size of a pancake, it had little linen flowers that could be held in place with pins. She put it on to one side at a jaunty angle, but Brendan turned the hat round across the front of her head. He stood back. 'Now yer look like a true bride and not a musical turn… yer look truly beautiful.'

Anna sat nervously awaiting the time to walk to her wedding. Then, to her surprise, Brendan hailed a passing hansom cab and helped her in. He looked at her and took her hand. 'Te'day is a special day an' I can say the happiest day in me life. Anna Ferguson, in a few hours' time yer'll truly be me wife, an' I'll never regret the day yer came ter me door, an' fer once in me life we're goin' ter do it in style.'

Anna sat telling herself, don't cry, don't cry, yer need yer face fer the wedding. Instead, she took Brendan's hand and held it to her lips.

They arrived at St Catherine's to find a large wedding in progress. Dozens of carriages were drawn up and drivers stood around in conversation. Not sure what to do Brendan and Anna approached the church steps. As they entered the west door, an elderly man dressed in a long dark tunic quietly called out. 'Are you Mr O'Neil and Miss Ferguson?'

They were shown to a seat at the back of the church and told by the warden he would guide them through the ceremony when the time came. Brendan held Anna's hand tightly; he knew what she was thinking. The bride, in a beautiful dress, with three bridesmaids, came down the aisle. The groom, elegantly dressed, carrying a top hat, smiled to his family and friends who filled the front part of the church. The bride, as she passed, gave them a smile.

Brendan and Anna listened to the clamour outside, then the sounds of horses' hooves as they receded into the distance. Silence settled.

The warden approached the couple sitting two pews in

front, and they followed him to the altar where their marriage was blessed by Father Nolan. As they moved to the registration office, the warden slipped in beside Brendan and Anna. In his hand, he carried a garland of flowers. 'The bride, you've just seen, asked me if you are to be married, and she wants you to have her garland and wishes you the same joy in life as herself.'

It was Brendan who responded. 'Sir, if yer ever have occasion ter see this fine lady again, will yer thank her and tell her she will forever remain in our thoughts fer such a kind act.' The warden told them that indeed he knew the lady, who was a devotee of the church, and he would pass on their message.

At seven o'clock, Mr and Mrs O'Neil signed the register and received their marriage certificate, and thanked the warden and his wife, witnesses to their marriage. It was at this point that Father Nolan made sure they were aware of the building maintenance box and Brendan, in an emotional state, put far too much in the box.

Outside it was a lovely evening, and the couple, with Anna clutching her bouquet, walked the two miles back to their barge. Anna responded to the many happy greetings from well-wishers with a wave and a smile, while Brendan tipped his bowler hat. On board, they looked at each other not sure what to do. This time it was Anna who made the decision. 'Bren, undo me dress and put it away. We head fer Queenstown te'morra'. Have yer forgotten yer planning?'

CHAPTER 9

The last stage to Queenstown, the port to Cork, followed the same pattern; many miles on foot, lifts by kind hauliers, and bribes to ease the journey. A few of the cheap lodgings saw them prefer the comfort of Brendan's bedroll rather than risk the flea-bitten beds. One night was spent in a barn, and this again was almost preferable to the accommodation on offer; it also balanced costs.

As they neared the port, accommodation was difficult to find with so many awaiting passage to America, while the inflated fees alarmed Brendan. They arrived late into the evening and once again their waxed bedroll was put to good use as they found a place under a boat on the beach; they weren't alone. Fortunately, it was a warm night.

Early the next morning, as they neared the main pier, they had their first glimpse of a steamship. They could not believe its size. 'Just look at her, Anna. Funnels as well as masts... steam power, can yer believe it?'

Anna was equally stunned. 'Yer mean if the engines fail yer've got the sails?'

Brendan told her, 'I think it's more ter do with the coal. Yer can only carry so much and America's a hell of a distance; it carries over three hundred passengers.'

'Three hundred!' Anna couldn't imagine such a number. 'Never mind the coal where do they put the food, and how do they keep it fresh fer so many days?'

'Ah, they must have ice bunkers, or something like it, but more ter the point, Anna, where the hell do they put all the passengers?'

After touring the shipping agencies, it was explained to them that most of the passengers leaving on the steamships were travelling on pre-paid tickets paid for by family or friends in America. And, even worse news, that it could be a month before they could get berths.

Despondent at this news, and with funds running low, Brendan was desperate. 'Anna, I had no idea things would be this difficult. I thought money was all yer needed. At this rate, we'll never get a crossing and I don't fancy another night on the beach with the change in the weather.' Anna looked at the angry sky and knew a storm was coming. Her eyes turned to the assembling passengers, many already moving up the covered gangplanks; the ship was to leave port that very evening

'Bren, try the office. Yer never know, they might be able to fit us in.'

It meant moving the sign across the entrance to one side, but Brendan was ready to try anything. They approached a man in a white and blue uniform who was working in a small bureau. Across the three serving windows, in bright red, were notices telling that the steamship *Trojan* had a full workforce and a complement of passengers. Anna gave a tap on the window. The man looked up, surprised. She gave him one of her wondrous smiles. He frowned but slid the window open; he didn't look too pleased.

Anna greeted him warmly. 'Dear sir, we're from Donegal, and we need ter be on that steamship and we have the money ter pay. Now I'm sure yer can find us a little corner.'

'From Donegal are yer? Well, so am I but can yer no read?'

'Sir, I've gorra the money here and a bit on top.' Brendan tapped his money belt. 'Sure, a man like yerself from Donegal can find a way ter get us a passage. All me savings are invested fer the other side, we've only pennies left fer this side.'

The man's attitude softened and he looked through a list of names and patiently explained. 'We have what we call a standing ticket, a few places not filled by the pre-paid, but these have been booked fer weeks.' He paused. 'But yer might be in luck, me friends, because *Trojan* sails tonight at six o'clock, and I've just been informed that a couple canna sail because of illness. So, I'm not about ter send runners all around the town ter look for a replacement when I have before me a couple from Donegal.' He reached for registration forms, smiled, and said, 'Fill these in. Because yer stand-by it'll cost yer four each instead of five pounds, and I'll make out yer tickets. Yer need ter gerra move on because yer must be on board by three o'clock, and it's near twelve now. Good luck ter yer both.'

Brendan went to offer Mr Callaghan a shilling, which was waved away, while Anna told him, 'Sir, wherever we go in this world we'll always remember yer fer yer kindness.'

'Kindness? Look, lady, yer've just made me work a wee bit easier that's all.'

Elated but anxious the O'Neils climbed the gangplank, and joined the queue aboard SS *Trojan*, to be checked over by a doctor. After a three-hour wait, the doctor quickly passed them, and they moved on to register their details and to hand over their baggage.

Brendan wanted to find their accommodation in gallery E4, but Anna was bubbling with excitement and joined the crowd lining the rails, watching the comings and goings. Ladies and gentlemen dressed in the most wonderful finery made their way up the gangplank to be met by the captain and senior officers. The quay was a scramble of activity, delivery men shouted to make way, men loaded huge crates into nets to be hauled aboard, porters carried huge containers to the holds. To their right, a frightened horse was causing mayhem. Friends of passengers were held back by a barrier, while authorised visitors and servants carried trunks up the gangplank, a band played traditional Irish tunes.

Looking up, Brendan could see that the people on the upper deck were well dressed; obviously the rich would be better catered for.

The blast on the ship's whistle made them jump and friends, visitors, and delivery men made their way ashore.

Down below, the gangplanks were removed, ropes cast off and slowly SS *Trojan* moved away from the jetty.

Anna waved to the many people on the quay, many of whom were crying. Next to her, a woman was sobbing, which brought home to Anna what a big step they were taking. A new life in a strange country: she thought of Da and Grandma Harriet, the tears came, more so as Ireland slipped out of sight. Brendan held her tight; when she looked up into his face his eyes were moist.

The crossing took twelve days, bringing a weather change and very high seas. Very few escaped seasickness; it lasted for five days. Brendan had had bad moments, but Anna had never felt so ill and miserable. Equally awful was the accommodation. Brendan thought that as they were a married couple, they would have some privacy, but instead, it was a narrow corridor with bunks stacked either side, with only a flimsy curtain between. Brendan and Anna were on the top bunk wedged together, and he slept on the outside to keep Anna from prying eyes. Below, a fat man from Killarney and his wife kept them awake with his constant snoring. Even worse was trying to get through the day without losing an item, and arguments broke out, even a few fights began over accusations of robbery. Anna, aware of envious eyes looking at her coat, kept it on most of the time. At night, she carefully rolled it and kept it between her and the bunk wall; the one thing she couldn't lose was her precious coat with her ring hidden away.

Meals were basic, and long queues formed each day in the cramped passageways to receive a never-ending variety of soups.

For Anna, it was the most miserable journey in her life. Sea, sea and more sea; would America ever arrive? She sat dejected on a seat huddled into Brendan looking out onto a foggy morning. Brendan, equally dejected, didn't dare tell Anna how nervous he felt, his seasickness had abated but now he was looking into the unknown; what would America hold for them?

They both jumped. Boom! Boom! Boom! The sound of gunfire echoed around the ship. There was a rush by the starboard passengers to the port side. Brendan grabbed Anna's hand and they followed. A sailor told them that a gun battery welcomed all arrivals; New York was in sight.

Brendan and Anna joined the throng at the guard rail and peered through the drifting sea mist. A tugboat came alongside, and passenger luggage was loaded, to be transported ahead.

Anna carefully rolled her coat and placed it along the top of her personal bag with the lining facing out; already the heat of a New York day was apparent.

As they approached the Castle Garden terminal, the mist lifted, and they could see the sunlit buildings of Manhattan and the many river craft in New York Bay. Anna gripped Brendan's arm. 'My God, Bren, an' we thought Dublin was big.' Brendan didn't answer – a sudden fear clamped his stomach.

One of the crew told their group that the large round red granite building ahead was the immigration terminal, a fort built by the British in 1812, the point of departure for the Brits after the War of Independence.

It took an hour for SS *Trojan* to dock, and a further delay came when a covered passageway was put in place. Shortly after, the first-class passengers were escorted into the building.

Anna and Brendan waited patiently before joining their fellow steerage passengers in a long corridor that led to a seated area beneath a large glass dome. High desks with numerous officials and police overlooked the nervous assembly. Finally, they moved to the desk and gave in their names, dates of birth, and their destination that Brendan had entered as New York. All details had to agree with their registration given to the captain of SS *Trojan*. Several officers from the Intelligence Department gave advice on accommodation, travel to other parts of America, and on employment. One warned them to beware of scalpers, boarding-house runners, and those who made a living feeding on the insecurities of newcomers to rid them of their money.

Anna nudged Brendan. 'I don't know if I'm just scared or excited.'

He gave her hand a reassuring squeeze. 'I'm a mixture of both. But I must say the organisation is wonderful.'

'Bren, why don't yer ask about employment? D'yer hear they can get us accommodation?'

'Ah, but look at the queue, we've already been here fer four hours. I think it'll be best ter make our own way.'

Brendan guided Anna to the luggage hall where he claimed his satchels. It was then the enormity hit them. Brendan breathed heavily.

'Through that door, Mrs O'Neil, is our new country and home, an' yes I'm scared; Donegal suddenly seems a long way away.'

CHAPTER 10

On the 27th May 1889, the O'Neils headed for the dock gates and followed the exodus of passengers. Outside, they stopped: this was indeed the new world, a different world, never had Brendan felt so unsure. Anna, on the other hand, exclaimed excitedly, 'Bren, just look at all the building goin' on. Yer'll find work here ter be sure.'

It was true, wherever Brendan looked all he could see were cranes and buildings higher than anything he could have imagined, but it was the people who drew his attention. He had never seen so many in his life, and for the first time, he was looking at people from different parts of the world. A man pushed by who wore a wide flat hat, and from his face, he thought him to be Chinese, or, was he Japanese? Loading a cart, three very dark-skinned men were having trouble with a lively horse. Were they from Africa? He didn't know. Another man wore flowing robes, a strange hat, and jewellery; his skin was lighter in colour. Indeed, wherever he looked there was a mix of people he had never seen in his part of Ireland. 'My God, Anna, just look at these people, where are they all from?'

Anna had read about America: she knew about its civil war, the conflict between the north and the south, that had only ended in 1865, and how slavery had been abolished in '84. Like Brendan, she had only known white people. This would be part of her new life, a strange new world where they would have to adapt. Now, however, she pushed such thoughts aside as she looked down the road. The number of horses and carts were unbelievable. Carriages and people thronged the gates from the dock; happy shouts of reunion as families embraced, names held high on placards as anxious relatives tried to find their loved ones. Sailors, eager to get back to their families, cheerily shouted greetings to those returning to duty. Lines of hansom cabs, their drivers touting for business, and carts of all descriptions, many displaying ware signs, were banked up and down the road.

Finding a quiet corner Brendan eased his carrying frame and satchels off his back and told Anna to rest for a moment. All his energy and know-how had been spent on getting from Donegal to Queenstown, but this was something extraordinary, beyond his comprehension, he needed time to adjust, to consult his map. Anna, for her part, was still reeling from days at sea with little sleep. Her initial excitement quickly turned to a feeling of overwhelming tiredness; all she wanted to do was to find somewhere to lay her head.

A voice made them look up. A man wearing a tunic type shirt locked into place by a broad belt, holding up trousers that once belonged to a suit smiled and said, 'Tell me ter mind me own business but I can tell yer from the ole country... have yer just arrived?' The relief at hearing his southern Irish brogue was music to Brendan and Anna's ears; if ever there was a time to ask for help it was now. Anna thought the man to be about fifty, and his ruddy complexion reminded her of an Irish farmer she once knew. His thick neck and face were both red from the afternoon sun, while his grey hair was thick around his ears but thin and bleached white on top.

'We've just arrived, and we'll be looking fer lodging fer the night, and if yer have somewhere in mind, not expensive, we'd be in debt ter yer.' Brendan picked up his satchels and helped Anna up.

The man seemed to be in no hurry and asked where they came from, and how their journey had been. He then added, 'Yer'll be mindful here that it's the dollar, no-one will take yer English money.' At this, he spat on the ground.

'Well, our first call must be at the Weston Union. In Dublin, I set up an account and I need ter transfer funds over here.' Brendan felt he could trust this man.

At this point, Anna broke in. 'Well, kind sir, we welcome yer help but haven't yer a name ter call yerself?'

The man laughed. 'Oh, everyone knows me just as Paddy, which I'm quite happy with because if I tell yer me real name yer'll mock me.' He went into a fit of laughter and it was hard not to enjoy the humour of this man.

He led them to a four-wheel horse and cart. Brendan sat up front and Anna climbed into the small wooden seat just behind. She clutched at the small improvised handrail as the cart pulled away. She tried to follow the conversation up front but felt too tired.

'Yer'll find the Weston Union up town itself. It's a fine building, I know it well, so, as I'm going that way I can drop yer off.'

Brendan relaxed and thought how fortunate they were to find a fellow Irishman who knew New York and its ways. He listened carefully as Paddy gave him all sorts of advice, on accommodation, finding work, how to be careful with your money and whom to trust. On one corner Paddy pointed to a tall building.

'That's one of the best hotels in New York, the Manhattan.' He then pointed out the bridge under construction away to their left, where a group of people huddled by one of its piers. 'Vagrants — scum!' Paddy spat from the cart. 'I've helped many a soul in trouble, but there's some yer canna help.' Brendan wasn't sure what to make of this as he had seen similar scenes in Ireland and England; people who were poor through no fault of their own.

Paddy pulled up a short distance away from the impressive Weston Union, a large brick building with terra-cotta decoration. Brendan helped Anna down, they thanked Paddy, but he waved their thanks away.

'Look, there's a clock over there. At seven I'll be passing this way again and if yer've got yer money me sister will be glad ter find yer a bed for the night.' He added, 'And, as I'm sure yer starving, behind the Union yer'll find Mick's place, and yer can get a good square meal there at little cost.'

Brendan thanked him for his kind help, while Anna waved as Paddy climbed back onto his cart.

Inside the Weston Union, there was a large tiled vestibule, and from this a series of queues led to windows set into a heavy dark oak secure framework. Over each window names from around the world were displayed. The longest queue told that it was for Dublin to New York transactions. Brendan and Anna waited patiently, and it was well into the afternoon when they moved to the desk. Brendan gave the clerk the certificate of transaction given to him in Dublin, and this was stamped and approved. The clerk looked at his watch and told them to return at 6 pm, and to the couple's delight he offered them a two-dollar voucher for meals, and this included Mick's place; the amount would be deducted later.

Not having eaten for several hours Brendon and Anna found Mick's restaurant and feeling at home with so many familiar sounds around them they relaxed for the first time; only the money caused a problem. Mick himself was very helpful and went through the various coins. He laid out a line and went through them: a cent, a nickel, a dime, a quarter, a half-dollar and a dollar. He showed them the menu written on a board over the counter. The familiar eggs and bacon with fried soda bread were too good to miss at twenty cents, and tea at ten cents. He took Brendan's voucher and gave him one dollar forty in change.

Feeling refreshed after their meal, at five to six, with the change buried deep in an inside pocket and the dollar in his money belt, the O'Neils returned to the Weston Union, hoping their transaction had come through. A sign told them to wait by a window until their code of three numbers was displayed for completed transfers; to be found on their receipt.

Brendan had never felt more lost. He had adapted well to life in England, but it had been simple; you worked and got paid. Now he was in New York dealing with affairs strange to him. Moreover, the tiredness he'd pushed to one side was closing in, and he could see that Anna could hardly keep awake. It was a great relief when his code came up and he was ushered into a small room where a Mr J T Watson went through the transaction and told him the commission was a half-dollar; that to Brendan seemed unreasonable. The two-dollar voucher was also deducted and Brendan's savings of thirty-two dollars were given to him with a warning from Mr Watson. 'We call you in here where no prying eyes can get. I suggest you hide this about your person very carefully; there's those outside just ready to take it from you.'

Brendan was prepared for this. He carefully loaded his body belt with the strange new money. 'Don't show me, friend, I don't wanna know.' Mr Watson turned his back.

Brendan rejoined Anna, and they moved outside. Anna gave a shiver, the May evening had cooled, dark storm clouds had moved in and seemed to be anchored behind the tall buildings. For the time of the evening it was quite dark, and a chill wind had blown up; Anna put on her coat.

'We'll look fer a cheap hotel but it's going ter be difficult with so many people after the same.' Brendan paused, not sure which way to go.

'Ah, there yer are. Now can I be of help? I hope yer Weston has delivered yer treasure.' Brendan turned to see Paddy's smiling face. Pleased, but tired with night coming on, Brendan nodded their success. Paddy put his hand on Brendan's shoulder. 'Me friend, the one thing yer need in this country is money. It's the only thing that talks. Now let me help yer. As I told yer I can find yer a cheap lodging at twenty cents, but mind, yer'll be scratching yerselves for days.' Paddy laughed and made a scratching motion down his arm. 'Me sister Cathy can put yer up for a quarter. Come on, it's not far.'

Brendan just wanted to escape the day, have a good night's sleep, refresh and begin anew with a plan of action. Anna, meanwhile, was only too pleased to have someone to help them after days of sickness and lack of sleep. Blindly they followed Paddy as he crossed the road and led them between two large dark tenement buildings.

Brendan didn't see the blow that felled him. All he felt was a numbing pain across his shoulder and neck that dropped him to his knees. He heard Anna scream, then he felt the knife against his throat. Paddy, his face now a vicious parody of earlier, hissed, 'Lie still or I'll stick yer. Now, where's all this money from the ole country.' As he said this, he lifted Brendan's coat. 'Surprise, surprise, surprise, a body belt. Now, who would have thought of that?' The second man, with a thin face marked by pox, missing front teeth, and wearing a leather overall, held his knife against Brendan's throat while Paddy cut away his money belt.

Another scream from Anna brought shouts from the tenement above, a voice answered, a light came on in a back room, a man looked over from a flat roof and began to blow a whistle. As Brendan struggled to get up, he could see the third man, a large balding brute, tugging off Anna's coat. Her frantic scream, 'Bren, me coat, me coat,' echoed through the alleyway.

Paddy and his thin pockmarked accomplice moved back ready to run. The large balding man, waving Anna's coat, joined them. Quickly they disappeared into the shadows of the tenement buildings.

Two men came running in from the street to help, and a group from the tenements gathered. Brendan, helped back to his feet by a man, went to go after Paddy and his accomplices, but strapped into the weight of his satchels, his legs still unsteady, all he could do was to yell after them. 'Yer lousy Irish bastards, I'll get yer fer this.'

Anna lay sobbing. 'They've taken me coat... me lovely coat.' Brendan, for once furious at her, shouted, 'Damn yer coat. We're destitute. Don't yer bloody understand, woman? We've forty cents ter live on.'

They explained what had happened and a woman, who could have been Italian, shrugged and told them how stupid they were. To Anna's request to go to the police, the man, crouched on the flat roof, told them that it was most likely the gang called the Irish Crew. They were well known to the police, but, they would have fifty witnesses to say they were playing cards in Brooklyn.

Anna came to Brendan: she had never seen him in such a state, he shook with fury, he held her tight, and as their helpers drifted away he said, 'Thank yer all most kindly. We'll be on our way.'

The man who had helped Brendan back to his feet warned, 'Heh man, keep to the main streets with folk and in the light. You'd better wise up quick or you'll end up in the river.'

Back on the main street Brendan looked at Anna and swore loudly, but mainly at himself. 'How could I be so stupid, stupid — bloody stupid!' He clenched his head in his arms. 'Anna, we've lost everything on our first day. Now what the hell will we do?' Anna thought of telling him about the loss of her ring, hidden in her coat, a safe place, their insurance against disaster, but if ever there was a time not to, it was now; suddenly she felt desperately cold and tired.

'Bren, we've got ter find somewhere ter lay our heads. I haven't slept fer three days… te'morra the world will look a different place.' Brendan was less sure but calmed down. He looked at Anna in her dress, pulled off his coat and tightened it around her.

'Well, we might as well join the people we saw earlier under the bridge. We should fit in fine.'

They walked back towards the docks until they came to the hotel they had passed earlier. Across the waste ground, they could see the new road bridge under construction, and people huddled around a fire. Brendan guided Anna to a place by the pier wall where some of the heat would reach; eyes looked at them suspiciously.

'I hope we can find a more friendly greeting here than we've found so far. This morning we arrived at the Garden from Ireland, and we've been robbed of every penny.' Brendan looked around the group to see the response.

A man, wrapped in a filthy blanket, with several days' stubble on his face and wearing an old cap, cleared his throat and spat. He stretched his mouth before speaking and when he did, he had an accent Brendan didn't recognise. 'We all have a tale to tell. What's yours?' Quickly Brendan told him how they had been tricked and robbed.

Blanket-man nodded; a murmur went around the group, he sighed and spat again. 'My friend Artem was killed for a dollar.'

Anna was surprised when a large blanket moved and a woman looked out, she then pulled a boy beside her who was no more than three years old. 'Two more mouths to feed?' She shook her head in disbelief; a murmur went around the group.

Blanket-man poked the fire, shrugged and said, 'It all depends – you can wait.'

Brendan stored his satchels behind his back against the wall and unfurled their waxed blanket to cover Anna. Immediately her head dropped onto his shoulder, within seconds she was asleep; soon he succumbed.

Voices brought Brendan awake, happy voices. When he looked up, a man whom he hadn't seen before was carrying a large box; delighted shouts came from the group.

Anna sleepily awoke to ask what was going on. Food was being given out while blanket-man took a large tin of soup and placed it in the fire's embers. Brendan and Anna looked on, not sure what to do. It was blanket-man who, after serving hot soup around the group, moved to them. He nodded in the direction of the hotel, its windows lit into a haphazard pattern that climbed into the sky.

'Alexi has a friend who works in the kitchen and the boss no mind. At the end of the day, he sends food because…' and he pointed at three of the men, 'we Ukrainian, he help us. Now you want soup?' Brendan had two tin mugs in his satchel. Its warmth helped to dispel some of their tiredness, and both could feel new energy seeping into their bodies.

Blanket-man pointed at the fire, then at Brendan. 'Andriv

keep the fire going for three hours; you after. No fire – no food. He wake you.' It was near to dawn when Brendan felt a hand on his shoulder, and he fed the fire with timber from a pile under the bridge.

CHAPTER 11

Anna awoke as Brendan pulled aside the blanket to take his turn at the fire. She drowsily watched him as he moved to the woodpile under the bridge. As the flames rose the glow caught his face; never had she seen him in such a state. His face was etched with tiredness, his mouth moved silently, forming words which she knew were reliving the disaster that had befallen them. But how could she tell him that it was far worse than he thought? It wasn't just the loss of her coat, inside was her precious ring, the one to bail them out in the direst emergency. She remembered Grandma's words. 'Don't even tell yer lover.' Now, when she looked at Bren, she felt guilty because he wasn't just her lover... he was her husband. Would he forgive her when she told him? The thought persisted that the ring had gone, so why add to their worries; only she would know. It had been such a good idea to hide the ring in the hem of her coat. Where else could you hide a ring? No wonder that Brendan, for the first time, had shown her such displeasure. Again, she wondered if she should tell him the truth, to ease her own conscience. Brendan's words, his anger, 'damn yer coat... we're destitute,' returned. Anna waited, her thoughts spiralling out of control, she wanted Brendan to come to her, but he still sat close to the fire poking fresh wood into the hot embers. She slumped into half-sleep, her mind still racing, out of control: crazy thoughts, her coat was out there – on somebody else's back; had they found her ring?

She felt Brendan move in beside her and pull her close; she relaxed.

'Have you ten cents?' The prod brought both awake. Blanket-man looked at them. 'We can get German sausage from the cafe down the road.' Brendan went through his money and offered twenty cents; he didn't get any change. They waited until a man they now knew as Oleg came back; a shout went up when he swung a line of sausages in the air. A large tin plate was put on the fire and a little woman they hadn't noticed before began turning them, the smell was delicious; another man they hadn't seen before arrived with a container of coffee.

Blanket-man explained. 'It's yesterday's but *gut*.'

Brendan liked the strong spicy sausage; Anna was less keen. However, it was hot and filling, and after mugs of coffee both felt refreshed enough to plan their day ahead.

The sounds of workmen arriving at the bridge interrupted their thoughts. Brendan leapt to his feet. 'Anna, I might find work, I won't be…' A laugh went up from the group.

A man who had joined them late into the night said, 'D'you think we've been sitting here on our arses all this time?'

Blanket-man patiently asked, 'You have card… no?'

An Englishman came over. 'He means a union card. Look, mate, getting work isn't that easy around here. You'll find Italian gangs, Irish gangs, German gangs, in fact, every nationality you can bloody well think of, and most have family ties, you've got to know someone on the inside.'

Exasperated, Brendan asked, 'And how the hell d'yer get this card?'

The Englishman laughed. 'I'm sorry, Paddy, but there's so many bloody Irish here ready to do anything at a cheap rate, that your lot aren't exactly popular currency.'

The lady with the child piped up, 'Heh, mister, who'll be looking out for your lady while you're off earning a buck? She's a pretty lass, you'll need a roof over your head… somewhere safe.'

The Englishman further explained. 'You need an address to work but you need to earn money to pay to find an address.' He waved his arm around the group. 'Which is why we're all here. Now, my Irish friend, do you understand?'

Anna sat silent. Bren had mentioned he had a letter from Merryweather and a testimonial from Mr Moffat in England, but it was seemingly of little use in New York.

Brendan sat down again, confused and disappointed, as the conversation changed to food. The man, Oleg, who had brought the sausage, joined them and told them he was from Estonia, but he had migrated from London, where he had lived for several years. He explained he had jumped ship and became a meat porter at Smithfield; his English was perfect.

'Have you a trade, my friend?'

'I'm a stonemason, worked in England these past two years building a mill in Derbyshire.'

'Well, you should find plenty to suit you uptown. The trick is to find the foreman or gangmaster, and a backhander might get you in; it all depends. It's no good trying to join a foreign crew. You'll have to find a building site with the Irish lads. Walk around and have a word and then find the office or foreman's hut, but I should warn you that it's no good going now as the work's all set for the day. And if you can find an address to satisfy, then all the better but I warn you, don't accept accommodation with a promise it'll be taken out of your pay. Some of the foremen have an arrangement that fills their pockets, leaving yours empty. Go this evening when the work is finishing. The foreman will know what he needs for the next day, and you might fill a dead man's boots.'

Anna was shocked and repeated. 'A dead man's…?

Oleg shrugged and pointed at the sky. 'They build it high here, land is scarce, there are many accidents.' To emphasise this, he gave his thigh a thump.

The Englishman, again showing an interest, pointed at the distant masts of ships moored on the Hudson River. 'Your best bet today is to join the labour pool and earn a few bucks. The foreign captains have no time for unions or cards. They want freight in and out for a quick turnaround. You look a strong lad and should catch an eye or two.'

Blanket-man gave a laugh, 'No more than your fine lady.'

The woman with the child added, 'Keep her in sight on the quay and you'll be alright.'

The Englishman, who introduced himself as Bob, said, 'To find work you need money. Everything here works on money, and you must find at least two weeks in advance for any landlord. Who can blame them? People scarper at night without paying their dues. Money talks, promises don't. Enough! You'd better get going if you want to find work. Just follow the street over there… It'll take you to the docks.'

Brendan and Anna set out, and though still early morning it was warm and promised a hot day. Half an hour later they stood in amazement. Ships flying flags from seemingly every nation under the sun were tied up. Huge barges were being loaded and unloaded. Cranes and hoists swung to and fro lifting or lowering huge nets with produce from all over the world. Men swarmed around on the quayside, overseers shouted instructions, lines of horses and carts waited their turn, others made off to the city. The smell of fresh horse manure filled the air, urchins shovelled it into bags to sell on.

'God, it's wonderful, Bren. I've never seen anything like it. Just look at all those ships and look at that blue and white paddle steamer, it's heading ter the other side.'

Brendan, with his map to hand said, 'That's New Jersey over there, come on, we need ter to follow these warehouses, the pool must be down here.' Ahead, Brendan could see a group of men outside a large warehouse. In the centre, a man wearing a top hat was calling and directing men to various gangmasters who stood to the side. As they approached, mutters came from some of the men. They didn't like a woman on the site.

Brendan told Anna to ignore them and was about to give in his name to the overseer when a man wearing a dark blue captain's uniform touched the overseer on the shoulder, turned to Brendan and Anna and pointed back along the line of ships, and called. 'Kom!' The overseer gave a brief look, gave a shrug, and waved him away.

The captain, a short, stocky man, possibly in his late forties, sharp-featured with a well-trimmed beard led them back to a large black sailing ship with four masts. Men were busily unloading and rolling barrels from a cart, and these were being loaded into the hold by a hoist. The captain pointed to the cart where a sailor was having difficulty lifting some larger barrels onto their sides for rolling. Brendan climbed up, heaved a barrel over and guided it down the plank to the quay; the captain nodded his approval.

'You work... I pay.' Brendan nodded in reply. He thought the captain could be Russian, while the men at work chatted away in a language he had never heard before.

The captain turned to Anna. 'Need woman. You kom.' Anna looked nervously towards Brendan; the thought came... *a woman fer what?* Brendan pointed and smiled, she looked up, a woman was busily hanging out washing strung on a line between two of the masts.

Anna joined her. The woman smiled and pointed to a second large washing tub. This was familiar work for Anna, but the pile of clothes was daunting. However, she set about it with great enthusiasm. Two hours later, her arms aching, her back stiff and sore she straightened up and looked for Brendan. He was doing stretching exercises, his grimace told her they both had the same problem. He held up his hands, someone had kindly given him large gloves to wear.

Another hour passed before the captain called a break, bottles of cold tea were passed around, and the sailors, smoking the longest pipes Brendan had ever seen, sat in the shade as the sun moved overhead.

Anna welcomed the break and enjoyed the cold tea. The woman sat beside her and pointing at Brendan, said in halting English, 'He your man?' Anna nodded. The woman pointed at the captain. 'He my man, Gregor,' and touching her chest said, 'I am Adela, and I am from Russia.'

Anna did likewise and said, 'Anna, an' I'm from Ireland.' From this moment the two women warmed to each other.

Brendan worked solidly: he had no idea what the men

around him were saying, but they were friendly. Near to one o'clock, the ship was loaded, the washing almost dry.

The captain waved Anna down onto the quay. He then spoke rapidly to his men. To Brendan, he said, 'Thank you, you strong man... gut,' and he pulled out a large silver dollar piece and pressed it into Brendan's hand. Turning to Anna he gave a little bow and pressed a half-dollar into her hand. The captain then took off his cap and moved around his crew who threw in any loose change. He smiled as he handed the odd bits of change over. 'We go... sail.' He held up five fingers. 'Dollar no good... Russia.'

Anna smiled, thanked him, and waved to Adela who waved back. Then, in turn, she thanked the eight sailors and shook hands. Brendan decided to do the same and this seemed to delight everyone. With a final wave to Gregor, Adela, and the sailors, Brendan and Anna left feeling a little happier at their improved financial situation, and how well they had been treated by the Russians.

Out of sight, Anna asked, 'How much have we got, Bren?'

Brendan slowly counted out the amount. 'With me twenty cents in me pocket, add a dollar, yer half, and the hatful, mainly cents, we've nearly two dollars, it's good. Some only get a dollar fer a full week's work. It'll find us lodging and food fer some days.'

Anna was shocked. 'A dollar fer a full week's work?' Brendan laughed. 'I wonder if our Russian captain knows the goin' rate?'

In better spirits, they followed the shoreline and the large warehouses until these gave way to more open ground and new wharves under construction. Ships were fewer while huge barges were anchored three abreast, many loaded with building materials ready for unloading. A dirt road ran ahead leading to a long low warehouse to their right. Outside stood a magnificent lacquered black coach, with two beautiful black horses, their livery shining in the sun. 'God, aren't they beautiful?' Anna could not resist going to the animals to give each in turn a scratch between the ears, and of course a few kind words.

As Brendan waited patiently, a man came around the corner of the coach. He was obviously very rich, and Brendan noted his fine top hat and his silver hair that he wore long. In his hand, he carried a silver-tipped cane. He stood talking to two men who were well dressed, possibly managers. The coachman, a black man, sitting in his high seat gave them a smile and a friendly wave.

Impatient to move on Brendan called, 'Come on, Anna.' As the men turned, Brendan acknowledged them with the tip of his bowler hat. In turn, the silver-haired gentleman raised his cane and nodded, while Anna gave the gentlemen one of her wondrous smiles; again, the silver-haired gent responded with a small bow.

'We'll follow the river, then cut inter the city centre, and look fer lodgings, then I can leave yer and go look fer work.' Anna said nothing, she didn't like the idea but there was little she could say. Getting to America had been one exciting adventure, indeed quite romantic, but now the reality was frightening.

Brendan could not believe the new buildings under construction. Buildings so high you needed to lean back to see the top. Offices, apartment blocks, lines of houses, some inhabited, some almost finished hidden between the multitude of signs and sale notices. Gangs of men worked at ground level, while others scaled scaffolding high in the sky. The early summer-burnt dry roads were full of carts, and the air hummed with the sound of human industry.

'Anna, listen out fer an Irish tongue. I'm sure ter find work here.' For the first time in a while, Brendan O'Neil's confidence was back.

Anna, looking riverside, at first admired the view over the Hudson; she loved the riverboats. Then her eyes were drawn to a gang of men, busily engaged in loading a long line of carts with bricks, not the usual kind, a sort of blue. Brendan had told her, when they were on the Liffey in Dublin, that they were a special type, resistant to water, and very expensive. As Anna looked down the line of carts, she came to the last one, where a man was holding a hod of bricks; he turned as he moved around the cart.

'Jesus!' Anna exclaimed.

Brendan swung round; it was the pockmarked knifeman. He put down his satchels. 'I'll have the bastard. Let's see how brave he is without his mates.'

'No! Bren – leave it. Gerra the police.' But she was too late.

Brendan crossed the road on the blind side of knifeman. As he came around the side of the cart, knifeman looked up; recognition was instant. He called to the group working further up the wharf and backed away. He tried to move left, Brendan blocked his path, he tried to his right, Brendan was in his way.

Anna looked for help, the coach she had seen earlier was coming, but so too were the men loading the hods and the carts. Hearing the shout, they had downed tools and were running towards them; they were only fifty yards away.

'Bren! There's ten of them.' It was then she saw the man pull his knife from his high boot; she screamed. 'Brennnnn!'

Brendan drew back as knifeman advanced thrusting at his chest. He moved quickly to his left, at the same time he grabbed a brick from the cart and threw it into his face. As knifeman swung his arm to deflect the brick, Brendan quickly moved in and sent a crashing blow over the top that landed between his assailant's nose and upper lip. Anna saw the squirt of blood and his two crooked front teeth fly into the air. Falling back, knifeman tripped over his hod, and Anna heard the snap of his neck as his head hit the pile of stacked bricks; he crumpled like a rag doll to the ground.

She was vaguely aware of her own scream and the coach coming to a halt.

'Miss... gerrin.' The coachman was slinging Brendan's satchels inside. She felt forcibly thrown in and looked out of the window. The silver-haired gent was shouting. 'Quick, man! Get in.'

Brendan was running, the coach was on the move. She could hear the coachman whipping his horses into a canter. She saw Brendan's arms reach through the open carriage door. The silver-haired gent pulled him in, and he fell partly onto Anna who pulled him onto the seat. A hand grabbed at the swinging door. Calmly the silver-haired gent pulled out a small pistol, leaned out of the carriage window and fired in the air. The hand released and all three hung on as the coach swayed and jumped over the rutted ground. Again, the gentleman leaned out to look back. Then he gave a tap to the roof, the coach slowed to a trot and then to a walk. Anna couldn't speak. Beside her, Brendan was shivering and nursing his right knuckle.

The silver-haired gent said, 'Further on there's a watering hole; we'll be safe there.' A few minutes later the coach pulled up outside a restaurant and bar. 'We'll sit here for a few minutes. I think we need a moment for reflection and recovery.'

Anna tried to speak calmly. She looked at their saviour and could see that he was elderly, his beautifully embroidered coat and waistcoat also told her that he was a man of substance. In a trembling voice, Anna went to thank him, but his hand stopped her. 'I think introductions are in order. I am Nathaniel Peabody.' He raised his eyebrows in question. Anna looked at Brendan, who was still in shock, breathing heavily and recovering his breath. Anna took over and launched into a rapid outline of everything that had befallen them since leaving Ireland.

Mr Peabody listened carefully. He leaned back and gave a long 'Hmmm!' He took off his top hat and placed it on the seat beside him; he addressed Brendan. 'Mr O'Neil, the man you despatched so efficiently with one punch is no loss to the world. Many will thank you. If we go to the police, I am sure that my word will absolve you of all blame but, the men you saw out there will not see it our way. They support their own, and right and wrong does not come into it.' He then looked at Anna and said, 'You will be easily found, the gangs of New York will put out the word and your flowing locks will identify you very quickly.' He added, 'If I hadn't by chance been this way then you could both be floating somewhere in the North River... some call it the Hudson.'

Nathaniel Peabody reached to a compartment under his seat and withdrew an elegant wooden writing case. He opened it, dipped his pen in the inkwell and began to write. At the same time, he explained that he would help them. He held the paper out of the window to dry, then he put the letter in an envelope and wrote a name and address on the front. 'My young friends, you will not be safe here, you need to move on. This is what I suggest: this letter will give you passage to a town called Scranton, thirty years ago it was a hamlet, now it is a thriving industrial town: coal, iron, steel mills. In fact, it grows by the day. With so much building going on I am sure you will find work. And as you are country folk you may also find something to your liking in the Lackawanna Valley. It is one of my favourite places, I have a cottage there, the river is beautiful but under threat from too much mining.' Nathaniel Peabody tapped the letter again. 'I am a trustee of the railway, The Delaware, Lackawanna and Western Railway, and we now have the Morris and Essex branch, which means we have a direct route from Hoboken to Buffalo. Scranton is about 120 miles down the line. You take the ferry across the North River and at the terminal you ask for Mr John Theodore Schulz, and you give him this letter; he will make all the necessary arrangements. In a few minutes' time, a friend of mine will run you to the ferry, it crosses every twenty minutes, then make your way to the station.' He pointed at Anna's rich brown hair cascading down her shoulders. 'However, you need some disguise.' He called to his coachman and a large square of reddish-brown material was passed in. Anna thought it was a shawl, but Mr Peabody told them it was called a bandana, used by the cowmen to keep dust off their faces and to cover their horses' heads during dust storms.

By this time Brendan had recovered. He took off Anna's bonnet, pulled her hair to the top of her head and tightly wrapped the material in place. Under her chin, he used one of her brooches to fasten the headscarf in place. He gave a nervous laugh, 'My God, Anna, yer look just like a turf cutter's woman.'

Mr Peabody turned to Brendan. 'And now for you, sir. I am sending my man to get you a sailor's sack, leave your satchels with me.'

An hour later the two stood by the coach. Nathaniel Peabody looked at Brendan in his white shirt, wearing his sailor's cap and holding his sack across his shoulders. His eyes turned to Anna. 'As you will be passing the scene of the so-called crime, I doubt that you will get a second glance.'

They thanked Mr Peabody and promised that once settled they would send him a letter. Nathaniel Peabody seemed moved. He addressed Brendan.

'Mr O'Neil, if I seem overly attentive to your lovely wife it is because nearly fifty years ago I came here with my new bride. She was from Sligo – she died three years later; she was called Kathleen.'

Anna took both his hands in hers. 'My second name is Kathleen; dear Mr Peabody, we will never forget yer kindness.' Nathaniel Peabody smiled through watery eyes.

'God bless you both, you'd better be on your way.'

A weather-stained cart with a cab built on pulled alongside. The O'Neils climbed aboard. Brendan helped his woman, obviously a peasant girl, onto the cart. At the ferry station, the two boarded the ferry to Hoboken.

CHAPTER 12

Anna and Brendan stood by the rails on the paddle steamer *Bergen*; both were thrilled by its sheer beauty and opulence. Its exquisite wooden interior and furnishings were quite unlike anything they had seen before. Brendan, forever an admirer of all craftsmanship, wanted to explore but Anna, captivated by the activities of the passengers, its mix of different people, was just thrilled by the spectacle. She could see on the lower deck carts, cabs, mules, and horses, while around her many passengers gathered to look back as Manhattan moved into the distance; she clung to Brendan's arm. He stood silent, his face stern, Anna knew what he was thinking. New York had been their dream, now it was floating away. Only weeks ago, they had watched Ireland slip into the distance.

'Bren, when yer think about it we've met more good people than bad. Let's put the bad behind us. The people around the fire, they had nothin' but took us in, then look at our Russian friends and Mr Peabody. He's funding us on our way, how will we ever repay him?' Anna added, 'We've just been unlucky.'

Brendan shrugged. 'Unlucky? We've been bloody stupid. How I didn't see through that Paddy I'll never know. An' now look at us. I've killed a man, an' we're runnin'.'

Anna drew back. 'Yer didn't KILL him, he tripped and fell, and remember he tried ter kill yer, and what's more if I could meet that Paddy again, and the brute who stole me coat, I think I could kill 'em both without te'much worry.' Anna pulled Brendan around to look into her face. 'And have yer thought what might have happened ter me if yer'd been killed? Would yer like ter see me end up as one of those prostitutes we saw in the city?'

Brendan gave a sigh, then a quiet chuckle and pulled Anna into him. 'Mrs O'Neil, what would I do without yer?' As he said this he took off his sailor's cap and pushed it inside his sack and put back his bowler.

The mile crossing soon brought up Hoboken and it was as busy as the Manhattan side with many ships at anchor and a mill of workers going about their duties. The name Lackawanna was in huge letters on the terminal. Ashore they followed the sign to the train station.

'Bren, I've never seen a steam train close up before.' Anna was now back to her excitable best.

'Well, that makes two of us.'

Brendan led the way until they came to the railway track and stopped in wonder at how anything could run so fast on metal legs. For a few minutes, they awaited the arrival of an enormous steam engine, with a tall chimney stack belching smoke. They marvelled at the size of its wheels and watched while the driver got down and squirted oil into boxes along the side. The engine then moved to a line of coal trucks behind the station.

At the front, destination markers told them Buffalo was the end of the line. Anna nudged Brendan when she saw the name, Scranton.

They found the office some distance away; it was empty. Brendan looked at his watch, it was close to four o'clock. Not sure as to what to do they moved around the corner of the building to find the shade. A man sat on a chair smoking a pipe. On his shirt was an insignia and underneath the name John Shultz.

'Are you looking for me?' As he said this, he saw the letter in O'Neil's hand and took it. Puffing on his pipe he read slowly, rested it on his lap, smiled and said, 'Ah, Mr Peabody, if all humanity were like him the world would be a happier place.' He got up. 'This way, my friends.' In his office he wrote out two tickets, put them in an envelope and added a smaller envelope, and chuckled as he did so. He shook the envelope and said, 'You can guess it's from Mr

Peabody. The train leaves at 8.30 am tomorrow morning. It's part freight on its way to Scranton. There's one car which will be full of engineers and you will join them. I see you are a kind of engineer in stone, Mr O'Neil?' Brendan nodded. Mr Schultz smiled, then looked nervously at Anna still wrapped in her bandana. 'If I may say so, without rudeness, Mrs O'Neil, you do not quite fit the image of an engineer's wife!'

Anna gave a squeal of laughter, removed her bandana and tossed her head to reveal her pride and glory, her long rich brown hair. She then put on her bonnet, fastened it, and asked. 'Is this more ter yer liking, Mr Schultz?'

Mr Schulz leaned back in his chair. 'I feel there's something here that I am not privy to, so we'll leave it there. You will need to find a room for the night. Not far from here, in West Street, you will find number nineteen and Mrs Becker. She looks after our station staff and visitors. There's no need to find payment, it will be taken care of.'

Outside, Brendan opened the envelope. He knew what he would find; four large dollar coins. He looked at Anna; tears filled her eyes.

Nineteen was easy to find and the O'Neils were invited in by Mrs Becker, a tall grey-haired lady who wore a long dark skirt, a ruffled blouse held at the neck by a huge cameo brooch. Her severe look was softened by a gentle smile and a slow melodious deep voice. Anna liked her instantly, especially when she drew back and exclaimed, 'Young lady, all my life I've wished for a wonderful head of hair and look at you? Magnificent!'

Brendan laughed. 'Madam, if yer've scissors I'm sure we can reach a deal.' Mrs Becker chuckled as she showed them to a ground floor room.

'It's lovely, Mrs Becker, really lovely.' Anna looked at the large bed that was covered in a honeycombed patterned quilt. Against the one wall stood a marble-topped vanity table and next to it a wardrobe, the curtains matched the colour scheme, a deep yellow ochre. Impressed, Brendan, clutching his bowler gave a small bow.

'Ma'am, we thank yer most kindly, 'tis the finest bedroom I've ever seen.'

Mrs Becker nodded a thank you and asked, 'Are you familiar with gas?' She then showed them the gaslight, took a match and lit the mantle. 'Whatever you do don't touch the mantle. If you break it, I'll have to charge you.'

Anna had never seen gaslight before; she was worried because she had read it could be very dangerous. Brendan, who had seen it at work in England, told her, 'It lights the streets in Manchester, it's much better than oil; yer eyes won't fall out.'

Mrs Becker went to the door. 'If you wish to eat, you'll find plenty of eating places down by the dock, I only serve breakfast.'

Brendan was pleased to put down his sailor's sack; he much preferred his turf cutter's frame. He stretched his arms and shoulders, still sore after the blow from Paddy and his barrel lifting and rolling, while his knuckle was swelling after his punch to knifeman.

'Come on, Anna, let's get out there. It's too hot ter stay indoors and I'm starving.'

Suddenly, for Anna and Brendan, the events of the morning slipped away. Hoboken had a charm that set it at a distance from their disaster in Manhattan. In the main street, they admired the rows of grand houses and felt the warmth of busy people who smiled as they passed.

'It's lovely here, Bren, it reminds me of Dublin.'

Brendan wasn't so sure. 'Aye, it's almost a pity ter leave, except it's like living in Germany.'

'Immigrants like us,' Anna told him. 'I thought it was only Ireland on the move.'

Returning to near the docks they found an open bar selling skewers of hot meat and cobs of bread. They sat on some crates enjoying the comings and goings of the many people using the ferry to cross to New York. It was hot under the midday sun and for once Brendan was pleased to have cool water instead of coffee.

Anna took Brendan's arm. 'Bren, d'yer realise we've not been husband and wife since Dublin? An' tonight we have a lovely room and I need ter buy some white vinegar.' Brendan shook his head in disbelief, but before he could say a word Anna told him, 'It's part of me secret!' By this time an intrigued Brendan had found out that the Romans had used Anna's secret. He smiled and shrugged; after all, it seemed to be working.

After a brief tour of the shops, and the essential item stored away, the two returned to Mrs Becker's establishment, where Anna pointed out that on such a hot evening it was an ideal time to get some washing done. 'Bren, in these clothes, te'morra we'll be thrown off the train smelling like this.'

Mrs Becker could not have been more helpful and pointed out that it wasn't only clothes that needed a wash, given that they had been travelling for over a month. She loaned them two dressing gowns, or, as she called them bathrobes, and led them to two bathrooms. Mrs Becker quickly checked the ladies' room and showed them two square fully tiled tubs with curtains for privacy. 'We have four baths here for the menfolk. It's rare we get ladies... we use both.'

Brendan had seen a bathhouse in Liverpool during his England travels, but to find a private dwelling with such facilities amazed him. Mrs Becker told them, 'This is for the rail men who can't get home, and when you've been on the footplate for six hours... well, a steam train can be a very dirty job, but I must tell you that your room is for...' she hesitated, 'more the officials.'

She showed them how to operate the taps. 'Mind you, take no more water than you need. It's cold but who wants hot in this weather. Outside, you'll find a washtub, drying frames, and a line. In this heat, your clothes will be dry within the hour.'

The days of staleness began to wash away. Anna wanted to babble away to Brendan. She could hear him next door exchanging greetings with someone, but the joy of the water and its purity made her lie back, relax, and think. *Truly this country invites everyone.* Her thoughts returned to Mollybeg, to her grandma and da. *What will they think when I tell 'em we're on our way ter Scranton? Should I tell 'em we've been robbed and there's a gang after us? No! I'd better not… they're worried enough.* Then, an image of the knifeman tripping over the bricks flashed into her mind; she shuddered and dismissed the thought. She told herself, America is a big country, and we'll find somewhere to settle.

Brendan, after a quick greeting with his fellow bather, sat and listened to him singing in a deep baritone voice. It was lovely to sit in cold water and wash the past month away. His thoughts returned to Mollybeg, to his farm, his work at Moynedale and his work in Derbyshire. Then the morning crashed in: he looked at his swollen knuckle. *Was it only this morning that I had me fight with knifeman? It seems more like a week ago… an' was it only yesterday that we arrived in New York? Mr Peabody – what a gentleman he is – he's said he'll notify the police about the knifeman and absolve me of all blame, but what about the gangs? We must move on, but where? Will Scranton be far enough?* Brendan pushed the thoughts away, and as he dried himself he had a chat with Giovanni, who was from Bologna.

In the yard Anna was waiting, a large basket of their clothes to hand. 'Bren, yer can help me, this morning I did the washing fer the whole Russian Navy.'

Brendan held up his hand. 'Now I would like ter help yer, me luv, but I canna.'

It was then Anna realised how swollen Brendan's right hand was. She thought to say something witty but decided against it. She did the washing and Brendan spread their garments on drying frames. He was struggling to shape Anna's dress when Mrs Becker came out with stretchers; she took over and hung the dress on a standing frame. She then lit a fire in a brick chamber and placed two irons to heat. She explained, 'We always iron outside in summer, it's too hot inside.' She added, 'It's not usually this hot in May.'

Back in clothes, the two returned to sit outside. It was a beautiful evening and as dusk fell, they found a bench behind the washhouse. Brendan sat deep in thought. At length, he quietly said, 'Anna, I feel as if I've lived a week in one day. Is it a dream or did we spend this morning sitting around a fire with strange people eating German sausage?' Anna snuggled in. 'Bren, as I've told yer many times, te'morra is a new day.' She paused. 'And I'll remind yer again, I'm yer woman.'

'Mrs O'Neil, I must tell yer that me desire is rather tempered by this heat.'

'Mr O'Neil, I remember that I made yer forget the cold so...!' She didn't finish. She was right!

CHAPTER 13

During the night they were disturbed by the sound of loud voices. At the breakfast table a dozen men looked up and said good morning, their curious glances made Anna, the only woman there, feel very uncomfortable. After breakfast, they thanked Mrs Becker and walked to the station waiting room to find four of the men from the breakfast table already there. The loud sound of escaping steam and the clatter of wheels brought Anna and Brendan outside.

People gathered to watch; children came from nowhere. Mr Shultz arrived and marked their tickets, and finally, a car was backed into place. Steps were lowered and the passengers climbed aboard. Brendan and Anna chose a seat just inside the car with their faces facing the direction of travel. A stack of cushions served to cover the wooden slatted seats. The seat opposite remained empty as the car filled with fellow travellers. Brendan noted that the eight men who had moved up front must be the engineers, already there seemed to be some sort of heated discussion as plans were laid out along the seats.

Mr Shultz came aboard to wish them bon voyage, followed by a boy carrying a large flagon of water and several glasses. The doors closed; the hoot from the engine and a jolt told the O'Neils they were on the move. Anna looked around to count the seats: eight in all; sixteen people to a car. A small crowd stood and waved as they pulled clear of the station; Anna waved back.

Brendan sat with a calm smile on his face, but his silence told Anna he was struggling with the situation. By now the engineers, in the heat, had divested even their waistcoats, and collars were open. A portly man, wearing distinctive checked trousers was arguing his case, and from time to time glances moved down the car to Brendan.

'Jeeze, I hope they don't call on me. They keep lookin' this way.' Anna could tell that Brendan was indeed the subject of some discussion.

She whispered back, 'We're a couple of Irish turnips. Just look at their clothes; they won't bother with us.' Brendan acknowledged the engineers as they made frequent trips to the water flagon. Anna whispered, 'Well, at least they are friendly.'

For a time, Anna looked out of the window and was thrilled by the countryside, in places it reminded her of the fields of home; but not so green.

At a halt, a man took the seat opposite to the O'Neils. He put down his case, smiled, and leaned over with his hand outstretched. 'I am Lars De Ridder – an old Dutch name, but I was born here.'

Brendan introduced himself and Anna.

'Ah, you are newcomers. Irish, I believe?'

For some reason, Anna took an instant dislike to the man, but couldn't say why. Brendan, as promised, gave little away. 'Fairly new.'

Anna noted his very modern short jacket, his slim trousers flared onto his very expensive looking boots. He wore a very high collar with a cravat in place, and even though it was stifling in the carriage he didn't remove his coat. Instead, he constantly mopped his hot face with a large handkerchief and demisted his rimless glasses every few minutes.

Brendan, feeling the need to be sociable, asked, 'Mr De Ridder, and what line of work are you in?'

'I am an industrial chemist, and you?'

'I'm a stonemason.'

De Ridder nodded wisely, sat back and pulled out a newspaper, the *New York Herald*. From time to time he gave them a tight little smile. Anna felt as if she was under surveillance as his eyes wandered over her body; she decided she didn't like him at all.

Brendan, still ill at ease at the interest shown in him by the engineers tensed when the portly man came down the car. He stopped.

'Sir, I hear you are a man of stone.' He gave a laugh at his joke. 'Will you please join us and give us your expert opinion.'

Brendan moved to the front, his heart racing. He looked at the plans and to his relief recognised the structure. He had studied such plans with his mentor Merryweather. It was a large type of warehouse, very much like the mill he had worked on in Derbyshire.

In his most professional voice and more careful use of English, Brendan asked, 'Gentlemen, what are you going to house in this space?'

A small man answered, 'A large steam engine.'

Brendan considered, and pointed to the girders set on the walls. 'The vibration will push the walls out. You need bigger pillars and pins set in concrete to give strength and stability.'

'What did I say?' A man who had been standing to the back of the group pushed forward but was blocked by a man dressed in striped blue trousers, who seemed to be less than pleased at Brendan's opinion.

'That'll put costs up by a fifth.'

Brendan looked up and replied, 'And if it falls down it will cost a lot more.'

'Thank you, sir. We value your input and you have given us much to think about.' The portly man shook Brendan's hand.

Back in his seat, Brendan listened to the ongoing arguments at the front of the car, and sat with a smile on his face, ignoring the digs from Anna. At length, he turned to her and said, 'Well, me love, I sorted that out fer 'em. When yer've worked on construction in England an experienced eye can soon sort out any problems.'

Anna gave him another dig in the ribs and simply whispered, 'Irish turnip.' However, her pride in her man soon saw her hand move into his and she gave it a gentle squeeze.

It was when the engineers began putting on their waistcoats and jackets, that the O'Neils knew that Scranton was in sight; minutes later their train pulled in. Lars De Ridder put on his bowler hat, tipped it to Brendan and Anna, smiled without a word and left. The two waited until the engineers filed past, each shook Brendan's hand and acknowledged Anna.

The O'Neils walked through the station annexe, turned the corner and stopped in amazement. For them railways were new but before them, cars of coal were lined up on several tracks that wound away into the distance. Behind, stood large factories belching smoke. A steelworks lay to their right and other buildings they could not identify. Brendan, who had visited Manchester in England, could not believe it. It was as he said, like his first visit to England.

Anna grasped his arm. 'Is this the small town yer talked about?'

Walking into the centre, they were amazed to see a vehicle coming towards them. It looked like a tram but, it wasn't pulled by a horse, or run by steam, and as it passed they could read the word electric on its side.

Further on they came to a run of shops and stopped to look at various items that seemed to have come from all over the world. As people passed, Anna gave Brendan's arm a squeeze. 'Bren, d'yer hear the accents? I've heard more Irish than anything and look, there's Paddy Mulligan's Bar.' Brendan's spirits soared; it was true!

Moving on they came to a building where several men gathered outside. They read that jobs were on offer, also accommodation. Inside they joined the queue, and Anna whispered, 'My God, it's like being in Ireland.'

Brendan moved up to give details, and the man behind the desk greeted them with, 'And how's ole Ireland?'

Mr O'Brian had several jobs he could offer and gave Brendan a chit to try at a new factory being built not far away, and he also gave them a list of apartments and lodging houses.

'I think things are looking up. There's work here.' Brendan was back to his positive best.

The building turned out to be a new silk factory that amazed them both. Brendan wasn't even sure exactly what it was, but he found the foreman, a man called Holmes, who told them he was a true American but second generation. His family originally came from Sheffield, in England. He eyed Brendan up and down and he could see his strength. 'If you're a stone man then cobbles shouldn't be a problem. I need a team to set out the yard. Start tomorrow at 6 am – sharp! Oh, the pay is a dollar and a quarter with a bonus for extra duties.'

Delighted, the O'Neils began to try the list of accommodation. The first three read full, the fourth was in such a state they didn't even try. The fifth turned out to be a tall apartment building not far from the town centre, set on a corner, with the name Chester Street fastened to the wall. Inside, in a small vestibule, a woman was busy cleaning behind the desk. She turned, smiled a welcome and said, 'I'm Yvonne, I've a room. You're in luck, a couple left this morning, a dollar down in advance, and pay every Friday.'

She showed them to a second-floor apartment with a kitchen. In the corner, there was a stove and an oven set into a fire-brick surround, with a large metal funnel anchored in the large chimney breast. The area was tiled, with two fire-buckets of sand in place.

'We've had one fire already so be careful. Oh, and mind how you use the gaslight, make sure you turn it off properly, we don't want any accidents. You'll find fuel down the road and we've just had a water supply fitted; there's not many with it around here. All washing is to be done on the ground floor, and there's a bathroom, but you must book a day and time with me. There are lines in the yard for drying, but no clothes out of the window or you'll be out! In winter there's a drying room but there's a twenty-cent charge.'

It was more in rent than the O'Neils wanted to pay but,

as Anna said, 'It's clean, and just look at the tenements we saw in New York and up the road – filthy! And washing strung from every window.'

They explored their apartment: the stove was fine, the oven had a crack, but nothing serious. The bed was hard with only one sheet, but in the heat, it wouldn't matter until colder nights set in. Indeed, the heat was the problem. Their corner room caught the late afternoon sun and even with the curtains closed the sun burnt its way into the room.

'Bren, we've gorra the money. With the four dollars that dear Mr Peabody gave us, and the two from our ship work. I'm boiling over and we haven't eaten since breakfast. Let's go out and find somewhere.'

At a small bar, Bren tried a root beer, his first, which he liked, while Anna had a ginger beer, and both enjoyed a dish of meat and potatoes, followed by an apple pastry with cream. Tired, but in better spirits, they slowly walked back to their apartment and found that the peace of earlier was broken. Shouts came from next door, a woman was swearing at her children, while voices could be heard out on the landing, men talking about their day and politics.

Both lay on the bed; little was said until near eleven o'clock when the sun had closed on their corner room.

Anna's thoughts returned to Mr Peabody. 'What a lovely man, Bren. D'yer realise that the four dollars he gave us is a month's pay. How will we ever be able ter pay him back?'

'Well, yer better with fine words and a pen than me, so, when we're settled do as yer promised and write ter him.'

Anna lay back, her thoughts on fire, life was so different after Mollybeg. She had always been, as her da had said, 'a busy bee'.

'Bren, I don't like the thought of being here all day with yer out so long. I think I'll have a look round ter see if I can find work.'

Brendan gathered her in his arms. 'One day soon, Mrs O'Neil, I hope we'll have a place of our own, so we can cut down on the cost of white vinegar!'

Anna said nothing, children would have to wait… when they had a nice home it would be lovely. She thought of her method, how well it had worked – so far – but for how long? She just said, 'One day.'

Brendan sighed. 'Me darlin', yer never know what life's goin' ter throw at yer. All I know is, life, 'tis said, has its ups and downs but is it all supposed ter happen in one day?'

Anna groaned. 'Jeeze, I now find that I'm married ter a philosopher as well as an expert in construction.' She turned; Bren was asleep.

CHAPTER 14

It was a tired Brendan O'Neil who crawled out of bed. He kissed Anna goodbye and began his short walk to the site of the new silk factory. On the way, he found, even at such an early hour, a roadside newspaper kiosk that also sold coffee and soup. He decided to have a bowl of hot cabbage soup and stood to one side as a continuous stream of workers chose their favourite newspapers.

It was then Brendan decided to buy the *New York Herald*. Anna was keen on reading; moreover, it was a way of finding out how their new country worked. With time in hand, he glanced at the headlines, a story of corruption, politicians involved. He turned to the inner page, read, and such was the shock he almost dropped his soup bowl. He could not believe it, there was a heading that read, LONGSHOREMAN, MURDERED. He read on, a young Irishman, possibly a new immigrant, had beaten a longshoreman called George Salter to death with a brick, while the young woman with him had looked on laughing; it seems an argument had broken out over money. There were two artists' drawings, the one of him could fit a thousand males, but the one of Anna with her long hair cascading from under her bonnet was more of a likeness. It was thought that the couple may have left New York. The police were checking all registrations at the Castle Garden terminal, any information on the couple should be reported to the police.

'Ah, we meet again.'

Brendan turned quickly to find Lars De Ridder standing there. He had that smug look on his face that had irritated Anna. He pointed at the *Herald*. 'Good news gets little attention heh?'

Brendan slowly closed his paper, put it under his arm, his casual behaviour belied the thumping of his heart. He smiled amiably. 'I didn't know industrial chemists made such an early start, Mr De Ridder.'

'Ah, and I didn't know that engineers, even in stone, rose with the dawn.' De Ridder smiled and added, 'I do hope that you and your lovely wife find what you are looking for. There are so many Irish people here you should feel quite at home.' He tipped his hat. 'Good day to you, Mr O'Neil.'

As he walked away Brendan could see he had a *Herald* under his arm. Brendan felt alarmed but he reasoned that with so many Irish in Scranton, it was doubtful that he and Anna could be identified. Would De Ridder make any connection with the newspaper story and them? Yes, he knew they had left New York, but many people were on the move. A further thought came as he entered the silk factory yard, would De Ridder even read the story, one of many criminal acts that newspapers liked to publish.

Putting these worrying thoughts to one side Brendan hurried on, at the same time he exercised his right hand. Fortunately, the swelling had gone down and wouldn't hinder his work too much; he joined Mr Holmes and met his new team.

Jack, from Liverpool, was friendly and humorous and Brendan took a liking to him. The second man was from Belfast, and while friendly, he had his colleague of a few years working beside him.

The cobbles, Brendan noted, weren't the traditional stone type. They were man-made, flatter and larger than the round cobble and cast in concrete with an additive of crushed blue slate, this made them easy to lay as they were regular in shape.

Brendan and his three new colleagues began on the minute at six o'clock. The four of them worked well and while Ed and Ronan did the levelling Brendan and Jack did the laying.

David Holmes, the foreman, was a good man and at a

break, he gave Brendan a large towel and string to tie around his head and warned him that sunstroke could kill you and told him to get a hat with a wide brim. He also admired their handiwork and warned that at the rate they were going they would finish within the month when six weeks had been declared. He added that he could not guarantee work into winter, but he would recommend their labour to anyone in Scranton.

As work finished for the day, Brendan looked down at his legs: his once decent trousers were stained blue and only good for further work; he would have to buy new. His colleagues were all wearing a type of trouser made from a strong blue material with heavy stitching; strong and cheap was Jack's description, and they could be bought at a store quite close. Brendan considered; would his budget allow a new purchase? Anna needed new clothes, he decided against it – for now.

On his walk back to Chester Street the dark cloud that had hovered all day returned. Should he tell Anna about his meeting with De Ridder? He decided not to, the story in the newspaper and its drawing of a young woman with long hair could be anyone, there were dozens of colleens in Scranton with similar hair, though he had noted a change in styles. Many wore their hair pinned up into a variety of shapes. Bonnets were less to be seen, in favour of large flat hats that shielded the sun. He wondered if he dared to suggest to Anna that she hid her pride and glory, he chuckled to himself. No! Life was difficult enough at present.

In the vestibule, Brendan left his *Herald* on a chair. Anna would have a fit if she saw her image in the newspaper. As he climbed to the second floor his thoughts turned to her and how she had passed her day.

After Brendan left for work, Anna felt nervous; it was the first time she had been on her own since Mollybeg. She tried the bathroom, but it was full. In a corridor leading to the yard, she found basins reserved for ladies. A single pump at the yard end sent water shooting along a channel where the user directed it into the basin. Two women looked up, muttered a greeting and carried on. Through the open doorway, Anna could see the men's basins sheltered under a canopy, while to the left eight toilets were housed in a brick building. The one woman, her head wrapped in a towel, stopped behind Anna.

'And where are you from, pet?' Anna knew she was English, but her accent was strange.

'I'm from Donegal, in Ireland.' She was ready for a chat, but the other woman called.

'Come on, Moll, we'll be late for work.'

Work! So, there were jobs out there. Anna, still feeling very apprehensive, made her way out of Chester Street. She turned the corner and passed new footings for a store; the site lay idle. Further on she came to crossroads and found, to her surprise, the rich living so close to the poor. On the far side stood an avenue of grand houses with palm trees in the gardens, while to her left an alleyway led to a tall squalid tenement building with washing strung from every corner. She walked to the alleyway and stopped by a pile of stacked rubbish where some children were playing. Women and men sat in the shade; their curious eyes, while not hostile, made her retreat.

Further on she at last found a little store, it sold everything. It even had a few tables and chairs outside with coffee and doughnuts on offer. Ravenous, Anna sat down and a little portly man with an enormous stomach came out to greet her. He was friendly and curious, and within minutes Anna was back to her full charm and blarney. He told her he was called Danilo and had arrived in America at the age of five.

Anna loved the doughnuts, and though not a coffee drinker its smell and taste were winning her over. He showed her his vegetable boxes at the side of his store, out of the sun. She chose potatoes, onions, a cabbage, and fresh pig's liver from Danilo's cellar store. Anna thanked her new friend, and he told her that if she came by at 9 pm the remains of the day would be hers at little cost. It was then that Anna told him she needed to find work. He pointed to a tall chimney about a mile away. 'Ryan's laundry, you can't miss it.'

Twenty minutes later Anna approached the yard. The smell of steam and soap was overpowering. Girls, no more than ten years old, were scrubbing away at miners' overalls. In the large open doorway, she could see women wringing out sheets and blankets. To the one side, a staircase led to a gallery with a large glass front that overlooked the steaming vats below. Anna could see a woman inside a small office and made her way up the steps. As she approached, the woman, without looking up, said, 'No work this week try next – three girls are leaving – you can guess why.' Anna politely thanked her, which made the woman look up; she made a hand gesture in reply.

Down below Anna studied the rules and pay structure and could not believe that the pay for women was three-quarters of a dollar for a weekly ten-hour day shift, while the few male employees were on a dollar and a quarter!

She returned to Chester Street and it was then she remembered she hadn't any fuel for the stove. Walking on she found the yard called Duggan's, the one mentioned above the fireplace. It listed timber faggots, coal and something she had never heard of before, anthracite. In the yard, she explained to a man, who only had one arm, her need and the type of stove and oven in her apartment. He listened politely and showed Anna to a long shelf with bags and told her that the Indians had discovered anthracite which they called Firestone because it was so hard.

'You must be a newcomer when you don't know that this area is the anthracite capital of the world. All the factories you see here use anthracite. It's harder to light but it gives a greater heat and lasts longer than the black stuff.'

His pack consisted of wooden faggots, broken down anthracite into small, what he called stove pieces, and larger pieces. However, the load was too heavy for Anna to carry, so she borrowed a small trolley and paid a deposit for its return.

Delighted at serving such an attractive young lady, the one-armed man, who asked to be called Frank, gave Anna some tarred hemp and newspaper at no extra charge. 'Start with this and then add the small pieces, it'll soon catch. Mind you, it's hot enough indoors without a furnace going.' Frank pulled a face.

Anna felt pleased with her day. She added Danilo and Frank to her list of new friends.

Back at the apartment, a man who lived on the same landing helped Anna carry her sack of fuel to their apartment.

She prepared their meal and moved to the stove. In Ireland, she had only ever used turf, which some called peat, for cooking. She lit the hemp and newspaper, added the wooden faggots, and waited. Nothing seemed to be happening when a knock brought her to the door. A rather worn, bony looking woman, wearing a thin shift stood there. Under an arm, she held a large contraption. She didn't say who she was but simply held out the thing under her arm and said, 'You'll never light anthracite without this,' she gestured to next door, 'you'll find me there.'

Anna pumped the handles of the large leather bellows and almost instantly the tarred hemp took hold, and a red glow formed. She added the small pieces of anthracite and pumped until her arms were falling off. Satisfied the fire was well alight for cooking, Anna knocked on number nineteen's door. It opened, a hand came through and took the bellows, and a voice said, 'Ta, I'm Sylvie, I'll catch up wid yer.' The door closed and Anna heard her scream, 'You little bugger; now sit down or...'

Back in her own apartment, the door opened, and Anna went to give Brendan a hug. She drew back. 'God, Bren, where've yer been?' She laughed. 'I've heard of the bogey man but never the blue man!'

Anna rambled on about her day as she made dinner. He would love the pig's liver. When she turned Brendan was asleep.

CHAPTER 15

The weeks passed quickly; Brendan put all thoughts of De Ridder to one side. If he had any doubts about them, then, surely by now they would have heard from the authorities.

For the first time, Brendan began to relax and embrace their new life, and while not exactly enjoying his work at the silk factory site, he did enjoy the camaraderie of his work colleagues. He got on well with David Holmes, the foreman. He now had his thick blue work trousers, and a hat called a Stetson, which Anna loved him in.

'My God, the wild Irish boyo has gone. With yer face, so brown, yer look as if yer were born here.' This quite pleased Brendan.

A bonus came when he escaped from cobbles to help lay a stone commemoration plaque to be set into the factory's wall. Along with an elderly Austrian/American called Klaus, an expert at cutting letters, together they finished the work and Brendan had the chance to practise an additional skill of engraving with chisels, not of course on the final work but on a piece of unused stone. Carefully he carved the name Donegal, which met with Klaus' approval. For his work he was paid a bonus of two dollars, then not knowing what to do with his Donegal tablet, David Holmes took it away and sold it to a small company called Donegal Post for five dollars and they shared the profit.

Anna for her part tried to find employment but couldn't find hours to fit in with looking after Brendan when he got home. She liked to cook and have a meal on the table when he walked in. Instead, she found a round of little jobs that often paid in kind.

Some early mornings she helped Danilo set out his vegetables and carry the rubbish up to the main street; this earned a hot coffee and a doughnut, plus some vegetables for her effort. On other occasions, she helped Danilo's wife, Maria – who suffered from back problems – to wash and iron.

One morning she decided to approach the house owners in the rich, palm tree-laden, Delaware Avenue to see if they had need of a maid or helper and was invited in by a Mrs Franco to see if Anna could cope with four children while she went shopping. She didn't ask for references but assessed Anna, as she said, on her gut instinct. And, although an older woman, Mrs Giulia Franco and Anna got on well. She listened, amused as Anna spelled out her life in Ireland, while the children, with ages from five to ten years, also loved to hear her stories; usually about horses.

Mrs Franco was a shrewd woman and quickly detected that possibly money wasn't most urgent to Anna's needs. One day she opened her wardrobe and invited Anna to try on a few of her dresses that she had no further use. She then asked Anna if she had a coat, as winter wasn't too far away, and handed her a coat with a built-in cape, perfect for wet weather. Anna loved it; it was lightweight and easy to carry. This brought back memories of her lovely coat – out there – and how her Grandma Harriet had gained it from a rich lady; life was repeating itself. She felt she had to tell Giulia about her coat stolen in New York. Giulia gave her a hug, placed the garments in a large bag, and money did not get a mention.

On other days, Anna would call but no work was on offer, but it was rare that she left without an item to supplement her kitchen. Mrs Franco had enough saucepans to furnish a restaurant, and she insisted that Anna could help her by throwing some away. Of course, both knew where they would end up, but the game was played out. Over tea, Anna learned more about life in America, and Giulia enjoyed her company as her husband spent so much time away in New York on business. She was also aware of Anna's love of reading, and the stories she told her children seemed to be having a very positive effect on their education.

At Chester Street, Anna, to her surprise, found that Yvonne wasn't quite as remote as she had first thought. Indeed, she was warm-hearted but kept up a business-like persona to deal with her many tenants. One day, after Anna had helped her sort out a blocked drain, Yvonne, over a cup of tea, told her all her troubles. Her husband, with an unpronounceable Polish name, had been killed in a building accident, and the company who owned the apartments had given Yvonne the job as the concierge.

In turn, Anna confided to Yvonne everything that had happened to them since arriving in New York; Yvonne was shocked. She told Anna that Peabody had been right, it was one thing being in the right, but the gangs had their own rules, and the police couldn't be everywhere. Anna decided not to tell Brendan: he would be furious as he often told Anna that not only did she use the confessional, she also told all Ireland.

However, the days were often long while Anna waited for Brendan to come home. Sunday was the one day they had together, though the occasional Saturday saw Brendan home by midday, to allow time for the cobbles to set for the Monday.

Anna had thoughts of going to church, but Brendan was adamant: she would be going on her own. He told her, ''Tisn't you who should be going ter confession but those evil bastards in New York.' He insisted that as they spent so little time together, they should use it to enjoy life, and this came about because of the large Irish community. Ronan introduced them to a club called The Irish Harp, where they could eat at little cost and enjoy some real music and dancing; they both found it wonderful.

In the town centre, growing by the day, they enjoyed a ride on the electric tram. Scranton was, as Brendan said, a town with a future and the amount of building going on would surely see him find further employment when his cobble laying was done. The problem was, finding the time to seek the work, as all factories closed on the Sunday except for the steel mills and furnaces. To this end, Brendan was indebted to David Holmes, who told him that he had put in a word for him, for the new courthouse that was to be built in the autumn. Stonemasons would be needed. Delighted with this news Brendan and Anna began planning.

On the 9th of July Anna told Brendan, 'Yer putting on yer best and we're goin' out ter celebrate.'

'Ter celebrate what?' he asked.

'Me birthday,' Anna told him.

Brendan groaned. He had a vague memory that he had been told, but birthdays were far from his mind. He had even forgotten his own when they were on the barge on the Liffey. He took Anna in his arms. 'I'm sorry, me darlin', I'll get yer somethin' when I can.' Anna wasn't too upset as she had almost forgotten it herself.

That evening, dressed in her new blue dress – well almost new – with the waist taken in, she looked in the mirror and felt pleased; Mrs Franco had good taste and money. Looking at Brendan, dressed in his frock coat and waistcoat, she felt less pleased. He really needed a new outfit, but getting him to spend on himself was difficult, he much preferred buying work clothes, once more she buffed his bowler into shape.

On a lovely evening, they walked to a small restaurant on the edge of the town called La Bistro. Inside they enjoyed a meal quite unlike anything they had ever tasted before. Veal cutlets served with a variety of vegetables, with crusty white bread and wine. The dessert was a choice of cheeses or caramel.

It was while they were drinking coffee that Anna noticed a man, seated across the room at the bar, who seemed to be taking a lot of interest in them, or was it her? At first, pride told her it was because she was female, and some men were very rude in their attentive glances.

However, when Brendan leaned over and said, 'Anna, don't look now but d'yer see the man at the bar in the checked suit? I'm sure I saw him at me site asking questions and he seems ter be very interested in us.'

Anna's anger was growing. Her birthday was being spoilt, their lives had settled to a pattern, now they were again looking over their shoulders.

'Bren, I'll go over and ask him ter join us as he seems so interested.' Brendan put his hand on hers.

'Fer God's sake, Anna, will yer calm down. I'll settle the bill and we'll go but we'll keep an eye on 'im.'

At the desk, Brendan paid the bill and asked Maurice, who had served them well all evening, if he knew the man at the far table. Maurice's face never changed, he smiled, shook hands and quietly said, 'He looks like a Pinkerton man, but I'm not sure.'

Outside, Anna had no idea what a Pinkerton man was. Brendan explained. 'It's a private security and police force set up by a man called Alan Pinkerton in the fifties. Agents are hired to keep an eye on people who step out of line, such as strikers, and anyone who acts criminal against the elected government.' Anna was curious.

'But what's it got ter do with us?'

'Cos the government an' the police use them – they can travel anywhere.'

In a more sombre mood, the two returned to their apartment, the magic of the evening dulled by the dark cloud that once more hung over their heads.

CHAPTER 16

It was a Thursday morning when Anna helped Danilo to sort the rubbish; the wooden boxes came in handy for fire lighting. She lingered over coffee and doughnuts and listened to Maria telling her all about the wonders of Italy, memories from her childhood.

Back at Chester Street, an agitated Yvonne called Anna to her office. 'There's been a guy here asking questions about you, your names. He says he's on government business. I had to tell him as it's in the book, and he knows you're Irish; he must be the Pinkerton man you saw. He'll be coming back. If I were you, I'd leave... move on somewhere.'

Anna was shocked. 'We canna leave in five minutes – we need time.'

Yvonne went to her desk and told Anna, 'I'll sign you out, if Pinkerton returns, you've left, and I don't know where. Clear your room and move up to forty-five. It's a storeroom but good enough for one night.' She added, 'I'll see what I can do.'

David Holmes was pleased. All the cobbles were laid. 'Well lads, you've earned yourselves two days' rest and as your contracts are up on Friday, I'm paying you now with a quarter-dollar bonus.'

Ronan staggered back. 'Ah, me luck has changed at last.'

Holmes smiled, he was used to the Irish, their wit, but he knew they were damned good workers. 'If you take my advice, you'll go down the road to the sidings, there's new offices going up and they need a yard just like this. I've put in a word for you so get there as soon as you can.'

Brendan bid a special goodbye to his foreman. 'Mr Holmes, I thank yer fer yer kindness, but in truth, I've had enough of cobbles an' I'm goin' ter try me luck in town until the courthouse comes up.'

Brendan hurried home, a little later than usual, the boyos had insisted he had a farewell drink with them at The Irish Harp. Tomorrow morning, he would go to a building site near the station where a new hotel was underway, and stone was being used. His thoughts turned to Anna. They could spend more time together, possibly walk out to the Lackawanna Valley, and find a nice place by the river. The moment he walked in he knew something was wrong. Yvonne's anxious face greeted him.

'Christ! Is it Anna?'

'Anna's up in the storeroom, forty-five, on the third floor; she'll fill you in.'

Brendan listened calmly while Anna told him the bad news. 'Yvonne knows all about New York? Christ! Who else have yer told?' Brendan wished he hadn't said it, but the shock brought it out. He saw the tears in Anna's eyes, he sighed and muttered, 'Just when things were goin' our way.' He drew Anna to him. 'Shouldn't we just wait and see? It may be nothin'. The Pinkerton man might be checking us out cos we're new.'

'Wait and see? And what if they take yer AWAY? Yer heard what Mr Peabody said... an' if the police get yer there'll be fifty willing ter swear yer killed him with a brick, and what about the gangs? I've read all about them in the *Herald*.'

The knock made them jump; they looked at each other. Brendan drew a deep breath and slowly opened the door. It was Yvonne; she was excited and spoke rapidly. 'There's waggons going up the Lackawanna Valley tomorrow morning, and I have a friend who's heading cross-country. Pinkerton has spies everywhere, but the chances are they'll be watching the trains. I'll be up before six tomorrow morning and I'll let you out through the back gate. Cut through the tenement opposite, out onto Glebe Street, then down to Coulter's coal yard on your right. Leni will be waiting with his horse and cart. He's a Lenape Indian. He'll take you down to the coal sidings by the river, you'll see the waggons, ask for Thomas Barnwell, and he'll know I sent you. Of course, he'll want payment, but he won't ask questions. With a bit of luck, you'll be able to make your way to Philadelphia; it's a lovely city.' She warned again, 'Keep off the trains.'

Anna looked at Brendan. 'Bren, yer've been paid early, yer contract's up, we've a wee bit saved, and yer've no job till October, let's move on as Yvonne suggests ter Philadelphia. There's work there ter be sure.' She held Brendan. 'I'll be on me own if they take yer away, then what'll I do?'

Brendan breathed deeply, inside his anger smouldered, yet at the same time, he asked himself if Scranton was the best place to settle down. Yes, there was work to be had but he would prefer the open countryside, near a town, but not in it. Yes, move on to Philadelphia, he had been told many times what a fine city it was, with plenty of work. Gently he pushed Anna aside and looked at Yvonne.

'Yvonne, I thank yer kindly. Yer've been a true friend ter Anna while I've been at me work, but I'm wondering as ter why?' Yvonne shrugged.

'Why? The law is the law, but they don't always get it right.' She paused, then added, 'My great-grandpapa found a stray horse, which he took in for the night. They hung him the next day for horse theft.' She moved to the door and said, 'Oh, by the way, I've a half dollar for you, your rent's clear.'

Anna nestled in Bren's arms. 'I know I've gorra gob on me, but if I hadn't told Yvonne she wouldna have looked out fer us.'

'Time ter pack, we'll sleep in our clothes, ready fer anything. If they want ter take me, it'll need more than one.' Brendan raised his fist, gave a grim sort of chuckle, and said, 'After all, I'm the killer from Donegal.' Brendan pulled down a mattress, sorted out all they could carry, and left saucepans and other cooking items just inside the door. He wanted to leave a few of Anna's dresses behind but her face told him to cram them in.

Anna had little sleep, but Brendan slept for a few hours after his hard week's work.

As dawn filtered into their room Anna lit the stove and used bits of wood and paper, enough to boil a pan of water for coffee, the noise brought Brendan awake and without a word he drank.

They collected their things. Anna now had a much bigger bag, full of her dresses, but she wore her coat as the morning was chilly. Brendan still had his sailor's sack, and he also wore a warmer coat bought second-hand from a street market. More importantly, he wore his wide-brimmed hat, both to keep the sun at bay, but also because it made him less conspicuous: his bowler with his sun-bleached hair, he felt, picked him out in the crowd; he had been wearing a bowler when he had hit knifeman.

In the vestibule, Yvonne was waiting. Without a word she led them through the yard to the gate which she unbarred and unlocked. She looked out, waited several seconds and then waved them through. She whispered, 'Good luck.' The door closed.

Anna couldn't hear anything as her heart was beating so loudly. They made their way through the tenement. A man moved from a doorway, looked at them but moved back without a word, Anna's heart beat even faster.

Glebe Street was much longer than they imagined, but as they approached Coulter's coal yard, a horse and cart pulled out, the driver called, 'You from Yvonne?' He moved over and Anna climbed up and sat close to him with Brendan wedged on the outside.

Anna decided to be her friendly best and cheerfully asked, 'You're Leni?' He nodded. She looked at him, he wore a large cape over overalls, but it was his hair that fascinated her. She had read that Indians wore feathers, but this man had his hair plaited high on his head and he wore a large three-fingered wooden comb to the back. He had a broad face with very dark eyes.

Brendan's thoughts turned only to what lay ahead. If they had to continually look over their shoulders to avoid arrest, it might be best, after putting some money aside in Philly to head for Canada.

On the way to the sidings the cart filled with workers; miners judging by their clothes. There was much banter about a woman and little notice was taken of Leni and his two passengers.

The coal sidings bordered a large rail depot with lines of empty cars standing silent ready for the new day. The occasional shudder, the clatter, and the distant sound of an engine told that soon the sidings would come to life. The river was so full of barges that it was difficult to see the water. The five men climbed out, thanked Leni and disappeared into the coal yards.

Brendan had already spotted the three covered waggons that were, in fact, what he knew to be called prairie schooners. A tall man seemed to be in charge who was supervising the storage of furniture in one of the three waggons; he looked up as they approached.

'Mr Barnwell?' Brendan put out his hand.

'Tom,' he replied and tipped his broad-brimmed hat to Anna. 'Got a message from Yvonne last night.' He again looked at Anna. 'Hope you can cook because you'll be travelling in the chuck waggon.' Turning to Brendan he said, 'No free ride here, my friend, and by the look of you, you're a strong young man.' He moved to the lead waggon that had four horses harnessed. 'Hope you know something about horses and mules. When we stop, we give them water and rest; it's hard-going in places. You look after the teams and put your shoulder to whatever I ask – no fee. Do we have an agreement?'

Brendan again shook hands. He judged Tom to be in his forties, his face was tanned which outlined the white stubble of his beard and the hair around his ears that had escaped from his Stetson. He wore what he knew to be a buckskin tunic, matched by his trousers and he wore traditional long riding boots but with low heels. Brendan's regard was instant; he felt he could trust Tom Barnwell. He didn't like being separated from Anna, and he had never worked with mules but it was the price to pay.

Anna climbed aboard the chuck waggon, equally unhappy at the separation, to be greeted by a woman who introduced herself as Alma Miller. Anna judged her to be in her late forties. She was dark in complexion and Anna thought her to be of Italian or Spanish heritage. She had brown eyes, and her hair was anchored in a net on top of her head and on this she wore a black Stetson with a ribbon of red trailing from the crown.

Within minutes any doubts disappeared. Alma was gently spoken and had a kind way about her which set Anna at ease. She explained that the day would be long, and they would prepare food for midday. She pointed to the store of flour, beans, potatoes and a dried type of meat tied in muslin sacks of salt. 'We need to get the salt out. Give it a good wash along the way; we're never far from the river. A good stew, that's what Tom and the men like.'

Alma's daughter Alice was up front to drive the mule team. She was fourteen, a tall girl with a pleasant face, spoilt only by scarring on the one side. As if to read her mind Alma told Anna that their cabin had been burnt down in a riot and Alice had been injured. When Anna asked about Mr Miller, Alma gave a snort of derision. 'Buggered off years back. Drunken swine's most likely dead.'

A little woman called Maggie drove the furniture waggon. Behind, a team of mules pulled an open waggon with seats down both sides. A canopy was slung over the top to give some protection from the sun; in charge was a man called Toby. It soon filled with men and Tom explained they were miners, mainly maintenance men working a Friday to Friday shift. He would drop them off at various points.

At eight o'clock the waggon train set out, and Brendan

found that his duties needed all his strength. On one steep incline, the miners quickly climbed out to help push the waggons over the steepest parts. However, it was the soft ground close to the river that caused wheels to sink, and it was here that Brendan, very familiar with the problem, quickly organised the men into attaching ropes to the back spokes and using bracken under the wheels to get clear. All this met with Thomas Barnwell's approval, and by midday, the two were on familiar terms, while Alma reported that Anna was, 'a dear girl.'

Under a canopy of trees, Tom brought the waggons to a halt for dinner. Anna had a quick word with Brendan. 'My God, Bren, it's really beautiful along here, much greener than I thought.' Brendan nodded.

'I could live here, just look at the soil, Christ, yer could grow vegetables three feet high.'

'Ah! Me farmer boyo's back, is he?'

'The man who has more than one string ter his bow will always find work.'

A fire was quickly made, and Anna and Alma began the cooking. While this was going on Brendan led the horses and mules down to the river for a drink and tethered them on a long-running rope to a tree. Tom helped but he didn't ask any questions. Brendan, after his misplaced trust in Paddy, decided that he would give little away.

After dinner, the cards came out. Brendan, who had never been a keen player, watched as the miners argued and passed over money. At one point he even stepped in to sort out an argument. Toby sat with the miners and seemed to be a winner.

On the move again, the waggon train followed a flat forest track, and Brendan had a chance to talk to Tom, to ask where they were heading.

'Harper's Drift; there's not much there at present but it will grow quickly once they finish the gravity railhead. It'll link with the canals and carry mostly anthracite. There's several mines scattered around the area. The coal will load straight into the barges, and I'm told there'll be a railhead all the way to Scranton soon.' He further explained that a few of the men would leave before Harper's Drift and walk overland to their mining villages. He would then return miners to the good life in Scranton, and to their families. He added that the coal mines of Scranton were overstaffed, mainly by Irish immigrants, and the pay was very poor. Tom laughed and asked, 'My friend, is there anyone left in Ireland?'

At a place called Twin Forks, four miners waved goodbye, and the teams were rested. Coffee was passed around, and Alma, with cooking finished for the day, told Anna to get Brendan on board as the track was good all the way to Harper's.

Late evening the waggons rolled in and Anna and Brendan climbed down to the most desolate sight they could ever have imagined. To their right, a huge incline was partly tracked with rail lines that ran past a half-built brick building, shovels and picks lay outside as if discarded in a hurry. In front stood a tall wooden building with the name Harper's Drift emblazoned over the top, underneath it advertised itself as the general store and hotel, and behind this lay a haphazard collection of shacks and tents; few people were around. The miners bid a noisy farewell and made their way to a track leading to the upper canal path and disappeared.

Tom and Bren followed the furniture waggon to a timber house in a clearing and helped Maggie, along with two men from the house to unload. For his last task of the day, Brendan led the horses and mules to an unscarred field some distance away, and taking Tom's advice, he kept the mules away from the horses.

Back at the waggons, Tom and Alma talked about their plans, and it was obvious, at least to Anna, that Tom and Alma were more than good friends. It was Alma who suggested that they stayed overnight and had a good rest before setting out for Philly.

Brendan looked around: could there be a more miserable

scene? He considered taking to the canal path, to find a barge for the night, but the thought of yet another night, possibly under the stars, had lost its appeal. Brendan didn't argue when Anna said, 'Bren, let's try the hotel, we need ter gerra our heads down.'

Tom shook hands. 'Good luck to you both. Who knows, our paths may cross again.'

He tipped his hat to Anna and climbed into the waggon to join Alma; Alice gave them a wave as they headed for the hotel.

The O'Neils entered the hotel and general store to find a large open room with a bar that also served as the reception. In one corner two men were playing a type of billiards. A staircase led from the other corner, and a sign, rooms 1–8 hung on a wooden frame. The restaurant was curtained off just past the bar. Brendan gave the handbell a ring and a large man, wearing an apron, came from behind the curtain. He had a rather surly look about him, but he gave a welcoming smile that changed his whole appearance.

'We'd like a room fer the night.'

'Sorry, folks, all the rooms are taken. However, you'll find empty tents behind here. Take your pick, the workers are off till Monday.'

From behind the same curtain, an elderly woman poked her head. 'Hi, I'm Alvira. If you're bedding down behind here, I can put you down for breakfast, from seven to nine.'

Brendan, always a believer in a good breakfast to start the day, agreed and Alvira wrote down their names.

Outside, Brendan turned to Anna. 'Jeeze, Anna, I've seen some places, but this must be…' he shook his head. By now Anna could read Brendan's moods and knew that his thoughts were back in Scranton. Life was beginning to feel good; they had made new friends, work was to be had, and their apartment was adequate, and with winter not far away he saw Scranton as a stepping-stone to something better. He had said repeatedly: 'Lie low fer a bit – save – and then move on.'

'Bren, things will look different in the morning. With a bit of Irish luck, we might reach Philly in two ter three days.' Brendan gave a shrug.

In the late evening light, they found one tent reasonably clean without clutter. Once again Brendan's waxed blanket served its purpose. He pulled Anna onto his chest; she loved his strong arms around her. 'Well, Anna O'Neil, d'yer wish yer'd never come ter me door in Donegal?'

'As I told yer then, Brendan O'Neil, what would yer do without me?'

CHAPTER 17

Both slept well until the early hours of the morning. It was Brendan who awoke first: lumps and bumps in the ground that hadn't existed before suddenly found his back and hips. Trying not to disturb Anna he crept out but in doing so he pulled the blanket away. Anna's eyes opened.

'What time is it, Bren?' Brendan cursed; he'd forgotten to wind his watch.

He looked out to the hotel where smoke was rising from the chimney, he could hear voices in the kitchen. 'Time ter move, I think.'

To the rear of the hotel, there was a yard for washing down the waggons and a pump that fed a trough; it was cold but refreshing. Anna tried to smooth her clothes into shape, she looked at Brendan and said, 'God, Bren, we must look like scarecrows. Brendan was less concerned, and they entered the hotel and stopped in surprise. The dining room was crowded, extra tables were spread across the room. Over thirty pairs of eyes looked at them in equal surprise, but it was a short, stocky man, who got up and greeted them. 'We meet again.'

Brendan remembered him: he had been on SS *Trojan* with his wife and two children on the Atlantic crossing. They had passed the time of day, but Brendan remembered that Anna had taken a liking to his wife. She was from Castlefinn, Donegal, while he was from Dublin. Brendan shook hands, while Anna and the woman embraced; their two children looked on smiling. The man smiled.

'I'm Dan O'Hara, and this is me wife Bridget, and that's Kevin and the little one is Sean.' As the two women moved apart, he patted his wife's stomach and said, 'We havena named this one yet. Pull up a table and join us.'

Alvira quickly brought up a table and chairs, and breakfast was served. Brendan and Anna received a plate of pancakes with a slice of bacon with beans. It wasn't to their liking but looking around, everyone had the same.

This brought Brendan into a long conversation with Dan. It turned out that their stories were similar. The O'Haras had lodged with a relative in New York before moving on to Scranton, where he had worked in a coal yard. However, finding pay poor and accommodation difficult, with two kids and one on the way, they had found out about a mining village called The Parade, three miles down the track from Harper's.

Brendan outlined their adventures since arriving in New York, except that he did not mention the attack and robbery by the Irish crew. He looked across at Anna who was animatedly talking to Bridget; he hoped she hadn't blabbed their full story.

Dan O'Hara looked around the table. 'I'll do anything to earn a penny, even mining. I've worked the coal barges at Queenstown, so it can't be any worse. With winter not far away, we need ter get settled and at The Parade, yer get a cabin. Where else will yer find a job with accommodation thrown in?' Dan O'Hara sat back to let his words sink in, then leaning forward he added, 'With Bridget in the family way we need ter find a place, but it's only a start. Once the baby's strong enough we can move on.'

At this, Bridget excitedly asked, 'Why don't yer join us? It'll be nice ter have friends, and yer'll have a roof over yer heads.' Anna looked at Bren. Mining? Bren a miner?

Brendan sat deep in thought without a word. Alvira busily moved from table to table collecting her dues. Brendan paid without really looking at the bill, he looked at Anna; he knew what she was thinking. A roof of their own over their heads with winter on the horizon and friends next door had appeal. He wouldn't have to do it for long, they could move on once winter was over. However, as he sat passively with a gentle smile on his face, a kaleidoscope of thoughts ran through his mind.

All I want ter do is ter be me own man. I'd love ter find a farm along the Lackawanna. I can use me stonemasonry as a back-up; both would suit me fine. I've moved from farmer to stonemason, labourer, and now it looks as if I will become a bloody coal miner. Surely in time, it will be fergotten, Pinkerton must have better things ter do than chase me. However, in the meantime, it might be best ter lie low. It's doubtful anyone will think of looking fer me here, it's such an out of the way place. At a guess, any search will move ter Philly.

Anna's thoughts were somewhat different. *Would the work be any more different ter that he was doing in Scranton? After all, he came home covered in blue slate dust. And, being a miner doesn't mean he'll be working underground, there are plenty of jobs ter be done above ground. I'm sure his stonework will find favour.*

In a confidential manner, Dan O'Hara said, 'When the waggon comes in just climb aboard, they're expecting twelve and twelve they'll get. A couple haven't turned up. I know, because they've stayed in Scranton. Just tell them yer've taken the place of the missing couple. There must be a cabin for yer, and I'm told the cabins are solid timber. We met a fella in Scranton, and he says they're okay.'

All this time Bridget looked on hopefully, the thought of a friend from Donegal was too good to be true, and Anna seemed to get on with her kids. She looked at Anna with a smile that told her to say yes, then she turned to look at Brendan.

Brendan had made up his mind, while he was away at his work a good friend to Anna was worth having. 'I think I'll give it a go till winter's over.' Bridget hugged Anna, while Brendan stood to one side. For some reason, he instinctively liked Bridget but there was something about Dan that worried him. Kevin and Sean caught up in the moment hugged the skirts of the two women, then, encouraged to play, they dashed outside.

Coffee was hastily arranged on tables under the sidewalk awning while Alvira and her team began clearing the dining room. As they finished, an open carriage arrived to take some of the diners to a village called Mogram, that lay seven miles away, and this disappeared down a track that ran away behind the hotel; all had been on a spree to Scranton.

The party of twelve bound for the mining village, called The Parade, assembled in the bright July sunshine. Brendan tried to take in his fellow travellers, but Dan kept up a monologue of grievances and injustices against seemingly only himself, all perpetrated by the English. Brendan didn't argue, he had reason to thank an Englishman for his new-found skill and his kindness.

Of those waiting Brendan had a quick greeting with the Welsh couple. Their boy, about eight years of age, was playing with the O'Hara children. The three single men, he picked up in conversation, were clay miners from Cornwall. The final couple, a young man with an older woman said little and sat some distance away. Brendan could see they were nervous and looked exhausted; later he found they hardly had a word of English.

It was when the three Cornishmen were talking to Dan that Brendan was shocked to hear the man, called Malcolm, complain. 'To get a cabin you have to sign a contract for at least two years; otherwise, you have to share a barrack.'

'Is this true? Did yer know this?' Bren challenged Dan.

Dan looked a little uneasy. 'Well, two years will soon go; it's nothin'.'

It was in this instant that Brendan knew that Dan was a windbag, with a careless tongue; not a man he would ever trust. The problem was his wife was a lovely girl, and he could see that Anna got on well with her, while their two children were respectful and under control.

Anna was equally shocked and shared Brendan's apprehension. Two years was a long time and she wished that Dan – and Bridget – had mentioned this before. The tension was relieved when Dan, to her relief, took this opportunity to sidle away to engage the Welsh couple in conversation.

Bridget, concerned at her new friend's dismay, told Anna.

'Dan never told me yer had ter sign fer two years.' She added, 'I leave these matters ter him.'

Brendan, needing time to think, moved away: he asked himself if he should tell Bridget and Dan that they had changed their minds, they would be moving on because two years wasn't in their plans. It was then the cloud of Pinkerton settled in his mind. He thought of Anna's distress. *What would happen ter her if he was arrested? He couldn't take the risk.*

Decision made his interest was aroused by a gang of men who appeared at the head of the gravity railway. He walked to the top and found a canal basin full of barges. Behind lay a landscape ruptured by shallow mining, and the remains of a forest. Some trees were struggling back to health, while other areas reminded him of a battle scene. The canal stretched away to a bend and disappeared behind a hilly outcrop. In the far distance, a range of mountains looked very blue in the hazy sunshine. Away to his left, a line of waggons on rails pulled by mules came from the forest of birch. The animals struggled to pull the loaded carts of anthracite round the knoll that climbed to the basin. Brendan wanted to see the loading but a shout from below told him the carriage for the mine had arrived.

In fact, the carriage was a converted waggon that brought forth admiration from onlookers, because it had cushioned seats with a padded handrail that ran the length on both sides, while the back folded down into a stepped entrance most suitable for ladies. Most eye-catching was the wooden canopy frame with a fabric liner and the name, Glenvale Mining Company outlined in red letters against a dark green background.

Two men sat up front and they were in a hurry. The driver was dressed in a long dark tunic and wore a bowler hat, while the second man wore a grey suit with an extravagant silver and black waistcoat; and he was in charge. 'My name's Henry, welcome to Glenvale Mining. As I call out your names you will fill up the seats from the front.'

Anna and Brendan waited until the name O'Sullivan was repeated, Brendan stepped forward and said, 'It's O'Neil, not O'Sullivan.' The man adjusted the name on his sheet and the two climbed aboard. Minutes later the waggon moved out and took the route they had come in on. After a mile it took a track off to the right that led them onto what Brendan could see was the coal run to the canal basin. In places, the route had been reinforced with shale and gravel.

The contrast between their colourful transport and the scene that met their eyes could not have been greater when they arrived at the village called, The Parade. A large weathered wooden store, with a sidewalk and a timber canopy, filled the small square. A water trough for horses stood in front, while an older model had been filled with soil. The sign on the building simply read Wozniacks General Store, with a notice listing all the wares on offer. A silence settled on those in the waggon.

As Anna said later, she had never seen such a drab, grey scene. The Parade was a line of log cabins that stretched down a slope, and any colour was hidden under a blanket of coal dust. To the right stood a large wooden hall with a small tower that suggested it could be a church. Around this, an effort had been made to create a garden, but with little success. Even the forest beyond looked dull and uninviting, while the road was a blackened strip. To the left, a dirt track ran off to a collection of buildings set amidst the stumps of trees and poorly filled mine workings.

As if reading the silence, Henry told them, 'Not seen at its best today but a good downpour will freshen everything up.' He then referred to his list and called out the names and cabin numbers. 'O'Neils? Number twenty; you're the last cabin.'

Brendan asked Henry, 'Can I see the contract?' He got no further.

'You'll find it in your cabin, sign and give it in on Monday and if you don't like it you've got two hours to get out.'

Anna grabbed Brendan's hand; she knew that disrespect

was something he would not ignore. 'Bren, come on, let's see our cabin.'

As they walked down the line of cabins, Anna felt a sense of panic. The thought of having Bridget and her two lovely children as friends had appeal, but now she wondered if they should move on; it wasn't too late. However, as they reached number twenty, Anna, ever the optimist exclaimed. 'At least we only have neighbours on the one side, we've a wee bit more space than the others.'

Brendan said nothing. He took the key from the side door and opened it. Inside, the two stood looking around their new home – if they decided to stay. The furniture was primitive: the single table was made from rough sawn timber, as were the two chairs; the bedroom was offset without a door, while the bed was attached to the wall and consisted of wooden slats. In a corner lay two large bed sacks filled with straw. To the rear, there was a scullery with a large brick-built chimney in the corner, and alongside a brick oven with the iron fire grate in the middle with an ash pit underneath, the floor was brushed earth to prevent fire. Just inside the doorway sat a metal tray, with two oil lamps and a small bottle of oil, and a note telling them that further supplies could be bought at the store. Outside, there was a small yard and another simple brick oven for use in the summer. A pile of anthracite lay piled up, and some kindling. A timber rail marked their territory.

Brendan pulled Anna to him. 'Jesus, after Scranton this is…' He was lost for words.

CHAPTER 18

A sense of panic hit Anna: she felt that it was because of her that Brendan had decided to stay. However, she looked around their cabin and thought that with a woman's touch it could be quite nice. 'Just look at the timber, it's got lovely patterns, I think it's very decorative.'

Brendan pointed out the chinks of light coming through the walls, and around the chimney. 'They'll need fixing before winter sets.'

On the table lay the contract: Brendan opened it and read it out to Anna. It could not have been more explicit. The accommodation was reserved for those signing for two years, agreeing to undertake duties at the behest of the company, the said Glenvale Mining Company. Work would begin at 6 am and finish at 6 pm. Wages would be paid on a Friday evening.

Brendan half-listened as Anna outlined her plans for their new home, but his thoughts were different. *We can do somethin' with the cabin, but mining underground all day, it's no way ter make a livin'. Jesus, one minute I'm a farmer, the next I'm laying cobbles, and now?* He looked at Anna and thought of her words. If he was taken what would happen to her? He didn't dare give it another thought.

He pointed at the contract. 'That is bloody slavery.'

Anna quietly said, 'Bren, it'll only take an hour ter get back ter Harper's an' like yer said we can move on ter Philly.' Brendan gave a sigh, opened his arms, then let them drop. 'So, we're staying?'

'Contract be damned, when the good weather comes, and we've gorra few dollars in our pockets we can slip away.' Brendan picked up the leaflet for the store at the head of The Parade, called Wozniacks. 'We need bedding, blankets.

Straw be damned, straw is fer animals and I'll not have yer sleeping on straw. We need food, and we have enough money ter cover it, let's go.' Brendan had made up his mind.

They walked past their new neighbours' cabins. At number sixteen they could hear the excited voices of the O'Hara children. Brendan wondered as to why any man would bring his family to such a place.

The store was a warehouse that tried to meet the demands of a people locked away from the normal intercourse of life. They looked around, bought potatoes, vegetables, coffee and flour, and then checked out the prices on bedding, towels, work clothes and on all the basics they would need for a long stay. It was when they found a corner with a sign telling them that goods could be bartered that Anna gripped Brendan's arm. 'I'll be back in a minute, wait here.'

Ten minutes later Anna was back carrying her bag and they joined the queue behind the three Cornish men, who were already talking about moving on. Brendan knew better than to stop Anna when an idea filled her head, once in her determined mood, nothing would stop her.

Mrs Wozniack turned her attention to them, the newcomers. Brendan judged her to be about fifty. Her grey hair was tied tightly in place by a red ribbon at the back. She wore a blue overall that reached the floor. Two large pockets on the front had embroidered motifs. She smiled a welcome. 'I can get you anything you want if you give me a few days.' Her accent was pronounced but her speech clear.

Hardly taking a breath Anna launched into her charm offensive. 'Mrs Wozniack, we only arrived here an hour ago and we have need of what yer might call essentials. I can only tell yer that we have a cabin I wouldna put an Irish pig in, and as I see yer have a barter corner, I'm going ter put yer in the way of two dresses straight from the halls of New York.'

Anna pulled out the two dresses she had never worn, given to her by Giulia Franco. 'They've never seen the light of day, till now, and all they need is a good iron, and just look at the hems, clean as the day they came from the couturier.' Anna drew back, spread her arms. 'Now, Mrs Wozniack, sure a good lady like yerself, I can tell, from foreign parts, can help us.'

Brendan stood impassive trying hard not to laugh, his mind flashed back to when Anna had first knocked on his door. He wondered where she had got the French word from.

Mrs Wozniack listened patiently, then clapped her hands and burst out laughing, tears sprung to her eyes, which she dabbed at with a loose apron. She shook her head and said, 'Everyone calls me Nadia. I need a laugh, but these dresses had better be good.' She handled them gently, then looked at the labels, and nodded approvingly. She held the blue and grey one against her body and sighed, 'It's years since I've seen this finery, what are you looking for in return?'

Anna moved to the barter corner and said, 'Nadia, I'll be straight with yer. We haven't a bean, and with winter comin' up we need blankets and anything yer can throw in.'

Nadia Wozniack looked around and gestured for them to follow her to a back room. She pointed to a pile of bedding: a mattress, blankets that looked like army issue, cushions, an old carpet only slightly worn and a cracked mirror. 'This has been here for almost two years. I have a ticket, but it should have been claimed a year back, I'd like it out of here.'

Brendan and Anna were delighted. The only problem was, as Nadia explained, that it would be better not to be seen with such a load, and she told them that Joe, her helper, would deliver all when it was dark. They thanked Nadia, paid for their groceries and were about to go when Nadia took Anna to one side.

'My little Irish lady, the dresses, as you say, need a good ironing, and I may have to alter one but...' She put her fingers to her lips. 'You've never seen them before.' Anna smiled and put her fingers to her lips.

It was near ten o'clock when a knock told them Joe was

outside. A boy of about fourteen, who wore a built-up boot on his left leg stood looking at them. Brendan helped him unload the large handcart. Joe told them that if they left a pan out in the morning, he delivered milk. He told them to pay Nadia on Fridays. Anna agreed and the boy slowly wrote their names in his pocketbook.

Within the hour the bed was made, the carpet down, the cushions in place on the crude chairs, with the two spare on the bedroom floor. In addition, they found a curtain that Brendan hung on nails to separate the kitchen area. From a nail already in place, they looked at themselves in the cracked mirror; suddenly, it looked more like a home.

Brendan sighed, picked up the contract. 'I suppose I'd better sign this.'

CHAPTER 19

It took a minute for Brendan to adjust to their new bedroom. He looked around its sparse furnishing, then at Anna who always slept with a slight smile on her face, as if she were having a lovely dream. Carefully he moved to the living area. He had slept surprisingly well aided by the coolness of their cabin. This he put down to the thickness of the timbers, and the absorption of heat. The thought came: *cool in summer, and possibly a bit warmer in winter.*

He looked at his watch – only 7 am. He moved to the yard; it was a lovely morning. He sat on the rough wooden bench enjoying its coolness, and the silence. Along the back of the cabins, there was a ridge covered in shrub, with wispy trees dotted here and there. In places, the ground fell away to reveal sandy, shale ruptures where someone had been digging. Brendan noted that the only green to be seen was along this ridge, obviously the water source that fed the two water pumps situated at either end of The Parade. His eyes moved to the path that led past their cabin: it climbed to a knoll that led only to the sky. Always fond of walking, Brendan promised himself he would explore over the rise.

He lit the fire in the yard and waited for the anthracite to take hold. It was then he realised that the flat rush woven shield, leaning against the wall, was for fanning the flames.

He was pouring the coffee, with the scrambled eggs and potato cake still in the pan when Anna appeared. She didn't speak, put her arms around Brendan's neck, gave him a hug, and sat down at the small trestle table. He moved behind her, swept her hair back, pulled it to one side, and kissed her neck; she loved this gentle show of affection. It reminded her of the first time Brendan had kissed her.

Brendan sipped his coffee, sighed and said, 'Anna O'Neil,

I look at yer and I want yer but we have a busy day ahead of us and I think we should call on our neighbours and find out what we've let ourselves in fer.'

Breakfast over, Brendan, dressed in his clean blue trousers held in place by a broad belt – instead of the favoured braces – a clean shirt, and wearing his broad-brimmed hat, placed Anna's arm through his and declared in his best English accent, 'Mrs O'Neil, it's time to inspect the local peasants.'

Anna felt less sure, her favourite blue-grey dress was still full of creases after its journey in Brendan's pack; she hoped they would fall out on their walk. Looking more closely into their cracked mirror she noted the redness in her face and chose her best large bonnet with a peak to keep the sun off her face. She looked at Bren: she loved him in his wide-brimmed hat, so different from the Irishman who had set out from Donegal.

Few people were out, but as they neared the top of the rise, close to the store a door opened, and a woman smiled and said, 'Welcome ter little Ireland.'

Her husband joined them, and they introduced themselves as David and Eileen Kearny from Tipperary. David explained, 'The cabins from one to twenty are Irish, around the corner yer'll find the Welsh, but not many, and the Scots are higher up. The large building yer see there is called the barracks, and yer'll find people from every corner of Europe. And if yer look behind the store yer'll find the stewards' houses and the even better houses of the police – much better than these.'

A worried Brendan repeated, 'Police?'

David shrugged. 'Private police who work fer the colonel, the only thing they do is look after the colonel's land. Best not ter get in their way.'

Eileen was quick to point out that the cabins were, in her opinion, good compared with other places they had been. David seemed content. 'I'm an engineer, not a miner, I have ter make sure the tubs and equipment are kept running; I'll be working this evening.'

They said goodbye and went into the store to say hello to Nadia. They thanked her for sending Joe with the bedding and other items. She put up her hand. 'Stop! We've forgotten the most important thing; you'll need a bath every day.' She pointed to a wall hung with a variety of large metal tubs. 'I'll have Joe deliver later today – the used ones are to the right, you can have it on tick, twenty cents a week, pay on Friday with your milk.'

They said goodbye to Nadia and walked in silence up the track, past the outbuildings beyond the store, and turned between stacks of seasoning timber. Across the track, a banner read, Glenvale Mine. Beyond lay a hillside covered with scrub and bushes, and underneath two tunnels cut into the side. Men were moving around at the entrance. Piles of timber stood to the one side, while the anthracite lay behind the hill in a miniature mountain. A line of coal tubs came from a side tunnel away to their right. Brendan wanted to move closer but was halted by the single pole barrier across the track; behind stood a large wooden office-type building. As they moved to go around the pole, a voice called. 'It's there for a purpose, you know.' A man stood in the doorway.

'I'm starting work here on Monday and I just want ter gerra a feel of the place.'

The man smiled. 'I'm Oliver Carew, assistant manager to Frank Crosby, who'll you'll meet on Monday, it'll save time if I find you a hat and a lamp, follow me.'

In a large hut adjoining the office, Brendan tried on stiff felt hats until one fitted tight. Mr Carew pointed out they used oil lamps, not candles; much safer he told him. Brendan signed, and both were placed in a box with his name and a number that he was told to use when he clocked in. He also signed the contract. 'Throw your cabin one away,' advised the assistant manager, 'you're all set for Monday.'

Mr Carew, possibly bored at so little to do and pleased to impress the delightful young lady before him, displayed his knowledge of mining in the area. 'At one time around here, you could scrape anthracite off the surface, which is why the landscape is so churned, but it's all long gone, and now there are drift mines all over the place. However, the colonel's mine is extensive and going deeper. You'll see for yourself on Monday.' Mr Carew paused before adding, 'The colonel will make a fortune when the railhead comes. Mark my words, you'll have a job here for no more than two years. When Harper's is up and fully running The Parade will close down.'

They thanked Mr Carew and slowly headed back. Anna didn't speak, she was alone with her thoughts, and couldn't think – for once – of any bright things to say. Brendan's only thought was, *how has it come ter this?*

Back at The Parade people were on the move, mainly the womenfolk. Anna suggested knocking on every door to introduce themselves. From number two, they worked their way down, but few answered. Were they out at work, or not answering? At number fourteen, a very harassed woman peeped out, pulled a child back and muttered, 'Good luck ter yer.'

At number sixteen Bridget came out and they swapped observations on their cabins, she insisted on showing them around. Apart from an extra bedroom on the back, that took all the yard space, there was little to see, though Bridget had been left curtains by the previous tenants, and she was pleased with these.

At number eighteen they had a warm welcome from Jonas and Millie Kelly. Jonas told them they had been in America since childhood; their parents had crossed in the twenties. Brendan took an immediate liking to the couple and it gave them an opportunity to find out more about The Parade.

'Anna and me are fond of a bit of rabbit, and I think there must be some in the forest. Surely this colonel doesn't mind losing a few?'

Anna added, 'In the store, all yer can find is fish and

we've had enough ter last us a good year.'

Millie shook her head. 'Don't go there, the colonel has his stewards, led by a man called Watts.'

Jonas shook his head. 'He's a brute, don't cross him, he'll shoot you on sight.'

'Yer mean all that,' Brendan waved at the forest, 'is all his?'

Jonas shrugged and said, 'It's all laid out in your contract – you'll find notices wherever you go.' Brendan tipped his hat back.

'I find it hard ter believe… hard work needs fuel in the belly.'

Millie nodded agreement, but added, 'There are much worse places than Glenvale. Many speak ill of the colonel but give him his due, he doesn't ask where you're from and you don't see notices, no Irish, no Catholics.'

Anna was shocked, she struggled to find words. 'No Irish?'

Jonas shrugged. 'We Irish aren't too popular, there's just too many of us and we take all the jobs.'

Millie broke in, 'Aye, the colonel asks no questions, you do your work, obey the rules and you should be okay. You'll do a twelve-hour shift and you get half an hour break midday. I know it's hard graft, but Frank Crosby and Oliver Carew are good men; we look out for each other.'

They said goodbye with the promise of a visit when they had settled. This left only number nineteen, but Jonas told them that the Murphys were away until Monday after their trip to Scranton.

Anna made soup at midday. Afterwards, Brendan set about work to improve their cabin. From the hillside, he found willowy young trees only finger thick. When trimmed they could be forced into any cracks between ill-fitting wall timbers, but it was the roof that worried him. The overlapping timbers would do well in the short-term to keep out rain, but around the chimney, he could see chinks of light caused by shrinkage of the timbers in hot weather. To solve this Brendan walked down the track to a notice fastened to a tree close to a footbridge called Kroos. He read that the property belonged to Colonel Jeremiah Caswell, and all that he had read in his contract was laid out in the notice. A big sign read PRIVATE.

Of interest to Brendan was a natural pool of thick black tar that oozed from a hole in the sandy shale close to the bridge. To stem the flow a bank of waste anthracite had been built that formed a vile-smelling pit. Brendan had worked with tar in Derbyshire to treat timbers; however, he had given little thought to its origin as it came in a barrel. To see it now, bubbling from the ground, was a strange experience; but one to put to good use. With a branch, he wound on a long skein of tar, and back on the roof he worked it into the crevice around the chimney along with a length of hemp Anna had found discarded across the track. Later, he told Anna he would use his grandpa's trick and lay turf on the roof.

There was little they could do indoors until they found the money to buy new furnishings, so Brendan turned his attention to the backyard, where he re-dug the privy and brought in lighter soil he'd found behind their cabin.

Late afternoon, they decided to explore the land behind their cabin, and climbed the slight rise to a dead tree that dominated the skyline, its branches clutching at the sky as if in pain; they stopped.

'My God,' it was Anna who broke the stillness. Stretching away over hill and rise was the most desolate landscape she had ever seen, only broken by the stumps of trees that stood like gravestones. 'There's not even a bird, never mind a rabbit.'

They walked on until they breasted another hill. 'Now this is better.' Down below Brendan could see the river and the forest. A rough path led down through a tangle of shrub and tree, and they followed this until they came out into a clearing. It was then they saw the camp, a collection of improvised huts and tents partly hidden by a grove of birch trees. A dog came running towards them and stopped yelping at their feet, Anna went to stroke it, but Brendan pulled her back.

The dog was called to heel by a man ahead of an approaching group of men. Anna froze, she could see they were Indians, dressed in a bizarre collection of traditional dress and western clothes. 'Smile and stand still,' Brendan told her. There were six in all, three boys no more than fourteen stood to the back, while the three men stood in a circle around them. The one wore an animal skin hat, a necklace of different coloured stones, while his jacket was western and his trousers of the hard-wearing type common to mineworkers and farmers. The other men wore skin trousers and hide waistcoats over a type of vest. Their arms were naked and adorned with an assortment of bangles.

They stood in front of Brendan obviously impressed by his height and build. Brendan smiled in a friendly way, his hands in his pockets; that is until the group moved to Anna.

Their leader, who had his black hair held by a wooden comb across the back of his head, went to touch Anna's bonnet. Brendan took his hands out of his pockets, Anna moved back, the leader laughed and said to his colleagues, 'Bon – net.

Brendan decided it was time to join in, laughed out loud and repeated, 'Yeah, bonnet.' In a second the mood changed.

In halting English, the western dressed man asked them, 'You from?' He pointed back to The Parade; Brendan nodded. The Indian translated for his friends, then pointed at the ground. 'We told go away, this white man land. Now you come here, this Indian land.'

Brendan explained they had come from far away and didn't know the ways of the white man, or the Indian. 'Why come now?' the Indian asked.

'We're hoping ter find a few rabbits fer the pot.'

At first, the Indian didn't understand but when he did, Brendan's answer could not have had a more rapturous response. As Anna said later, 'It could not have had more laughs than in a Dublin theatre.' The men and boys howled with laughter. The leader pointed behind them.

'No cottontail here; cottontail over there.' Brendan decided not to tell them that they could not catch rabbits there because it was owned by a white man.

It was Anna who confirmed an uneasy friendship. She took off her bonnet and the Indians gasped in appreciation as her hair spilled out. Anna held out her bonnet to the Indian and said, 'This is a present fer yer wife.'

He took it as if it were a precious ornament, looked at them, then he slowly shook hands with Brendan and said, 'Very good for fishing.' This brought forth another burst of laughter, the Indian smiled, 'You go now.' The men turned, obviously in good humour and ran back to the camp, headed by the black and white dog.

Brendan and Anna retraced their steps to the top of the hill and turned to wave; no one was in sight. 'Well, I must say that went well, I don't mind losing me bonnet but me scalp's another matter.' Anna tried to laugh, but Brendan was serious.

'Anna, there's a hell of a lot we need ter learn ter exist in this country.'

On the way back Brendan was in an angry mood. 'Anna, Colonel bloody Caswell has rabbits – or should I call 'em cottontails – eating his land away, everyone knows it and says it, so we will have rabbit. How can one man decide he owns nature? Does he own the birds that fly over?'

CHAPTER 20

Anna had always loved Sunday mornings and church. It was time to put on your best dress and meet your friends, but this time she felt nervous. At Mollybeg she knew everybody. St Patrick's was a fine stone building that served a wide parish, and people came in from several miles away, indeed during summer days many brought a picnic and made a day of it, while others met with relatives. And, though it was frowned upon, some of the men met at the only tavern, Murphy's Bar. The door remained closed all day to meet the needs of the Sabbath, which did not explain the drunken singing late at night, said to be private parties held by George the proprietor.

All these memories flooded through Ann's mind as she looked at herself in the mirror. She loved her favourite green dress with a black panel down the front. Brendan's idea to hang the dress and weight the bottom hem had indeed pulled out many of the creases. She put on her second bonnet and groaned: its best days were past; it had seen every type of weather since Mollybeg. She thought of her best bonnet which she had given to the Indians. It had seemed a good idea at the time, now she regretted it. However, she couldn't go to church in her best dress with a faded hat on her head. Bridget came to her rescue and loaned her a dark green one that matched her dress perfectly. She told Bridget how she had lost hers on their walk after a gust of wind had taken it away into the river; she didn't mention their meeting with the Indians.

Brendan, for his part, though never keen to attend church saw it as an opportunity to meet his new neighbours. As they walked the short distance to church, he told her, 'Just think, Anna, the number of fish that yer bonnet will hold. I doubt a trout in the Lackawanna will escape and we've made Indian friends fer life.' He got a dig in his ribs.

The church was a timber A-frame structure built by volunteers and it was used by all denominations. On a mound, to the one side, a huge cross made from tree trunks told of its purpose. The Catholics had first use from 9 am until 10.30 am, the Protestants until midday, while the few Methodists used a small room added to the main structure. All came together after the services when all religious insignia was hidden away. This was the signal for the ladies of The Parade, regardless of their religious persuasion, to bring out tea, coffee, and cakes.

Attempts had been made to create a garden, but the poor covering of soil encouraged only the weeds to show their faces.

Early to arrive Anna and Brendan sat in the church and watched as the pews filled up. People filed past, some pausing to whisper a welcome, and Brendan was up and down shaking hands. Bridget, Dan, and their children joined them, and the two ladies whispered compliments to each other. Bridget said how much she liked Anna's dress, while Anna responded in kind but in fact thought Bridget's dress far too fussy with ruches around her expanding waistline that suggested she could give birth at any minute. Brendan listened politely while Dan outlined his plans, and his intention, as soon as the baby was able to walk, of moving on to Canada.

There were far more people in the church than Brendan had thought possible and as carriages pulled up outside, he could see through the large window on the village side that many had travelled some distance to attend; one family he recognised after a brief glimpse of them at Harper's Drift.

The area outside the church door was patrolled by two church stewards to keep it clear, and into this Brendan saw the Glenvale coaches arrive, the first an open landau with house staff, the second, a very smart coach with its hood up. From this emerged a lady holding a dainty parasol above her head. Her dress was lime coloured with a black trim around the neckline, her hat observed the latest fashion, a wide, flat, lacy creation that partly hid her face. Anna had seen similar ones advertised in the *New York Herald*. She whispered, 'Isn't she beautiful,' and decided that at the first opportunity she would rid herself of her bonnets and buy the fashionable large flat hats she had seen in Scranton.

Brendan's interest was on Colonel Caswell. He was tall and powerfully built. Brendan thought him to be in his forties, his hair was shorter than the fashion and he was bald on top. He didn't wear a moustache though he had a small well-trimmed beard that greyed in places. His impressive lightweight brocaded coat shone as the silver and gold caught the morning sunlight. His trousers were anchored, and V cut to cover his elegant shoes. In a whisper, Brendan said, 'Here comes God, ruler of the universe.'

At the entrance, they could hear the church elders welcome Colonel and Lady Caswell. Their entourage, servants, and employees moved to seats to the front right.

Lady Caswell, on the arm of her husband, moved regally past. Behind them, two boys aged between five and eight, holding hands, were guided into their seats by a nanny to the front left. A small harmonium set on a platform, played by an elderly red-faced man, began to play a piece of music. A notice informed the congregation that it was by Handel. Two boys, wearing surpluses and holding candles, passed by followed by the priest who announced in his welcoming address that he was Father O'Brien. His gushing acknowledgment of Colonel Caswell's generous support led Brendan to whisper, 'He's even bought God.'

Anna enjoyed the service but was aware that Brendan's faith was more dutiful than devotional; Anna went to Mass, he stayed in his seat.

The service over they waited until the colonel and his entourage departed before filing out into the sunshine. Some stayed behind to discuss their week while others returned home to wait for the Protestant service to finish at midday.

As the last worshipper left a team of volunteers prepared the room for the social occasion.

Brendan, by now convinced that he did not like Dan O'Hara, moved away to engage his new neighbours in introductions; this caused a little friction between him and Anna.

Anna knew that Brendan liked Bridget and the children, but his dislike for Dan was growing by the minute. Anna agreed with him that Dan did seem to complain too much, but she told him that it was just his way, Bridget was her friend and sometimes you had to… well, make allowances! This left Anna, Bridget, and the children, to happily share stories about their new homes. Bridget was pleased because a school ran most days, run by Gwen Owen from Wales.

It was while Brendan was returning to Anna that he was approached by a man he had never met before, who held out his hand and said, 'I don't think I've had the pleasure, I'm Frank Crosby. I believe you are starting work tomorrow.' He laughed in a friendly way. 'At work, I'm your foreman and Mr Crosby, but at social events like this please call me Frank.'

Brendan instantly liked the man. However, the question in his mind was, is he his own man, or, does he feed the ear of the colonel? He decided he would wait and see but gave him the benefit of the doubt – for now.

'Mr O'Neil, I must say I'm surprised that you haven't found work in New York, or Scranton. I'm told that you are a stonemason by trade and there's a hell of a lot of building going on.'

'Ah, there's plenty of work ter be sure but look at the pay. And if yer Irish yer don't always find a welcome. We'd all like a nice place ter live but yer've gorra pay the bills. Scranton's a fine town but me work ran out and I've no wish ter end up in debt.'

Mr Crosby smiled affably and told Brendan, 'There are many reasons why some men choose the isolation of mining out here.' He laughed. 'Some are running from their wives, some from debt, and others – who knows?'

Brendan took in the meaning. Obviously, Frank Crosby thought there were reasons, possibly not within the law, that brought some men to the Lackawanna; he shrugged and said, 'Ah sure there's many a story ter be told.'

'See you tomorrow, Mr O'Neil.' Brendan shook hands.

As the groups dispersed Anna and Brendon explored the upper track past the barracks, and greeted a few families who, in some cases, had very little English. Further on, to their surprise, they reached a large pool fringed with reeds. This could be used in all sorts of ways, and Anna's thought was to make reed mats for the scullery.

After a quick lunch, Anna and Brendan returned to the church and found that from every corner of The Parade people were on their way there. Inside, the hall was packed: tables were arranged, and groups sat around discussing their week, telling stories, meeting friends. It was, as Anna said, a wonderful atmosphere. Bridget waved to them from a corner and they joined the Irish group. This was a feature: nationalities congregating together. On the opposite side a group of eastern Europeans was celebrating, possibly a festival, or a birthday.

The ladies of The Parade moved about serving tea, coffee, and cakes to the adults and lemonade and cakes to the children, at the same time reminding people about the bucket at the entrance asking for contributions; whatever they could afford. A large notice thanked Colonel and Lady Caswell for their kind donation.

As the afternoon wore on, the tables in the centre were moved to the sides and a concert began. The Welsh group began with a medley of traditional songs, then, from a side room, a Russian trio, in traditional costume, performed a wild dance. This was followed by ballads from an Italian tenor and his wife. A highlight came when Mrs Owen and the children from her school performed a mime while she narrated.

Anna was delighted by the children's performance, but

this turned to shock when a man told them that, as newcomers, they were expected to perform something! This brought forth roars of approval and rowdy clapping.

Brendan sat stunned, he had nothing to offer. To his surprise, Anna moved to the centre and sang 'The Rose of Tralee'. An accordionist quickly picked up the melody and the silence as she sang was extraordinary. Brendan had a lump in his throat, he had no idea Anna could sing, though she often, as he called it, warbled while she worked. He looked around, handkerchiefs were out, and it wasn't only the Irish who were affected. The Russians came from their seats and danced some form of appreciation on their knees; the applause was thunderous.

Bridget then recited a poem that few understood while Dan asked if he could perform next time, but he didn't say what he had to offer. This brought the concert to a close, and Mrs Rossini, a true American lady whom they had spoken to earlier, thanked everyone for a wonderful day and reminded them again about the bucket at the door.

It was time for dinner, and Brendan and Anna joined the happy Paraders as they slowly walked back to number twenty. Anna took Brendan's arm and said, 'It's a strange ole world. One minute yer heart's in yer boots, the next, it's in the clouds; it's been a lovely day.'

Brendan laughed and held Anna tightly. 'Anna O'Neil, te'night no man could have been prouder, yer truly an incredible woman.' Anna fluttered her eyes.

'Brendan O'Neil, did I not tell yer all this when I first came ter yer door? Yer truly are a doubting Thomas.'

CHAPTER 21

Early Monday morning Anna stoked the fire, made porridge, not the kind she was used to, a type of yellowish rather gritty meal; she was told it came from India. Brendan ate with few words passed and gulped down his coffee. He gave Anna his watch, a mine wasn't the place for such a delicate instrument, took her in his arms and whispered, 'Love yer, see yer later.'

O'Neil joined the men making their way up the rise out of The Parade. At Wozniacks', the eastern European workers joined the file, some had English and exchanged greetings while many spoke in their mother tongue. A murmur of conversation ran around the various groups, but it was subdued.

Mr Crosby and Mr Carew waited at the gate. As the miners passed by, they checked in on a tally-board fixed to the office sidewall, good-humoured banter was exchanged, and it was clear that Crosby and Carew were respected by the miners.

The experienced teams moved into the mine, leaving the newcomers to hand in their contracts and choose suitable headwear from a large box; lamps were checked and handed out. Mr Crosby explained that they would be working in teams of four or five, and an experienced ganger would be in charge. The shift would be twelve hours with a break of half an hour to be taken at the ganger's discretion. Brendan, who had never been below ground in his life, listened carefully trying to imagine what it would be like to spend so many hours in the dark and dust with only an oil lamp for illumination. He noticed that many men chose to carry bottles of water to dampen cloths to hold over their faces to keep out the anthracite dust. Others chose to ignore the hazard; Brendan hadn't thought of this.

When his name was called, he found himself working with two other Irish men, Seamus from County Kerry and Roy from County Armagh. The third man, Olly, was a tall powerful-looking man from Nottingham in England. Brendan noted that similar nationalities made up the gangs.

Seamus looked at his team and said, 'Tubs 'tis me, lads,' to Brendan. He explained, 'We're hauling the coal trucks, better than at the face, 'tis hard but at least yer can stand up most of the time. As he said this he waved to a boy of no more than twelve years. 'Young Brian, yer with us today.' The boy smiled and picked up a metal can with a spout. 'He's our oil monkey, don't let yer lamp go out, hand it ter young one and he'll fill it.' Seamus led the way into the mine.

Brendan was surprised by the huge cavern cut into the hillside. There was a large apron where pit supports were ready for use, and this was well lit. Seamus moved to a ladder and they climbed down to a darker, lower level, and followed a short tunnel that brought them to a further ladder-drop of about eight feet. This was where the darkness closed in on Brendan, his lamp caught only the rear of Olly as they moved to a larger gallery. He could just make out the narrow rail lines running away to a tunnel to his left, and it was here that the face workers called goodbye and disappeared. Seamus followed the lines to their right and a halo of light grew bigger as they approached the tunnel opening. On a loop line stood the empty tubs, wooden bodies set on metal carriages, with four small metal wheels. Seamus showed Brendan how the tubs tipped up, and the ratchet to release the load. He put his hand on Brendan's shoulder.

'Now yer know me, boyo, why yer've been chosen fer the tubs. I can see some strength there, an' we'll need it. It's our job ter haul the tubs ter the face, help with the loading, and then push them back ter the loading bay. It's uphill ter the loading bay and downhill to the face. We have a brake tub, yer pull on this large lever here which will slow the wheels, but mind if this lot gets on a run, everyone's in trouble.'

'Shall I go and fetch Barney?' Olly asked.

'Aye 'tis time.'

Brendan thought another man would be joining them, instead, Olly returned leading a horse. Roy explained that he could only use the larger gallery, just high enough for the animal, but he was needed on the steep incline. Barney, a mixture of brown and white patches, with large hairy fetlocks liked fuss and got it.

In the smaller galleries, the team pulled the tubs using ropes with padded harnesses while Barney, in the larger gallery, knew exactly what to do. As soon as he was in harness he put his head forward and heaved, and with the help of the men, ten tubs at a time could be hauled up the steep slope. Once over the rise, it was a case of controlling the weight so there wasn't a run-back and danger.

Barney had a stall to himself, cut into the larger gallery, with hay and water. Olly laughed and told Brendan, 'He's better looked after than us.'

The hillside was cut away to give a broad shelf and on this, a loop of rail brought the tubs round so that the side gates could be opened to tumble the anthracite into the waiting carts below. Men and a team of mules stood by to cart the loads to Harper's Drift on a crude rail line that ran away into the woods.

Brendan found the work hard, but the humour of his colleagues helped the time pass more quickly than he thought. Moreover, as the tubs came out into daylight this lessened the sensation of being entombed; and the feel of fresh air was most welcome.

On his first run to the face, Brendan was appalled at the conditions, men lying on their sides picking away, while the prop men stood by to do their work. The dust was thick, and the oil lamps gave out little light. More frightening were the groans and creaks as timber and anthracite settled from its disturbance. Seamus told him, 'Yer lucky, Brendan, the small men gerra most of the cutting.'

For their break, the men joined Barney in the wider gallery, and over cold tea, Seamus explained to Brendan the workings of the mine, in particular the work of the prop men.

'They have to move in quickly when a cut is made, mind you a good fall means we can load the tubs more quickly, and we gerra a bonus at the end of the month.' Roy took over, explaining to Brendan, 'As soon as the cut is made yer need ter gerra the roof support in quick but, the pine from the forest is ter willowy; it's an accident waiting ter happen.'

Olly added, 'Two men have been killed this past year – prop men – the timber's too green, it bends like a straw in the wind.'

Roy butted in, 'It's all about profit, get the anthracite ter the big cities as soon as yer can. If yer lose a few men, there's plenty ter fill a dead man's boots.'

Brendan said nothing, it was the same story he had heard in New York, but here, there was a bitterness he hadn't felt before. Roy told him about how the Irish were the lowest paid and exploited by the mine owners, and he mentioned the Molly Maguires. Brendan knew that they were a secret Irish network who had set out to improve the lot of the Irish immigrant workers, who were paid less for their work than other nationalities, or so it was believed. It had been a constant topic at his Scranton workplace.

'D'yer know that in seventy-eight twenty of our lads were hanged fer so-called insurrection?' Roy was trembling with anger.

A calmer Olly warned, 'Bren, if I were you, keep your thoughts to yourself, you never know who's listening, there's rumours that Pinkerton is moving in.'

Seamus shared Roy's anger. 'I wouldn't be surprised if the colonel hasn't already brought them in.' Brendan listened with growing alarm; all he could think of was that he was here to avoid the Pinkerton men. He decided not to tell Anna.

Near to six o'clock, the team made their last haul to the loop. Brendan was delighted to feel fresh air on his face, though within minutes the heat of the day hit him, and he looked forward to his cold bath.

Olly was quite happy to leave Brendan to field Barney. He showed him the track that ran around the hillside and down a ramp past the vent tunnel; here he said goodbye. Further down lay the field, a mixture of burnt grass with some greener patches near a brook; behind stood the mining office and a soil privy. Barney, as soon as he saw his field, picked up speed, while Brendan enjoyed the freedom to stretch his legs. As he strode along, he beat the dust from his clothes.

The gate lay open and Barney stepped through, then turned and pressed his muzzle into Brendan's hand. This was when his emotions got the better of him. Just seeing his eyes looking at him took him back to Donegal, and the life he had left behind; he had had such hopes that his skills would find favour in America. Even the field reminded Brendan of his field in Donegal, stony with little grass coverage. In a corner, there was a shelter, but Barney remained at the gate watching him as he left. Brendan laughed to himself; once he mentioned Barney to Anna, she would forget all about his day. His thoughts turned to her and he quickened his pace. He would be home soon.

Anna was waiting; she had his bathtub ready and two buckets of cold water standing by. She drew back in mock horror. 'Well, I've seen the blue man and now yer the bogeyman.' Brendan made a face, stripped, climbed into the tub and watched the dust settle into a pattern around his body. Anna went outside and he could hear her beating his clothes.

When she came back, he said, 'Anna, I've been working on the coal tubs with Barney the horse.'

Her eyes lit up. 'Ah, that's lovely, so yer've no had too bad a day?' Brendan laughed and laughed as he looked at her puzzled face.

CHAPTER 22

In mid-August, the full heat of an American summer hit home. For Anna, the coolest place was their cabin, and Brendan's idea to turf the roof did seem to have some effect.

For Brendan the heat below ground was unbelievable, even the air coming in seemed to be on fire. Most welcome were Anna's bottles of ginger beer: the root and yeast had been given to her when their next-door neighbours, Beth and George Murphy, returned from Scranton. George explained they had relatives who had bought out their contract, and they were going to make a fresh start, moving on to Boston. Beth handed the plant over to Anna, and though sugar was a problem, Anna quickly had a small business going, with Nadia supplying the sugar.

Below ground, cold tea was still popular with the Irish, but ginger beer, for Brendan, seemed to have a bite that dulled the dust. Fortunately, a spring came from the hillside behind the cabins a short distance away, and though the main water source was the two pumps, the spring was constant and seemed to have a purity aided by its journey through sand and gravel.

Brendan formed a collecting area by gouging into the hillside to make a platform where several leather bags were stored in the cool. Each day Anna filled the bags, took them to the yard, boiled the water and added the sugar before adding the ginger beer plant. The storage bags were then returned to the cool waterhole and left for two days. Every evening Anna filled the smaller hide bottles, bought from an elderly Indian who regularly visited The Parade, and these were sold from the store; Nadia and Anna shared the profit. Anna soon found out not to fill the bottles to the top because in hot weather the wooden plugs could fire off like a rifle. Brendan realised the importance of a liquid intake and took two bottles with him every day.

Hauling the tubs was hard work, and in the heat Brendan had lost weight. Also, he now wore a scar to his temple after a minor roof fall; accidents were common and blue scars were a common sight among the miners. What the men needed was meat but any that came to the store went to families with children. Nadia was apologetic, but as she pointed out, the small amount that came in she had to decide who got it, and to her, the children came first.

Brendan knew from the gossip in the village that the forest was overrun with rabbits, and he had tried several times to explore, but each time he been foiled by the presence of the stewards. Several local men had been caught, including one Scottish miner, who had been thrown out of his cabin along with his wife and two children.

Anna was equally frustrated. 'Bren, much as I like trout, I'm fed up with fish. It was fish at home and fish here, I'll be growing gills if this carries on and what I'd like ter make is a nice Irish rabbit stew. There's land the other side of the colonel's, perhaps yer can try there.'

Brendan sighed and spread his hands. 'Out there? Where? Seamus tells me that a lad from Harper's shot a jackrabbit and was arrested by the stewards. He told them it wasn't on the colonel's land, but it made little difference. They took it off him and threatened him with the magistrate and we all know who that is; yer just canna win.'

However, it was a thoughtful Brendan who searched through his sack and took out a small canvas folder and laid out its contents on the floor. 'God knows why I brought these with me, me da gave them ter me.' He laid out two rabbit snares; Brendan had made up his mind. 'We'll have meat and, Anna, yer'll have yer Irish rabbit stew. There's plenty of it over there, I'm told that Watts was seen with a bagful the other day.' Brendan pointed. 'Why is it the bloody colonel doesn't know that his workers need food ter do his work? After dinner, I'm off ter do a bit of lookin', I'll be damned if I let that man own every bird and animal that God created.'

Anna was frightened. 'Bren, yer know the stewards shoot on sight if they find poachers?'

'Aye, but they've gorra find me. I'll be careful, they can't be everywhere. And, it's mealtime, so it's a good time ter go – I'll eat when I get back.'

Brendan climbed the rise behind their cabin. To any onlooker, he was out for an evening stroll. At the dead tree, and out of sight, he made his way around to Kroos Bridge. All was silent; he waited, listening for any sound before moving on. The smell from the fetid brook, along with the tar pit, was awful but possibly it was one to keep others away.

For a time, he followed the track, then pushed his way through the dense undergrowth of tree and bush. In the next clearing, Brendan froze. At least a dozen wild turkeys were pecking away, he watched thinking of a way to catch one, but it would be difficult. He dismissed the idea; rabbits he knew about.

Avoiding the paths Brendan headed for the river, he knew that on such a lovely evening this would be the place to be careful, it was, he estimated, about three-quarters of a mile. Cautiously he looked out to find a wide part of the river lined with trees that came into the water. Centre stream, there were small stony-marooned islands with bushes and vegetation and in places deep pockets of water. An even deeper stream ran by an old wooden jetty and tied to this was a rowing boat. Brendan could see the jetty was in use but decided against moving into the open. Again, he listened for anyone coming down the river path; all was still. He was about to leave when he saw, snagged on a bush downriver, a length of netting lost by fishermen; it could be useful. It meant crossing into the open, but he took the chance. The net was snagged in several places on a spiky bush. However, he managed to cut away a good section.

Back under the cover of the trees, he took a different

path to see where it led. Suddenly, approaching voices made him hide. He was just in time, two stewards he knew by sight, talking loudly, headed for the river; both carried shotguns. Even more cautiously Brendan moved on and came out into another clearing, where a sandy hill rose and then fell away into an area of twisted roots where trees had been felled. This was rabbit country and as he cautiously moved to the side, a large rabbit came out of its burrow and crossed his path. As a late sun broke through, more rabbits came out, as if to play; he could have been back in Donegal. For some minutes he enjoyed watching them dance and leap about, entering burrows only to come out some distance away. It was everything Brendan wanted to know, rabbits could be caught at night and that would make catching them easier. Turkeys would be far too difficult, daylight was needed, and would they feed in the same place?

Brendan made his way back to Kroos Bridge and waited until he was sure that no stewards or guardians were in the area. Returning by the same route he sauntered back from his walk to find Anna anxiously waiting for him in the yard. He asked her what was for dinner.

Anna put her hands over her face and said, 'Fish pie!' Brendan burst out laughing and took her in his arms.

'Yer gonna have yer Irish stew. There's enough rabbits out there ter feed an army. I just need ter wait fer the right night, and I've an idea.' Later, in bed, he outlined how he would go about it, and asked for Anna's help; she listened without saying a word.

Brendan, as usual, after his work quickly fell asleep but, for Anna, sleep would not come. She lay awake, her mind casting back to New York. *Ter be robbed on our first day; that brute Paddy and gang could have killed me man. I could have been a widow at twenty! And now we're in this godfersaken place. Why did I listen ter Bridget and Dan? And now me man could be killed because of a rabbit!*

Anna's last thought was, *we must gerra the hell out of here.*

CHAPTER 23

On Monday Brendan's first task was to fetch Barney, the part of his day he looked forward to. He loved to see his head go up and his gallop to the gate. Brendan scratched him between his ears, then offered him a crab apple from the bag Anna had given him for his lunch, along with bread and cheese.

Anna had found the loaded tree not far from their cabin and was excited by its possibilities. She didn't know what type it was, but its fruit had a bitter-sweet flavour, unlike the rather sour variety she had known back in Ireland. She could use them for cooking, baking pies, but above all, she could make crab apple wine. Storage was a problem but once again Nadia came up with the answer and supplied brown paper and a corner in her store, while Anna used the space under the bed.

Brendan, to his surprise, found he quite liked the bitter taste; it would lessen the slime of anthracite in his mouth, but would Barney? He held out an apple and Barney took it from his palm. His mouth opened, he rolled the apple between his teeth as if to spit it out, then his eyes widened, his ears went up, and with a big crunch, the apple disappeared. He liked it and pushed his muzzle for more. The two entered the mine with Barney following him up the slope.

The day passed without incident. In conversation, Brendan found out that Seamus had finished his contract and had other plans. 'I'm out of here soon; there's railway work ter be found at Harper's, that's the future, boyos, railheads.' Brendan was sure that he was right. He joined in the banter and listened to the stories about home, but only one thought occupied his mind – rabbit stew! The problem

143

was, how he could snare a few rabbits without getting caught, or even worse – shot!

Work for the day over, on a glorious evening, Brendan led Barney to his field and gave him his last apple. He had never seen such joy on a horse's face. His eyes were ablaze, his mouth moved left and right, the juice squirting in sequence. Brendan laughed and gave him a last pat and hurried home.

Anna had his tub and his clean clothes ready. 'Fer dinner I've a salad with omelettes,' she told Brendan, but his mind was elsewhere. Dressed, he moved to the yard and sat under the canopy he and Anna had made from reeds from the upper pool.

'Have yer managed ter collect what I asked yer?'

Anna smiled. 'I'll show yer after dinner.'

Dinner over, Anna pulled a sack from under the bench, opened it and pulled out a handful of leaves. Brendan wasn't sure what type they were, but they were strong and pliable. He bent one between his fingers and it gently returned to its natural shape. Brendan nodded approval. 'Perfect an' more than enough.'

Anna said, 'I can sew them on, but it'll take me some time.' Brendan shrugged.

'No need ter sew, we can use twine and tie them on. If a few fall off, no matter.'

Anna spread the fishing net that Brendan had rescued from the river on the ground and using a nail she carefully pierced a hole into each leaf. Brendan began at the bottom tying the leaves to overlap as he moved up the net. It took them far less time than they thought. Finished, Brendan pulled the netting over his head while Anna shaped the leafy mesh around his body. He crouched down. Anna laughed.

'In the dark yer'll look just like a bush. I'll finish it off te'morra, and I'll make a peephole – yer'll need ter see where yer goin'.'

Brendan was pleased, this was exactly his intention. He looked at the sky, brought up in the countryside he could read the weather better than most. 'There's a storm comin', we could do with rain ter cool things down.'

In the early hours of Saturday morning, Brendan's prediction came true. Sooner than he had expected, thunder and lightning of an intensity he had never known hit The Parade, followed by driving rain. When Brendan rose the worst was over, but angry dark clouds still swirled and rolled across the sky. It was time to wear his fisherman's cape, and on his walk to the mine, he fell into step with Dan O'Hara. However, as they approached the barrier, which was down, others in front were turning back, and the call came... flooding! No work till Monday; a cheer went up from some, for others, it meant no pay. Dan was keen to get back, while Brendan carried on to the field; he had a few apples for Barney.

He was surprised at how the field had greened up in such a short time. Barney was waiting and seemed to be enjoying the freshness. Brendan made his usual fuss of him, but his mind was in the forest; Saturday was perfect. There was every chance that the stewards would be otherwise occupied, dealing with their flood problems; it all depended on the weather.

Brendan hurried back. All down The Parade people were busy mopping water and putting furniture out to dry; roofs had leaked. Bridget came out to tell him their curtains were ruined.

Anna was mopping up a trickle down the one wall when Brendan entered.

'Yer did the trick, what a clever boyo yer are.'

Brendan looked at the roof. 'Aye, the tar has done its job, and the turves have absorbed most of the water, once the sun's back it'll soon dry out. The only problem is the weight, but it's pretty sturdy and should hold.'

'The second yer left I heard the mine was flooded...' Anna stopped, she knew Brendan too well, that look on his face; she waited.

'Te'night I'm off a hunting. But first I'd better check the

brook out.'

'Bren, that brute Watts is back. I hear that last year an Irish lad was taken to Delaware and hanged. Nadia tells me that one of the stewards shot his own man in the dark, but they blamed the Irish lad, they said he was deer hunting, but he was after a turkey.' Brendan had heard the story. Watts was feared and the one man to keep well away from.

'Ah well, with me snares they'll have a job pinning that on me.'

Anna made coffee, the thought came, *yer've already told me they can pin anything on yer, gun or no gun. Those brutes will set yer up.* She sat down and said, 'Bren, why don't we do a moonlight flit and gerra the hell out of here? I'd rather risk the Pinkerton men than lose yer because of a rabbit.'

Brendan shrugged. He didn't like to admit that it was a challenge that he couldn't give up. To put one over the stewards and their boss, the colonel, had an appeal. However, this wasn't something he wanted to tell Anna. Instead, he said, 'It might be a good idea; we'll talk it over later.'

Towards midday, the sun was back, and Brendan walked down to the footbridge. He wasn't surprised to find it flooded; for once the smell had gone. Even as he watched the water level was falling. Pleased and enjoying the freshness, he walked back to find his neighbours talking to Anna. A big laugh went up when Jonas pointed at their roof which was steaming like a pudding. 'Yer cooking nicely.' Brendan gave a bow.

As the afternoon wore on more clouds rolled in from the north. It was a long afternoon. After an early dinner, Brendan returned to the bridge to find the water level almost back to normal. Cautiously, he hid his camouflage underneath.

As the light faded, Brendan put on his work boots, a type of clog with stout leather uppers. He couldn't use his waterproofs as they were too bulky. He moved to the yard and he could see that Anna was nervous and frightened. He took her by the shoulders. 'It'll be a long night but as daylight breaks, I'll be at the tree… yer know me signal.' Anna nodded; she had helped to make the crow's nest.

At the footbridge Brendan put on his leafy camouflage and waited until the shadows lengthened. Cautiously he made his way to rabbit hill. It was open to the front, with a stretch of sandy soil that rose in three levels until it met a mound of scrub and small bushes. He listened for any movement or the sound of voices; all was quiet. The only sign of life was the rabbits who, sensing his presence, disappeared down the many holes. Carefully, he set his two snares and lightly covered them with a scattering of sand in the hope they would be invisible to any passing steward; it was then the rain returned.

In a small avenue of trees, that gave him a clear sight of rabbit hill, Brendan found a clump of bushes and crouched down. Leaning back against a tree he pulled his leafy camouflage around him and waited until it was dark. It would be a long night. He looked at the sky, it was clearing. Suddenly, the moon made an appearance; the strong shadows would help. He ignored the trickle of water running down his neck; his thoughts turned to Anna.

Anna tried to read, but the words disappeared; her mind was in the forest. She tried to think of the positives, all the good things that had happened. She promised herself that she would write to Mr Peabody and Yvonne – soon! She looked forward to the next day, Sunday, to see all her friends. There was a kinship between the miners that made life worthwhile, well almost. She loved the once-a-month concerts and enjoyed singing her Irish songs. She thought back to life in Donegal, how safe it was. She shuddered; Brendan was out there, risking his life to catch a rabbit! It was all so stupid, unbelievable; how had it come to this?

She moved to the yard to enjoy the freshness. The clouds were still scudding across the sky, chased by the moon. A shower of rain sent her inside. She sat in her favourite place on a cushion leaning back against the wall; again, she tried to read.

The hours passed slowly: she looked at Brendan's watch; it was almost midnight. The sound of a gun made her leap awake – what time was it? She looked again at Brendan's watch: two-thirty. Oh God! Her hands went to her face. *Oh Jesus, was it an animal stalk, or was Bren in trouble?*

She forced herself to keep calm and told herself that shots often rang out from the forest. Sometimes it was done to frighten would-be poachers. At other times the stewards added to their pay by selling venison to a butcher from Scranton who called once a week at Harper's Drift. She wondered if the colonel knew what his stewards were up to, and how his so-called police turned a blind eye. Watts reported to him but no doubt the story he told was far from the truth; someone ought to tell him.

To keep awake Anna made strong coffee and waited for first light. Never had dawn taken so long to break: several times she went to the yard to see the sky lighten behind dead-tree hill. She searched for the crow's nest – no sign. A sense of panic came. Should she knock Bridget's door? No! Dan had a blab of a mouth. She put on the kettle; another coffee might help. She forced herself to drink slowly, put down her cup and went to the yard. A crow's nest was in place; she gave a quick wave and waited just inside the door.

The sack was lifted in, Brendan's face came around the door. He gave her a smile of triumph. Now she wanted to cry, to hit him, instead, she nestled in his arms. He was home safe. Anna drew back. 'Yer soaking – go and change. I heard the shot, thank God yer okay. I don't want yer ter die of pneumonia.'

CHAPTER 24

The tears came. 'Brendan O'Neil, d'yer realise what yer've put me through? We've gorra get out of here.' Anna sat at Brendan's feet. 'God, when I heard the shot, I thought yer'd been taken.' She put her head on Brendan's lap, she couldn't stop crying. 'If anything happens ter yer, what will I do?'

Brendan sipped his coffee and stroked Anna's hair. He couldn't bear to see her so distressed. 'Yer right, Anna, 'tis the first and last time. I just find it hard ter believe that yer canna catch a rabbit without an army manoeuvre. Someone needs ter tell that colonel what's going on in his name. I doubt he even knows what his stewards are up ter. Fer Christ's sake back in Donegal if yer didn't see off a few rabbits yer'd be overrun.'

Brendan looked back over his night and tried not to smile; he had come through. Watts and his gang would be furious they had been outwitted by a – he remembered an expression he had picked up from an American – a dumb cluck from Ireland. Anna lifted her head.

'Brendan O'Neil, are yer laughing? Yer enjoyed it didn't yer?'

Brendan couldn't help it, he dissolved into a fit of laughing. He explained it was the relief after a very dangerous night and told Anna all that had happened. She listened without comment; finally, she got up, wiped her tears, and told him her news.

'There's no church today; it's flooded, and they want helpers ter mop the place out. Yer can have a rest and I'll cook the rabbit when I get back.' Brendan sighed.

'They'll know someone's been in the forest, so if I don't appear it might point a finger. I'll go and yer stay and cook the rabbit. Use the clay pots I made yer or the smell will

149

carry fer miles.'

At the church, the mopping was well underway. The small wooden tower built to give some sense of dignity to the building had acted as a funnel to carry the rain inside; however, it was only water damage. Brendan helped to carry the furniture outside and chatted to friends while Mrs Williams, a Welsh lady who regarded a cup of tea as of the same importance as the breaking of bread at the Last Supper, was on hand with her special brew.

Brendan didn't feel particularly tired, but he knew it was often the day after that fatigue kicked in. By midday he returned home to find a note from Anna; she was at Jonas and Millie's.

Anna skinned both rabbits and cut them into pieces, then placed them into two fire-hardened clay boxes made by Brendan. She lit the fire under the cooking pot in the yard, adjusted the reed canopy to keep out the worst of the August heat and settled until the rabbits were cooked. Then, with one rabbit on a plate and well hidden in her bag, she called on her neighbours.

Millie was midwife to The Parade, and because of her skills, the couple was granted free accommodation after Jonas' accident in the mine. A badly secured ladder had sent him tumbling into the shaft, and he had broken his shoulder, injured his right leg and broken three ribs; he had never fully recovered. He could use his left arm for menial tasks, but his mining days were over. Fearing the worst, that they would be forced out of their home, it came as a surprise when the Paraders petitioned the colonel for them to stay, because Millie treated all, regardless of social class. And now she was not only the midwife but also the nurse who attended to anyone who was ill or injured. It was said that the colonel's wife, Leonora, had persuaded his agreement.

Behind their cabin, Jonas had created a little vegetable patch that he kept watered from a spring close to that of his neighbours. In danger of drying up during the hot months,

Brendan had helped him dig a waterhole which they puddled with clay from the mine. This worked well, retaining the water, and Jonas grew his carrots, onions, and parsnips, which he didn't mind exchanging for the odd treat; a rabbit was much to his liking.

Both were in when Anna called, and she stopped for a coffee. The rabbit was passed over, no questions asked, and Anna came away with onions and carrots.

Brendan was back when she returned. 'Now fer me rabbit stew. God, in this heat I'll be stewed myself. Bren, sit yerself down and have a drink.' Brendan sipped his crab apple wine, now a special Sunday treat. He watched Anna preparing their meal and his desire for her grew by the second. For some reason he didn't feel tired, in fact, he felt a sense of elation. As if reading his mind, Anna waved her wooden spoon at him. 'I can see yer looking at me. Yer supposed ter be dog-tired – not on heat – so yer'll have ter wait.'

Brendan laughed. 'Is it so obvious?'

''Tis, but yer've chosen the wrong time of the month, and another thing, I'll be needin' some white vinegar, soon!'

Brendan shrugged, time and time again his thoughts had turned to children. He would love to be a father, and he daydreamed of Anna being pregnant. But he was worried because although the measures Anna took had worked well so far, he had never heard of a foolproof method. The thought came – *could there be a problem?* He didn't put this to Anna, as her temper, at times, could flare like a gorse fire. But she was right, if they had a child while living at The Parade, he would be a miner for life; much better to wait. Time was on their side, though at twenty-one it was unusual to find a girl without issue.

Brendan's thoughts turned to her Catholic faith. She seemed to draw from it what she wanted and ignored the parts that didn't fit in. Birth control was a new subject, something being talked about in the newspapers – well certain newspapers, not Catholic. Anna, on Sundays, sat through Father O'Brian's hell and brimstone denunciation of

151

such an act. Giving birth was God's will and had nothing to do with earthly protestations. Indeed, lust was something to be beaten from the breast of man. When Brendan had put this to Anna she had sniffed and told him that the church didn't get everything right, and she wasn't going to spend half her life flat on her back. Then she had wrapped herself around him in a very provocative way, and in a deep, breathy and sultry voice had told him, 'But I like the lust part.'

'Brendan O'Neil, what are yer laughing at?'

Brendan wasn't aware he was. He looked into Anna's face. 'Ah, just a few thoughts.'

Anna gave a long, 'Hmmm,' shook her head and moved to the oven.

Brendan sat back. *Yes, children, one day.* He looked around their cabin yard, *but not here... it's time ter move on.*

'Dinner's ready.'

Brendan fetched the chairs and adjusted the reed canopy and sat down. Anna placed his meal under his nose and the smell brought home his farm in Donegal. He tried to speak, but his voice broke, he tried again, nothing came. Anna moved to him, gave him a hug and whispered, 'Bren, we're back home, just fer a few hours.' Brendan held her, how on earth did this girl always seem to know what he was thinking? He thought back to the very first meal Anna had made. He smiled to himself; it was fish! He ignored this and instead recalled the soda bread with gooseberry jam.

Brendan ate with relish and finally pushed his plate away very satisfied. 'Mrs O'Neil, I've had many a rabbit stew, but I must say I've never tasted better.'

'Ah, Mr and Mrs O'Neil, I'm sorry to intrude but I've been knocking on your door.'

Brendan almost fell off his chair. Anna's hands flew to her face; Mr Frank Crosby smiled at them.

'I had no idea you were at dinner. Mr O'Neil, I need to have a word with you.'

Brendan went to pull up a chair, still stunned to find his foreman in his backyard.

'Rabbit stew; well, well, it smells delicious.' He smiled amiably, then added, 'I see one crossed your path.' It was Anna who reacted first and served up a dose of her blarney.

'Ah, well ter be sure, Mr Crosby, as yer know we're from Ireland and we have a special way with rabbits, and this one ran out of the forest yesterday and ran up the hill yer can see there. An' I was quick enough ter throw some salt on his tail, which stopped him in his tracks. I don't suppose there's many who know this trick in America.'

Crosby went into deep thought, then looked up and said, 'Mrs O'Neil, I believe you, but there's many – with more authority than myself – who might not do so and for this reason, I shall remain mute on the subject.' Crosby smiled in a friendly way.

Brendan found his voice. 'Will yer have a coffee with us, Mr Crosby?'

'Thank you, I never refuse a coffee.'

Brendan waited, his heart still pounding, while Crosby, who insisted his Christian name Frank was used, talked about the storm and his wife whom he had left in Scranton. Finally, he looked at Brendan. 'I remember you telling me that by trade you are a stonemason and you also have knowledge of building and construction.'

Brendan didn't quite remember the conversation in the same way but decided to see where it led.

'Brendan, I have mentioned to the colonel that you might save him some money before he brings in an expert from Scranton. It concerns his house and a problem that has arisen. Tomorrow, with your agreement, you will report to me at ten o'clock at the mine and we will have to walk the two miles to the colonel's estate. After the storm the road is impassable. You'll be paid your normal day's pay.'

Brendan nodded agreement, thanked Frank, and walked with him to the front, and shook hands.

As he was leaving, Frank turned with a very serious look on his face. 'By the way, Brendan, I hear that someone got away with a deer last night and Mr Watts is very annoyed.

Your rabbit didn't have antlers by any chance?' Brendan thought carefully before replying.

'Eh, no, Frank, I can say that ours was female.' Frank walked away up the track laughing.

Anna joined Brendan. 'Well yer said he was a decent man, and I think yer right.' She looked at Brendan. 'And te'morra yer meet the colonel.'

CHAPTER 25

Brendan slept well and had a lie-in. He joined Anna for breakfast but said little. Anna knew that Brendan was an afternoon and night person, who rarely had anything to say for at least an hour until he had had his cup of coffee; buttermilk was now a distant memory.

After breakfast, he dressed in his Sunday best while Anna tried to give his bowler hat a better shape.

Brendan took a deep breath; now that he was to meet the colonel face to face, he felt nervous, not helped by Anna's advice to give him a piece of his mind.

At the mining office, Frank Crosby was waiting. He looked at O'Neil's boots and brought out a pair of large riding boots. 'Put these on, shove your pants in, we could end up knee-deep in water.' Brendan was pleased to have the boots; they were an ill fit but coped well with the pools that crossed their path. Storm water had rushed down the hillside and in places the hillside had slid into the forest leaving a morass of mud. They passed the notice that warned they were entering private property. Ahead lay Mount Tahoma, the home of Colonel Caswell.

'Frank, what does it mean, Tahoma?'

It's an Indian word meaning water's edge, and you'll see why when we turn the next corner.'

By this time Brendan felt he could trust Frank Crosby. 'Frank, I've a story ter tell, but yer must keep it ter yerself.' He went on to tell Crosby about how they had been robbed in New York, and how he had been attacked and had defended himself resulting in the death of knifeman. 'Frank, we're here because we believe the police have Pinkerton men after us.'

Frank stopped and shook his head. 'My friend, I know

the ways here better than you. I was born in Scranton when it was a village. I can't believe New York police would be bothered at losing one of its scum.'

'Frank, it's not only the Pinkerton. I'm told the gangs look after their own.'

'The gangs won't leave New York to come here; you're a flea bite. And the police haven't the time or money to send Pinkerton agents all the way to Scranton. It doesn't make sense. There's something here I don't understand.'

They turned the last corner, and their conversation was forgotten; Mount Tahoma stood before them. A large wooden house with an overhanging shingle roof to give shade to the open balconies that led from three parts of the house. Its weathered wood gleamed white in the bright morning sunshine, even whiter against its green setting. In front lay a paddock that ran around the one side of the house where several horses were being attended to by two grooms. Adjoining was a block of stables. To the east lay the Lackawanna River, a beautiful section, wider than many parts Brendan had seen.

'Really beautiful; you won't see finer in these parts,' said Frank.

Brendan agreed, but added, 'So, this is how the rich live.' Crosby put his hand on Brendan's arm.

'A word of warning, there's talk of the Molly Maguires spreading through this part of the mining industry, be careful what you say, just being Irish raises a few heads.'

Crosby moved to a side entrance and asked for the colonel and they were directed to the stables adjoining the main building.

Jeremiah Caswell, to Brendan's surprise, was cleaning out a stable dressed in breeches, riding boots, and a shirt. At close quarters Brendan realised he was older than he had thought, possibly nearer to fifty. He stopped when he saw them. Crosby introduced O'Neil and he went to shake hands, but Caswell held up his hands, went to a water pump, washed them and returned. He led them into an office part of the stable where there were chairs and a small table.

'Mr O'Neil, I'm told by Mr Crosby that you might be able to solve a problem I have. Now, what experience do you have in building, especially wooden framed structures?' The colonel spoke using very correct English but with a slight accent that Brendan didn't recognise.

Brendan smiled and using his modified use of the English language, that is, a little less of the Irish, which he had found an advantage when dealing with professional people he replied. 'Sir, none at all, but the principles are the same. However, it is difficult for me to make an evaluation until you have shown me the problem.' Brendan felt the stunned silence. Caswell looked at Crosby, who raised his eyebrows.

'Well let's get to it.' Colonel Caswell led them to the back of the house.

Brendan knew the problem before another word was uttered. He had dealt with many Irish farmhouses that were traditionally built into a bank; damp was always a problem. He listened carefully while the colonel showed him the rotten timbers at ground level and the stone piers that supported the house. The colonel questioned the ability of his builder. He paused, and waited for Brendan's judgment.

'Colonel, who decided the positioning of the house?' asked Brendan.

'My wife wanted the balconies to overlook the river. It is a most wonderful view, is it not, Mr O'Neil?'

Brendan turned to look up the rising slope of green grass that ran into a copse of trees, then continued to a high ridge above the house. The colonel followed Brendan's gaze. 'The ridge shields the house from winter winds.' The colonel waited, while Brendan moved to a better position. 'Well, man, have you something to tell me or not?'

His tone annoyed Brendan, the man was showing him disrespect. However, he remained calm, pointed at the high ridge and said, 'It's a collecting point for water, and it's running downhill under your house. Every time it rains it adds to the problem, and the piers are sinking; it's a simple matter of drainage.'

The colonel gave a sarcastic laugh. 'And what do you suggest? That I pick my house up and carry it over there?'

Brendan gave it long and careful consideration. 'It is one answer, but it would be very expensive.'

The colonel couldn't control his exasperation. 'Mr O'Neil, I take it this is part of your Irish sense of humour.'

Brendan was enjoying himself and replied, 'My colleague in England, Albert Merryweather, master builder, and stonemason who worked on Lichfield Cathedral, moved a stone chapel several feet on rollers, so it can be done. But in this case, we must find the water level below ground and dig a trench around the house and clay line it – we call it puddling – as you would a pond. Then fill it in with aggregate, that is gravel, brick, and stone.' Brendan couldn't resist adding, 'And of course, you can use anthracite if there's any to hand, then finish with a layer of soil; the grass will quickly recover. The water will then move around your house and drain to the river. Your house will soon dry out when the sun is back. The piers need packing out; I suggest slate. I also suggest you replace the timbers with new, treated in tar. You have a tar pit close to your mine and it has worked well for me.'

Frank Crosby, feeling he had to make some contribution if only to ease the tension said, 'Colonel, we have the manpower. I can recruit more men from Scranton. It sounds a straightforward job. Along with Mr O'Neil, I'm sure the two of us can sort this out.'

Brendan could see that the colonel was far from pleased. No doubt because here was a man, not a professional man, one of inferior social rank who worked in his mine, daring to tell him what he should have known in the first place, indeed daring to poke fun at him. He could see the colonel struggling with his assessment.

Caswell turned to Crosby. 'Well, as you say it sounds simple enough. You are my foreman and I will leave it in your capable hands.' He turned to Brendan. 'Thank you, Mr

O'Neil, I see no point in taking you away from your duties at the mine.'

As the colonel turned away, this dismissal was too much for Brendan; now was his chance to tell this man – this so-called colonel – what was happening in his name. 'Colonel Caswell, as I have been of service to you, perhaps you can return a service. Your workers work hard, and they need food – good food – meat, and you control the source. Your stewards shoot anyone on sight who puts a foot on your land. And your land is overrun with rabbits and turkeys. Surely you can relax your hold to allow your workers some benefit.' There was a long silence.

At length, the colonel turned to Crosby. 'Mr Crosby, I think it best we conclude this meeting. Mr O'Neil, it would seem, is using my invitation to insult me on my own land.'

Frank Crosby stood, head bowed, as if in deep deliberation. He looked up and said, 'Colonel Caswell, as your foreman I have served you well for six years, and all my consultations with you concern the running of the mine. Mr Watts is your head steward who reports his business to you. Mr Pedersen is your head of police and does likewise. I cannot speak for them. Mr O'Neil has raised a matter without my prior knowledge but, the fact is, I believe your stewards are not following your directives. I am sure Mr O'Neil means no insult. He is one of your excellent workers, and he is a man I trust. He speaks out because he believes it may well be that certain information is withheld from you.'

The colonel turned away, put his hands on his hips, gave a shrug of irritation, turned back and calmly asked, 'What information, Mr Crosby?'

Brendan knew he had put Frank in a difficult position. The colonel had sought to divide and rule, believing that his man, Crosby, would back him. Now it would be a difficult walk back to The Parade. He decided to stand back and leave any further discussion with Frank.

Crosby paused for a second and responded. 'Colonel, you agreed two summers ago that rabbits, woodcock, pigeons, and turkeys, of which there are many on your land, could be given, or sold, at low cost to your workers as an additional reward for their work at certain times of the year. A rota was to be kept so all would benefit and this would be kept by your head steward, Mr Watts, and he was to arrange and display this at Wozniacks' store and—'

The colonel interrupted, 'Mr Watts informs me that he follows my directive but tells me that poachers are on my land every night shooting my deer and this I will not allow. I will decide when a cull takes place.' The colonel turned to Brendan, and with a hint of sarcasm said, 'Sir, you have suddenly lost your tongue. Would you like to add to Mr Crosby's narrative?'

Brendan decided he had no option. 'Watts is a violent man, his stewards are frightened of him, and the game of which you speak does not reach the village, it is sold on to a butcher he meets at Harper's Drift, and any profit is shared among his particular friends.'

'Do you know this for a fact, man, or is this just rumour? Envy because of his position?' The colonel turned to Crosby and raised his eyes in question.

'Colonel, I cannot verify what Mr O'Neil says, but it is a fact that not one rabbit, woodcock or turkey has found its way into The Parade for a very long time.'

Colonel Caswell walked away, turned and said, 'Say no more. I will deal with this, and THIS conversation remains between the three of us. Agreed?' Crosby and O'Neil nodded.

The colonel, sensing he had lost the argument and seeing Brendan as the instrument of his discomfort, seized the moment to remind him of his place in society. He came close, too close for Brendan's comfort, and said, 'Mr O'Neil, you consider me rich and yourself poor, and that may well be the case, but we are no different. Does the Irish farmer allow others to walk on his land, help themselves to his crops, his animals? I think not, do you not defend what is yours by right?'

Brendan was about to respond when he saw Crosby shake his head. Instead, he decided to mellow his response.

'Sir, I thank you for the opportunity to speak to you and it is now clear to me that you have been deceived by some people in your trust, and as you have said that you will deal with this, I am happy to leave matters in your hands.' Colonel Caswell drew back and for the first time smiled. He addressed Crosby.

'One minute we have a stonemason, the next a miner, now an expert in drainage, and on top of this I perceive a politician.' Caswell raised his eyebrows and added, 'I do hope we don't have another Irish agitator.' Crosby laughed, possibly one of relief but the atmosphere changed.

Brendan listened while Crosby and the colonel moved on to discuss mining matters. However, to imply that he was an Irish agitator brought home to Brendan that he and Anna now had another unfair situation to deal with. He counselled himself to keep calm and stood back, out of the conversation.

It was the colonel who again addressed him. 'Mr O'Neil, not all information passes me by. These are difficult times, indeed dangerous times and I have been warned that my life could be at risk from some of your countrymen. And, it comes to my attention that your friend O'Hara speaks against me. Should I keep him in my employ, Mr O'Neil, hmmm?'

Brendan was shocked. All his warnings had been ignored and now he was being tarred with the same brush, no wonder the colonel was unsure about him. He responded. 'O'Hara is no particular friend of mine, but his wife is a good friend to my wife. He is a windbag who blows hot air over anyone who has bettered himself. He is no danger to you; it is the man who says nothing you need to fear.'

The colonel, now in a more genial mood, laughed, turned to Crosby and said, 'My God, Crosby, I shall add philosopher to my list.' He shook hands with both men and told them he had affairs to attend to and walked away.

On the walk back Brendan decided to leave any further comment to Frank. They walked in silence for several minutes before Frank gave a chuckle and said, 'In his own way, he's an honest man. He was born into money and knows no other way and you cannot expect a man to give up his wealth to make other people happy; it's not human nature.'

Brendan asked, 'Frank, what do you think will happen to Watts?'

'The colonel has advisers who will no doubt verify everything we have told him. The truth will come out, and I wouldn't like to be in Watts' shoes, or for that matter his stewards. But we can say that things will now change for the better, and I'm sure your lovely wife will not have to dig buckshot out of your arse.' As they entered The Parade, Frank laughed and said, 'All together it's been a very good day, but Brendan, the colonel is a proud man, so it's back to the tubs for you.' Frank laughed again before adding, 'Here you are, back home at two-thirty, no work to do and you'll get paid. I'll get O'Hara to drop your boots off; see you tomorrow.'

Anna was waiting. Brendan told her about the drainage problems, and how Frank Crosby would be in charge and he would be back on the tubs. Anna was about to react when Brendan added, 'Anna, yer must go and see Bridget te'night. Dan has shot his big gob off once ter often. The colonel thinks he could be a Molly Maguire and we're implicated. They could be thrown out of their cabin, and Dan could end up in jail; or even worse.'

Anna's hands flew to her face.

CHAPTER 26

Brendan unbound his aching hands and removed the lengths of old curtain bindings that Anna had made for him. He wriggled his fingers to get new life into them. Pulling on the rough tub handles over twelve hours was hard both on body and hands. His shift over, with Barney's head dropped over his shoulder, the two made their way through the vent tunnel.

In the entrance, a large bellows was under construction, and canvas tubes lay stacked against the side; Brendan wondered if they would work. As the seam went deeper the men were complaining of lack of oxygen made worse by the heat. For the thousandth time that day, Brendan told himself, *it's time ter move on, or this job will be the end of me.* Even more worrying were the rumours sweeping The Parade, that Watts and his gang of stewards had been brought to heel by the colonel. And who was behind it? Well, it could only be Brendan O'Neil.

Brendan couldn't believe that it was only a week since his visit to see the colonel. Obviously, he had been seen in his finery walking up the track with Frank Crosby. There was only one place to visit – Mount Tahoma. Crosby was a regular visitor and no changes had occurred under his watch in the past, which left only O'Neil as the man who must have had the ear of the colonel. For most this was good news, but would Watts just slink away without retribution? He lived in a superior house, the far side of the barracks. He had six children, and it was said he had two wives, although Watts claimed the one woman was his sister. True or not, no-one was going to question this arrangement. If he had been fired where would he go and where would he find a better position? Whatever anyone said about the colonel, he gave employment and demanded loyalty in return.

Brendan told himself it was only a rumour, too early for the colonel to act, but already looks in his direction on his walk to the mine early in the morning, had warned him of problems ahead. And Frank Crosby wasn't around to ask as he was at the Mount, sorting out the drainage, leaving Oliver Carew in charge.

Brendan made his usual fuss of Barney and began his walk home. It was the last day in August, and the heat caused the track ahead to shimmer like a mirage. He thought of Anna and quickened his pace; she would have his cold tub ready. How lovely to get home out of the heat.

Waiting in the doorway a very distressed Anna told him, 'Christ, Bren, Bridget's been around ter tell me she's heard that Watts and his family have been told ter get out, or he'll be arrested. He's on the warpath and he blames you.'

As they moved inside Millie joined them. 'A notice has gone up at the store, it's from the colonel, there's going to be big changes; you'd better read it.'

Brendan dressed and helped to scrub the potatoes. He kept his conversation light-hearted; he didn't want to make Anna any more nervous. After dinner, he sat outside and drank a cool ginger beer. When Anna joined him he got up. 'Well, we'd better see what the colonel has ter say.' The notice was just inside the door; it read:

To the workers and residents of the Glenvale Mining Company.

It has come to the attention of Colonel Jeremiah Caswell that duties undertaken by stewards under contract to him, and under the leadership of Josiah Watts, to safeguard his woods from poachers and trespassers, have been negligent in their duties. Part of their undertaking was to make available at convenient times, to the residents of The Parade, namely those who work to contract for the said owner, Colonel J Caswell, such game: rabbits; woodcock; pigeon and turkeys that are in abundance in his woods.

Colonel Caswell has been made aware that such game has been misappropriated by J Watts and accomplices, and sold to a third party, thus denying to the inhabitants of The Parade his benefice.

This was contracted to disavow those who believe they have a right to enter the private grounds of Colonel Caswell and take illegally any of the above-named game.

Please note that anyone not adhering to this notice risk a loss of work and abode.

Further, anyone shooting deer risk a severe penalty. Colonel Caswell will determine the time when a cull will take place, and how any benefice will be shared. This is usually in the autumn, and it is his promise that three carcasses will be delivered to the church authorities for a festivity to be arranged by them.

A new head steward will be appointed, and he will be responsible for the supervision of five stewards. The head steward will carry arms: his five assistants will carry cudgels. He will report directly to Colonel Caswell and to the elders of the church. A committee of all dominations will decide on a rota for the distribution of the said game to the most in need. In addition, the church elders will be making representation to butchers in Scranton to see if an assortment of meat can be delivered to Wozniacks General Store. It is well understood that meat during the heat of summer will perish quickly, but it is hoped that some kind of cool store can be in place by next year.

Colonel Jeremiah Caswell

'Well, I suppose 'tis a lot fairer,' said Anna. Brendan was less impressed.

'Ter the neediest; that means just about everyone with families. Anna, it looks as if we are back ter fish, there'll never be enough ter go around.'

Nadia, feeling that somehow it was partly her fault said, 'I can get meat in during winter but in this heat, it's a waste of time. I'm told the colonel has in mind a stone underground pit that will fill with ice during winter, and last over the summer.' Brendan had heard about icehouses in England, built by the rich to serve their great houses. Nadia turned to Brendan. 'You're the stonemason, you might find work.' Brendan shrugged but his thoughts were elsewhere. His visit to see the colonel was to point out his damp problem. Now, not only were they in danger from Pinkerton men but also from Watts and his gang. However, he said nothing; he didn't want to frighten Anna.

It was while they were leaving that a woman they knew by sight as Mary, stopped them and said, 'You've done a fine thing, Mr O'Neil, but I fear for you. All the talk is that Watts is looking for you. If I were you, I'd move in with friends or move out. Your cabin is at the end of the line where your friends can't easily keep an eye on you.'

Brendan was annoyed, the very thing he was trying to protect Anna from was now out in the open. However, he smiled and thanked her. He also wondered whether his so-called friends would stand by him. He took Anna's hand and walked her back to their cabin. He knew she would say little until they were in bed. For some reason, this was the place where she liked to unfold the day and any worries.

Brendan sat in his favourite chair and dozed, while Anna read her book borrowed from the church library. However, Brendan was planning for every eventuality. His first thought was to do a moonlight flit, but he rejected this on two counts. He needed to collect his wages, paid on a Friday, while the three miles' walk to Harper's Drift was a perfect place for an accident. Brendan ruled this out and then turned his mind to the colonel's police. Surely, they would be at hand to protect them. And would Watts dare to go against the colonel? If so, he would be arrested.

Later, in bed, this was the argument he put to Anna, who seemed reassured.

Brendan's thoughts now turned to his worst scenario: *If Watts comes a-lookin' fer me I'll confront him. Yes, he's big, but he's about forty and just look at the gut on 'im. I can tell he's a drinking man. The first time I passed him in the village yer could smell the whisky. He'll be slow on his feet and I know I'm damned quick. I can put 'im down.*

Brendan tried to sleep but his mind wouldn't settle. His thoughts turned to when he was seventeen when he had walked four miles to a travelling fair, and he had paid to see a professional boxer take on all comers.

My God, that was some night: how many challengers did the English champion put down? It must have been six or seven. What was his name? Ah, Joe Martin. When that farrier from Wicklow got in the ring, I thought it would be murder, if ever there was a mismatch that was surely it. But, lookin' back he was short but my God he was strong; yer have ter be ter do his job. I don't think he got hit once: he circled the ring and taunted the big man ter get 'im mad. Yer not supposed ter lose yer rag but Martin certainly did. When he went in, I can see it now… farrier dropped on his left knee and sunk his right fist into Martin's guts, I thought his eyeballs were goin' ter land on me lap. What a punch!

Brendan laughed out loud.

'Jesus Bren, will yer settle, I need me sleep.'

Ter be sure it was a low blow, but if the promoter hadn't paid up the £5 stake, there would have been a riot. Will it come ter this? Watts can't use his gun or a knife, he's a fist man and he brags about how many he's put down, but at a guess, that was twenty years back. If he comes a-callin', he'll want an audience, his reputation is at stake.

For some reason, Brendan knew that the confrontation could not be avoided. *I've run twice. First New York, then Scranton. I'll be damned if a thug like Watts is drivin', me – us – out.*

CHAPTER 27

After a restless night, a tired Brendan fell into step with Dan O'Hara. From the heads that turned his way he knew he was the subject of rumours sweeping through The Parade.

'Bren, what are yer goin' ter do? Bridget's beside herself with worry.' Dan waited.

Brendan shrugged without reply. 'The colonel sent in his police yesterday ter throw Watts and his family out. I'm told he's moved downriver to Mogram.'

Brendan shrugged again and replied, 'Dan, what's it gorra do with me?' The one man he would not share a thought with was Dan O'Hara. He knew that Anna had talked to Bridget and told her that Dan's indiscreet comments had attracted attention, that both families were under suspicion as possible Irish agitators and Molly Maguire sympathisers. Bridget was aghast – she had no idea – her words must have finally hit home because Dan, for once, was quiet on expressing his views on the colonel and people like him. They parted company at the entrance. Dan moved into the mine to work on the face while Brendan went to fetch Barney.

Brendan worked automatically. He listened to the banter of Bryn Reagan, and his stories of finding a good woman until the conversation turned to the colonel's new contract.

A man called Gibbons, new to the mine, cynically remarked, 'I've as little trust in the church elders as I have in the colonel.'

Rob Llewellyn sniffed and said, 'A rota will mean – if we're lucky – one rabbit and a turkey a year, we need a supply of meat coming in.'

Brendan agreed and added, 'How the hell can it be right ter kill a man fer taking a deer when his family's starving?'

Gibbons spoke up. 'Ah, they don't shoot you for killing a deer; it's just another accident, a gun went off in the dark.'

Rob Llewellyn joined in. 'Have any of you seen a deer? I'm told the only place you'll see them is in the valley close to the colonel's spread.'

Bryn Reagan, who had listened but said little on this more serious matter, now had his say. 'We all know who did the shooting when the Irish lad was taken, it was Watts. He killed the steward by mistake, but he put the blame on the lad and those cowardly ruffians with him backed him up.' The name Watts caused a silence, there were a few uneasy looks at Brendan before work resumed.

It was a longer day than usual for Brendan. He took Barney to his field and trudged home alone. As he walked down The Parade, he could feel the tension as people spoke to him; he knew something was in the air.

Anna was nervous and chattered away about nothing. After dinner she and Brendan sat outside; it was a beautiful evening. The nights were closing in and a brilliant red sky bathed The Parade in a russet glow. It was then they heard a commotion coming from the barracks area and feet running in its direction. Millie came around to tell them the police had been called to restore order. Brendan walked to the front and found groups of people standing in doorways trying to find out what was happening. He returned to Anna and settled to cleaning his Sunday boots.

Both jumped when they heard a voice bellow.

'Are you there, Brendan O'Neil? You snivelling Irish piece of shit.'

Instantly Brendan was calm: the moment he had feared had come. He took both of Anna's hands and quietly told her. 'Look at me, Anna. Anna, at ME!' She looked into Brendan's eyes and couldn't believe any man could be so calm and in control. Her mind went back to New York; he had been shocked, dithering after his fight with the knifeman. 'Anna, I'm not running. Yer wait here and I'll be back. I want yer ter to bind me hands in me mining wraps.'

'Jesus, Bren, yer no goin' out there ter fight that brute?'
Brendan gave her hands a squeeze.

'He's a fat slug. I'm not going ter fight him but I'm goin'
ter put him down, now bind me hands.' Brendan's calmness
affected Anna. She fetched the bindings and strapped them
securely. Brendan moved to the door and opened it a few
inches.

'Are you coming out to fight like a man, you Irish snitch,
or shall I come in?'

Brendan could see Watts; he had three men with him.
Undoubtedly, he had other friends who had caused a
disturbance at the barracks. The police would not be
arriving, at least for some time; he was on his own. Brendan
waited; the insults came. He peeped out to see Watts take a
slug of what looked like whisky. Watts was drunk – fighting
drunk! This was the very thing Brendan hoped for, drink
dulled the senses. Coarse insults, followed by sexual taunts
against all the Irish brought people down to the corner.
Brendan knew that this would enrage his Irish neighbours,
he could hear the clamour as more Paraders came down to
the corner, joined by the Scots and Welsh.

Anna sat down; her hands clasped in her lap. She
listened, shocked, as Watts shouted.

'My kids have lost their home. But you, O'Neil, where are
your kids? Can't you get it up? Why don't you send your
bitch out here and I'll show her a real man.'

A woman's voice answered. Brendan thought it was
Eileen Kearney. 'And d'yer know the father of yer kids? Yer
too fat ter get down.' A ripple of laughter ran around the
growing crowd.

Looking out Brendan saw that the three men with Watts
had drifted away: this wasn't what they had come to see, a
fight was one thing but taking on the Irish community was
quite another matter. He listened to the angry exchanges and
he knew he had support. It was time to confront Watts. He
opened the door and stepped out, moving to his right so that
the last rays of the setting sun were in Watts' eyes. Without

saying a word Brendan stood with his hands on his hips. Watts moved to his right, swaying and breathing heavily. Then, he slowly took off a heavy belt from his waist and wrapped it tightly around his right hand with its metal buckle facing out. A murmur of apprehension swept the watching group, a voice called that the police were coming.

'I'm going to smash your fucking Irish face in. By the time I've finished with you they'll need a shovel to scrape you up.' Watts' words were slurred. He stood, not sure what to do. He lurched forward but stopped when Brendan quickly stepped back.

'Stand and fight like a man, you Irish shit, or are you going to run to the colonel and tell him more tittle-tattle?' At this, Watts laughed and looked around for support, but found only silence from the watching group.

This was when Brendan moved forward and leaning from the waist towards Watts, he gave out a long, 'BOOOO!' The crowd laughed, and Watts, enraged, rushed at Brendan, swinging wildly at his head.

For Brendan this was the moment he had waited for, Watts was out of control. He sank to his left knee and felt the metal of Watts' buckle scythe through his hair, at the same time he drove his right fist into the midriff of Watts. In his mind's eye, he saw the farrier's fist sink into the boxer's gut.

Those who witnessed the so-called fight told that the sound that came from Watts, as every inch of air left his body, could be heard in Harper's Drift. It was described as a giant rush of air after a tornado. Watts fell on top of Brendan, who pushed him aside. He was shocked at the sounds coming from Watts, his eyes stood out, his face contorted as he tried to suck oxygen into his diaphragm. He sank to his knees, then was violently sick.

Millie, recognising the danger of Watts choking on his own vomit, gave him a cup of water and patted his back encouraging him to breathe deeply and steadily.

Brendan walked back to Anna, who stood in the doorway

held tightly by Bridget. To the onlooker, Brendan was nonchalant in his manner as if he had swotted a fly that was pestering him. He knew all eyes were on him, and he forced himself to walk slowly. Inside, his mind while ordered, presented an angry exchange with his conscience. *Christ why has it come ter this? All I want is a peaceful life. Knifeman was an accident. I didn't mean ter kill him, but he did try ter kill me. Yes, I mentioned Watts ter the colonel but all I was trying ter do was to get more food fer The Parade. Watts came after me – what else could I do?*

It was at this moment Brendan's downing of Watts entered folklore. Cool as a cucumber, ice-cold was another description, a warrior with a right punch that would have felled an ox. It was Anna who knew that Brendan O'Neil was the gentlest, the most thoughtful man alive, but he was also a proud man whose sense of fairness would not see him bow the knee to anyone.

Brendan gently took Anna's hand and led her back inside their cabin. Bridget joined Dan, who was trying, with Jonas' help, to comfort their excited children who had followed them to see what was going on.

For a time, onlookers stood outside number twenty; cheers of solidarity rang out around The Parade. With one punch Brendan O'Neil had demolished the hold Watts and his gang of stewards had held over their lives. Three policemen arrived and arrested Watts for breaking his exclusion order from The Parade. Pedersen, head of the police, told the onlookers that the colonel had sent Watts packing on the understanding that if he returned to The Parade he would be arrested and come before the magistrate; the very colonel himself.

As night settled, Anna lit the lamp and turned to look at Brendan. He sat, his hands folded in his lap, looking utterly miserable; her curtain wraps trailed from his hands. She sat at his feet and folded the tapes to put with his work clothes. Brendan looked at her and quietly said, 'Well, Anna O'Neil, yer wanted excitement, and I hope I'm fulfilling yer needs.'

Only Millie and Jonas next door heard the laughter that

came from number twenty.

CHAPTER 28

Brendan didn't know it at the time, but his life had changed. He had a hint of it when he walked to work the next morning. As the miners converged on the track to the mine fists were raised in his direction. He knew it was a symbol of solidarity; his fist had put down Watts, but it made him uneasy. He had never considered himself as a leader of men, and now he wondered if it was an invitation for others to see him as leader of the pack, ready to be challenged and dethroned.

At the entrance, Mr Carew read out notices for the day. Then he drew Brendan to one side to tell him that the colonel had been informed of events the night before, how Watts had abused him and his wife, and the good people of The Parade. All these would register in the charges brought against him. Brendan asked about his children. Carew shrugged and said, 'He should have thought of that before. Did he think of The Parade's children?'

Brendan had no answer, but he knew Anna would tell him that the sins of the father should not be held against innocent children. However, Frank had already told him that the eldest of Watts' children was, in his words, a thug in the making. Pushing these thoughts to the back of his mind he organised the tubs and welcomed the cooler day. September heralded what he had been told was called "the fall". Winter would soon be upon them, and the thought of spending months in their cabin wasn't a prospect that he wished to think about. Pinkerton or no Pinkerton it was time to move on. He would tell Anna about his plans when he got home. They would leave on a Friday evening after he had been paid and make for Philadelphia.

Brendan led Barney to his field and gave him his apple

treat; he would miss him. On his walk back home, he realised he would miss more than Barney. The camaraderie, especially the socials on a Sunday, had been wonderful. His heart leapt at the vision in his mind of Anna singing her Irish ballads. He quickened his pace, he had made up his mind, he would tell Anna they were leaving.

He had barely reached Wozniacks' corner when Anna came running towards him; he could tell it wasn't bad news. Her face was laughing, her teeth gleamed in the sunlight, her hair was flying. She looked gorgeous; she flew into his arms and babbled away in his ear.

'Christ, Anna, will yer slow down and take a breath.' Brendan laughed.

'I've got wonderful news, yer just won't believe it. We've had a letter from Yvonne.' Anna pulled at his hand to speed him.

'And?'

'Wait till we get back but, yer won't believe it.'

Brendan took her hand and swinging along they returned home. Anna held out the letter and told him, 'Alice rode in from Harper's Drift. Tom and Yvonne both thought we'd gone on ter Philly. Then by chance, Tom bumped into Seamus who told him we were here. When Tom got back ter Scranton he told Yvonne and right away she wrote this letter; just read it.'

Brendan sat down on the bench in the yard, looked up and said, 'How about a glass of ginger beer, I'm parched.' The folded letter lay on his lap.

'Brendan O'Neil, yer'd put years on a saint.' Anna gave an exasperated huff and went to get his ginger beer.

Brendan drank slowly while Anna hopped up and down. Finally, he unfolded the letter and held it up to the light to read.

Dear Anna and Brendan,

I got your letter which arrived a month late, half the address and part of the letter was missing. I could make out that Brendan had turned his hand to mining, but I assumed you were in Philly.

In June I tried to do right by you but instead, I caused you mischief.

Just after you left the Pinkerton man turned up and told me that he had been sent by a Mr Peabody, the kind friend you mentioned. I told him that you had run because you thought that the New York police were after you, but in fact, the police want you to return to New York to give evidence in a trial against one of the men who robbed you.

You must get in touch with Mr Peabody, but it must be before the 20th of September because you need swearing in as witnesses. The Pinkerton man, J L Sawyer, suggests that you get back to Scranton, go to the station and send a telegraph to the station at Hoboken. A rail warrant will get you to Hoboken, arranged by Mr Peabody.

Tom arrives every Friday evening at Harper's Drift. When you get back to Scranton, I can find you a bed.

Yvonne

PS Mr Peabody is searching Philadelphia for you.

Brendan put down the letter and smiled. 'Anna, I was coming home ter tell yer we're moving on ter Philly. God! Now we're heading back ter Scranton, I don't know ter be pleased or not. New York? Well! I thought I'd seen the last of that place.'

Anna moved to Brendan and took his still dirty face in her hands and said, 'Bren, there's a lovely man out there who's not only saved us, he's funded us, and all this time he's been lookin' out fer us, d'yer mean yer'd let him down?' Brendan sighed.

'No, we've no choice – but I've broken me contract, so I'll lose me bonus, an' we need every penny.'

Anna was insistent. 'Why don't yer write a letter ter the colonel and explain. Seein' yer on the side of law and order he'll understand.'

Brendan thought for a second. 'Yer better at fine words than me. While I'm having me bath, write a letter and I'll give it ter Frank. He's up at the Mount every day now and he can pass it on. But whatever happens, after I get paid on Friday we'll meet up with Tom at Harper's.'

After dinner, Anna set about the task and read it to

Brendan.

To Colonel J Caswell, Glendale Mining Company.

Sir, I have been called as a witness in a trial to take place in New York at the end of this month. Therefore, I am obliged to tender my notice from working in your mine, and this, of course, means that I must break my contract with you and forego my bonus.

Mr Nathanial Peabody of the Lackawanna Rail Company has been searching for me for several weeks. Therefore, with my wife Anna, we need to leave for Scranton on Friday 14th September, to arrive in New York no later than the 17th.

I wish to thank you for your prompt attention in dealing with the matter of your stewards, and your new contract for the people of The Parade. I also hope that the work at present underway at Mount Tahoma will see your home secure in all weather.

Yours sincerely

Brendan sat back. 'Anna O'Neil, yer've a way about yer, and words I'd never find but I must say it's kinder than me thoughts.'

Anna looked at him. 'Bren, we're trying ter humour him, not annoy him. A kind word goes a long way.' Brendan signed the letter with a flourish.

In the evening Brendan walked to Frank Crosby's lodge, a smart timber building on a track behind Wozniacks' store. To his surprise, a young woman, whom he knew was from Russia, answered the door. She invited him in, and Frank looked up from his chair very surprised. Brendan told him about the letter and Peabody wanting them to return to New York.

'Didn't I tell you Pinkerton wouldn't waste a minute on you unless it was something really important?' Crosby seemed pleased. 'I'll give the colonel your letter. Crosby got up and walked Brendan to the door, shook hands, gave a wink and said, 'Every man needs a woman,' then added, 'Tahoma's looking good and the colonel has been very fulsome in praise of you, not to mention putting Watts down. My God, Brendan, things have changed overnight –

for the better – thanks to you.' Brendan smiled, shook hands again and thanked Frank for being such a good friend, and said goodbye. Back with Anna, he decided not to mention the Russian girl.

It was a difficult night for sleep. Brendan could only recall the smiling face of Paddy, his evil and snarling true face as he took his money belt. Had he been caught? And why was it so important for them to return to New York as witnesses? Anna was less disturbed. For some reason, she felt it was the beginning of something good.

CHAPTER 29

On Friday morning Anna saw Nadia at the store and told her they would be leaving in the evening. She was both surprised and disappointed. Anna felt compelled to tell her the full story; Nadia listened then embraced her. 'What will we do without your bright smile about the place? And your man's a hero.' Nadia waved her hand around the store. 'And whatever's said about the colonel he's making changes, though from what I hear the railhead will soon come here and who knows what will happen.'

It was at this moment that Mrs Feeney came in and told them, 'Watts has been charged with murder and he's on his way to jail at Delaware. Two stewards, I'm not sure which two, have said that Watts shot the steward. He meant to shoot the Irish boy but missed. All the lad had was one turkey, and there wasn't a deer in sight. The boy's shotgun was discharged by Watts afterward, and he told them to keep quiet – or else! For sure he'll drop.'

Anna's hand flew to her face, the thought that Bren was responsible, that Watts would be hanged coming after knifeman's death, was just too much.

Nadia sensed this and took her arm. 'Remember the Irish lad, he was only nineteen, and I wouldn't be surprised if Watts hasn't killed a few in his time. And what about the brute who attacked you in New York?'

When Mrs Feeney had moved away Nadia folded her arms, looked at Anna, smiled and said, 'Come on, my little Irish girl, no more dark clouds. Now, what deal have you in mind?' For once Anna had no blarney to offer.

'Nadia, we can only take what we can carry which isn't much. I think it best we return the bedding ter yer. In fact, we'll give yer the clay cooking pots Bren made. Send Joe down later and we'll load the cart. Oh! And I'll pass on me ginger beer plant, everyone seems ter like it.'

Nadia shrugged and said, 'I can't do much for you, but you can forget your milk and oil bill.' She embraced Anna again. 'You will call in and say goodbye before you go?'

Anna was in tears. Yes, mining was a short-term measure to avoid the Pinkerton men but, the people – well most of them – were wonderful. She would miss her friends in The Parade. She loved Sundays and singing her Irish songs. And she wouldn't be there for Bridget, due in early October. She pushed these thoughts aside: how long would it be before Bren was hurt at work? It was time to pack.

On the way back Anna called in to say goodbye to Bridget, who could not believe the news. She was shocked, leading Anna to tell her they were returning to New York to give it another try; she didn't mention being called as witnesses in a trial.

Her next stop was at Millie and Jonas', who listened quietly while Anna explained their quick departure. Millie just gathered Anna in her arms and said, 'Life's an adventure; yer young, and there's nothing here for yer. God bless yer.'

The cart arrived and Anna helped Joe, and an older man she didn't know, load their possessions on the cart and watched them move to the store. Inside, she turned to look at her now almost empty room, the home they had made was no more. She could hear the echo of her voice and her mind went back to their first evening. Brushing away her tears she packed Brendan's large sack and sat down on the hard chair to wait. They would dine at Harper's. The moment Brendan arrived home they would walk the three miles and hope to find something to eat.

Brendan led Barney to his field and felt sad when he turned to see him still watching as he walked up the track to the office. He hated mining and equally the thought that Barney would see out only the days when he was of use. He joined the queue to receive his wages and found himself last. As he moved to Mr Carew's table, to his surprise, he was given two envelopes. Brendan took the small brown envelope with his name written on it, but it was the larger cream coloured envelope with the printed heading of the Glenvale Mining Company on it that made him nervously take it from Mr Carew who shook hands and said, 'I hear you are moving on to better things. I wish you good fortune.' Brendan thanked Oliver Carew and wished him the same. He waited until he was well down the track before opening the envelope. It was from the colonel addressed to him and Anna; he read:

Dear Mr and Mrs O'Neil,

It has come to my attention that your return to New York is to further the cause of law and order. On your behalf, Mr Frank Crosby has informed me that this is at the request of Mr Nathaniel Peabody, a name well known in the business world and respected by all.

Therefore, I wish you and Mrs O'Neil Godspeed in your endeavour.

As regards your employment it is unusual to receive such a courteous letter informing me of your intention, and I reciprocate your good wishes. This being so I am waving your contractual agreement and you will find enclosed the bonus of two dollars that would have accrued to you over the given time.

My wife and I wish you good fortune in this wonderful country and hope you will find fulfilment in your new life in America.

Colonel Jeremiah Caswell.

Brendan was delighted and couldn't wait to get back to Anna; many thoughts moved through his mind. What a strange man the colonel was. Ruthless on the one hand, ready to execute a man who stole his deer, believing that once the law was set then every man had a choice, obey or take the risk. To be poor was something he didn't understand, he believed he had worked hard for his riches, and every man had the same chance in life. Brendan pondered at how Caswell had become a colonel, no-one seemed to know. Had he fought in the Civil War? Or had he decided to title himself to gain prestige?

Pushing these thoughts aside Brendan returned home. Anna's letter and Frank's support had landed two extra dollars, now they could live in style, at least for several days, and with winter coming they would both need warmer clothing. He opened the door; Anna was sitting with both their packs at her feet. He looked around the cabin and felt the same emptiness. He said nothing and handed her the letter. She read it and immediately her face brightened. 'God, Bren, that's a good omen; d'yer know I feel it's a turning point. Things can only get better.'

Later, as they walked up The Parade, neighbours came out to say goodbye. At the store, Nadia was waiting. She shook hands with Brendan and gave Anna a hug. 'Send me a letter when you've got a minute.'

On a glorious evening, the two set out for Harper's Drift. It would take just over an hour to get there, and they hoped that Tom would be there with his waggons.

Harper's had changed. It was hard to believe it was the same place. The new gravity railhead was almost finished, its rails running up the steep bank to the canal basin above. Brendan just had to see what was happening. Anna, less curious after hauling her bag three miles, knew she had packed far too much but the thought of throwing garments away was unthinkable. She sat on some stacked timber and then decided to try and lift Brendan's sack. She could barely lift it two inches off the ground. Again, she marvelled at the strength of her man but consoled herself that a good marriage was about bringing to the table what both had to offer.

Brendan was amazed to find barges tied up and coal hoppers in place for loading. The railroad ran away into the distance following the canal until it branched away to the left and disappeared behind a hillock. Mountains of anthracite awaited the coal cars, still to arrive. Dozens of mules were still doing the carrying from the mines on the lower reach, but he knew that soon steam locomotives would be employed to do the work. Seamus was right, this was the place to find work, but not for him. Turning back Brendan waved to Anna and looked beyond the hotel where the forest was being stripped to allow rails to be laid. Soon they would reach The Parade and further on connect with Mogram and other mining villages. He recalled Mr Carew's words that very soon that Harper's Drift would be part of Scranton.

Back with Anna, Brendan searched for any sign of Tom's waggons. Disappointed not to find them they were about to cross to the hotel when a shout came; it was Alice. 'Ma thought you might be here. We're settled behind the new houses. I'll tell 'em. The hotel's full, you can use one of the waggons; come when yer ready.' They told her they were starving and would see them after a meal. With a cheery wave, she ran back down the track.

The hotel had also changed. A new section was under construction, while the tents behind had been replaced with log cabins. Inside the lamps were lit as night crept in. To their surprise, a new team ran the hotel and they were told to go to the improved restaurant, find a table, and their order would be taken. A girl dressed in a green costume with a white apron moved from table to table.

Anna whispered, 'I hope ter God it's not trout.'

'Evenin', mister and missus, you can have trout, marinated beef or German sausage, with boiled potatoes. To drink we have root beer, lemonade or ginger beer. Or, at the bar, you can order whisky, German beers or German wines.' They ordered the beef.

Bren whispered to Anna, 'D'yer want ter bet the new people are German?'

Along with a basket of bread and a jug of lemonade they ate well. Brendan was well satisfied and declared, 'It's a long time since I ate beef. That's what workers need.' At a small cash desk, he paid and then turned to find Tom grinning at him.

'Ah, when I met Seamus, I thought we'd meet up again.

If you want a free ride I need your help to do a bit of loading. Tomorrow, you look after the teams and Anna can help Alma with the cooking – same as before.' Brendan was tired but pleased to meet up again with Tom and Alma. However, he had found that tiredness could be put to one side. Tom's cheerfulness made him forget his aching limbs; he followed him to a house. As night settled lamps were hung from the trees to sort the furniture; it took an hour to load the waggon.

Further down the track Anna found Alma and Alice, and they set about making a fire; suddenly the nights were getting colder. Later, with both families together, warmed by the fire, they recounted their adventures since parting in June. Brendan decided to tell them they were returning to New York to give witness against a gang who had robbed them; he mentioned Nathaniel Peabody. Tom took an immediate interest.

'My friend, he's an important man in the freight business, he's an investor in the canal you can see up there and he's something to do with the Scranton Steam Locomotive Company.' Anna was impressed.

'Is there anyone who doesn't know Mr Peabody? He was our saviour. He's a lovely man.'

It was Alice who spoke up. 'Aren't you going to tell us about putting down Watts? It's all the talk around here – one punch – you're quite famous. He was a big brute, and no-one liked him.'

Anna sat quietly thinking, *two punches – the New York one and The Parade, but my Brendan is the gentlest man I've ever met.*

Tom held up his hand at Alice. 'Kids, ignore her.'

Brendan smiled, shrugged and said, 'He was drunk.' This finished the conversation.

Alma stood up. 'Come on, folks, we're leaving at six in the morning – time to hit the hay.'

Again, Brendan's Donegal bedroll came in handy. It was a cool night, but they were quite snug in the waggon; morning came too soon. Tom rattled the water barrel attached to the front board. Brendan quickly came awake, less so Anna who was always a bit slow to rise.

Alma had the fire going and after a breakfast of beans, eggs, and coffee, the waggons were hitched. Tom took the first with Brendan beside him, Alice the second, while a man called Able took the reins of the third seated waggon, with Alma and Anna in the chuck. Tom explained that he would be picking up several men at points along the route, as well as two horses from a farm near Scranton.

For Anna, working with Alma was agreeable, however, she had a feeling of moving backward rather than forward. Suddenly, she felt nervous about the future. What did a witness mean, would she be involved, and what would they face in New York? Brendan, on the other hand, was enjoying keeping the waggon train moving, and he worked happily alongside Tom. The outdoor life had an appeal he had thought he could put behind him. After all, he was now a stonemason and towns offered work and living. His thoughts returned to Ireland, to the farm he had left behind, stony, unworkable fields, and little to be had in the way of work for miles around. Too many men trying to find a living. He wondered how his brothers were doing at their fishing.

In discussion with Tom he pointed out that you could claim land for a registration fee; the government wanted the land worked and settled but you had to go to the Mid-West. Tom grimaced. 'It's too far out for me. It's undeveloped, and from what I hear it can be a dangerous place. You'd be far better off settling in the Lackawanna.' This was everything Brendan wanted to hear.

'Yer know, Tom, I tell everyone I'm a stonemason, but the truth is, at heart, I'm a farmer, and just look at the soil along here, yer could grow anything yer wanted.'

As they passed the homesteads dotted along the riverbank, Brendan could see himself in a cottage with Anna and their children. He could build their home; he had the skills.

The jolt as Tom brought the team to a halt broke his

reverie. Six men joined the waggon train. A man called Uriah took over the reins from Tom, leaving him to ride the spare horse to check out the track ahead. Further on, four men joined at Fork Creek, having walked overland from a drift mine.

As midday approached Tom rode up and shouted, 'We've got trouble.'

CHAPTER 30

Tom reined in and stopped the waggon train. Anna, at the back, had no idea what was happening. Brendan at the front could see the track ahead; seven Indians stood barring their way. Three of them carried rifles crooked in their arms. They looked a motley crew, dressed in a variety of clothing, part western, part Indian. The leader had his hair fastened back with a large black and red wooden comb, and although the weather was warm, he wore an old grey army coat with the insignia removed.

'Brendan, stay here, I'll deal with this.' Tom got off his horse, took a small blanket, walked towards the group and sat down several feet away. The leader with the wooden comb sat down to join him.

Alma and Anna moved to the front, while Able warned the miners to sit where they were; one false move could see lives lost.

After a discussion, Tom got up and walked slowly back with three of the Indians. 'Alma, these men want flour, whisky, a few blankets, and can you sort out the knives we've put to one side.' From this Brendan understood that this had happened before. He watched while Alma spread three blankets on the ground to await approval. One Indian threw them over his shoulder, and the three moved to the chuck waggon where Tom lifted out a half-sack of flour. This didn't seem to please the Indians and Brendan could hear the argument. Tom moved deeper into the waggon, brought out a cloth and spilled six long-bladed knives at the feet of the Indians, the type used by hunters. The Indian with the blankets picked one up and waved it in the air to show his delight. The Indians conversed and it seemed to Anna that they wanted more. Several times she heard the word whisky mentioned but she knew Tom and Alma were against what they called the evils of drink. Brendan looked on concerned, more so when Tom undid his tunic shirt to reveal he had a holster and revolver tucked into his trouser top. He stood squarely before the Indians; the time for talking was over. Anna was equally alarmed when she saw Alma reach inside the waggon with her right hand; she knew a Remington rifle was strapped just inside.

A call came from the elderly Indian in the grey army coat, he gestured to the forest, and without a further word the Indians collected their goods and the group disappeared into the trees alongside the river.

'That's the third time in two years. I've told them that the next time they will be hunted down and put in jail. Poor bastards, they're starving and can't get work.' Tom shrugged. 'But I have a living to make as well as them. Come on, let's get going.'

Another few hours brought them to a shady clearing, close to the river for dinner; but it was a subdued atmosphere.

Anna and Alma served the stew. As the men waited for their share a short man, who wore the scars of mining, a series of blue creases that anchored at his mouth and ran behind his withered left ear, thumped his chest and declared, 'I'm starving, I could eat a horse.'

Alma replied. 'An' if you wait a minute, you'll get your wish.' Anna looked dubiously at her stew. Horse? Brendan just laughed.

After dinner, Brendan discussed with Tom what the future held, with so many wonderful inventions coming out every year. Alma listening in laughed, 'We have about two years before the iron horse ruins us.'

'Nonsense!' Tom replied, 'and who's going to get the goods to the railheads and what about the passengers? Trains need rails, I can go anywhere, there's more money to be made when the trains come, you wait and see. And how will people get to the trains out here er?'

The miners sat in a group and played cards, while Able sat to one side and entertained everyone with his harmonica. Anna joined him, she just loved music, and Able described some of his sad songs, but he didn't know 'The Rose of Tralee'!

'Come on, we're running late.' Tom broke up the party.

The journey to Scranton passed without any further problems. Near to the town they made a detour to a farm and two horses were tied to the chuck waggon for delivery to a large warehouse on the outskirts of the town. An hour later, horses delivered, they pulled up at the railhead.

Brendan and Anna said goodbye and promised Tom and Alma that they would keep in touch – when they could, while the miners paid their dues before going their separate ways.

Anna looked forward to seeing Yvonne, but Brendan's thoughts were elsewhere. 'I think we must go ter the station first, we need ter send a telegram to Mr Peabody. It's already past six and we may have ter wait till te'morra.'

A shortcut past Brendan's old workplace brought them to the station, and in the office, they found a young man called Oliver who listened carefully to Brendan's request to contact Mr Nathaniel Peabody by telegraph.

'I'll send it on to Hoboken and he'll pick it up there.' He looked at his watch. 'Bit late now; he may not get it until tomorrow, but I'll mark it urgent.' They thanked him and watched while he tapped out the message.

The walk back to Chester Street made them both a little nervous. It was, as Brendan said, a repeat of their lives. As they entered the vestibule Yvonne was waiting.

CHAPTER 31

'I still feel guilty when I think back. If that Pinkerton man had mentioned your Mr Peabody the first time, well, it would be a different story.' Yvonne was still angry with herself.

Brendan shushed her, 'Yvonne, yer weren't ter know; yer did yer best as a good friend and Anna and meself appreciate yer kindness.' Anna nodded agreement.

Later, after spending an hour with Yvonne and recounting all that had happened to them since their hasty departure, they climbed to room forty-five on the top floor.

After a long and arduous day, Brendan looked forward to bed; however, sleep wouldn't come. He lay awake thinking ahead to their return journey to New York. He felt apprehensive, not knowing what to expect, but one thing was clear to him, he didn't like cities, he liked the countryside where a man could breathe. Again, the Lackawanna Valley filled his thoughts. Yes, it was the place for him, Anna, and their children.

Anna wondered if it was the stew at midday that was keeping her awake. Was it horse meat? She felt a bit queasy. She turned to look at Brendan, he was breathing deeply. *Ah, nothing worries Bren*, she thought. *He takes everything in his stride.* Her thoughts turned to their return. She could see dear Mr Peabody, what a lovely gentleman he was, and she knew, even in the short time they had met, that he was fond of her. No doubt she reminded him of his late wife, but no matter, sometimes it takes only an instant to like someone; and she liked Nathanial Peabody.

The loud knock on the door made her start. 'It's gone eight, make hay.' Yvonne's voice brought Brendan out of bed as quickly as if it had caught fire.

'Christ, Anna, we need ter get ter the station; move yer clogs.'

The usual queue at the washroom saw the two dash along to the yard to use the outdoor facilities, and a hasty return to their room to grab their belongings; breakfast would have to wait.

In the vestibule, Brendan found Yvonne. 'We'll settle up with yer when we can, but I don't know if we'll be coming back fer another night... ter tell the truth, we've no idea what the hell's goin' on.'

Yvonne pointed at the door. 'Go sort yourselves out, but when you get a minute let me know. I'm part of this you know, and I hate a story without an ending.' Yvonne was close to tears. Anna gave her a hug while Brendan, never a demonstrative man, impulsively took Yvonne's hand and gave it a kiss.

'Yvonne, yer a friend fer life.'

Anna and Brendan walked quickly to the station. Inside, a clerk introduced himself as George. He looked through the telegraph messages.

'Ah! Here's one from Oliver – you're to catch the noon train. I've tickets here for train and ferry; someone will meet you at the landing. Don't lose them.' He looked at the clock. 'You've three hours to kill.' The relief was enormous.

Brendan smiled and took Anna's hand. 'Now we can go fer breakfast; I need a strong coffee.'

'And I know just where ter go.' Anna led the way.

Danilo gave a whoop of pleasure when he saw them. His vegetables were laid out neatly along the pavement, and his small coffee table was free. 'Sit down, my friends.' Without any introduction, he grabbed Brendan's hand, and pumped it up and down. 'Your good lady here, we do good business together. My wife, she go to market. I get you coffee and doughnuts.'

Brendan had to agree that the hot doughnuts were great, but he wasn't used to, as he called it, a sweet breakfast. However, the coffee was the best he had ever tasted and as his cup emptied Danilo refilled it. Near to noon they headed back to the station and arrived with time to spare. For both, the iron horse was fascinating, and they watched as the large engine moved onto a bridge over a deep circular pit, and in amazement as three men with large levers slowly turned the enormous engine to face back the way it came. Slowly it moved into position and the cars were joined; this solved for Brendan the question as to how you moved such a great weight.

The passengers boarded. Businessmen moved to the first car, while the second was quickly taken by families. Brendan guided Anna to a seat to the front, and unlike their first rail journey, the seats were cushioned. A number of excited children lined the windows waiting for the train to move. The third car was taken by a team of railway workers. Behind lay a long line of open waggons filled with building materials. At twelve the train left Scranton and Anna and Brendan settled down to the four-hour journey.

Anna was thrilled at the changing scenery; she remembered her thoughts from their first journey. Nudging Brendan she reminded him. 'I could live here.'

Brendan shook his head. 'If we live anywhere, it'll be the Lackawanna Valley.'

'So, yer back ter being a farmer's boyo are yer? What about yer stone?'

'As I see it, Anna, I can do both.'

It was warm in the car, and the babble of conversations slowly reduced until only the rumble of the wheels played a sleep pattern that most of the passengers gave in to; even the children succumbed. Brendan tried to keep awake, but with Anna's head on his shoulder he gave up.

The hoot from the engine brought them awake. A stout little man called out, 'Just in time for the ferry.' In the general rush to get aboard, Brendan and Anna were swept along in the melee and found themselves crushed against a railing. 'Jesus, I think everyone's goin' to New York,' said Anna. Twenty minutes later the ferry began its turn to align with the landing, and for the first time, Anna could see the terminal. She grabbed Brendan's arm and shouted. 'I can see Mr Peabody's coach.'

Many passengers made for the city-bound train but, as far as the eye could see carriages awaited those who lived off the city and main routes. Brendan stood on a bollard to see if he could see Mr Peabody's coach but failed.'

'He's there, I saw him.' Anna tried to push on. Brendan held her back.

'He'll find us as soon as this crowd moves on.' They waited until gaps appeared in the line of carriages and the nearest moved away.

'There he is.' Brendan guided Anna to the end of the landing and Anna recognised the shiny black lacquered coach with Mr Peabody's emblem on the door, the coachman grinned a welcome as he reined in.

'Heh, Irish, we meet again, thought I'd seen the last of you. Climb aboard, folks, and hang on, the road ain't too good.' Brendan reached up to the driver's hand.

'My friend, we're pleased ter see yer again, but we don't know yer name.'

'Isaac Walcott, sir, I remember your lady's name, but I forget yours.'

'Brendan, but Bren will do.' They shook hands and Brendan climbed in and shut the door.

As the carriage headed north Anna hung onto Brendan, who in turn anchored himself to a strap as Isaac kept up a steady pace over, in places, the heavily rutted road. Away to their left, they caught glimpses of the river, and factories under construction and the masts of tall ships. On one hilly section, Isaac gave the horses a breather and a drink from a roadside trough. He explained that the smell from the river came from the whaling station. Further on huge sawmills came into sight. Ahead they could see a town, its tall church spire an impressive sight.

Isaac called down. 'Yonkers!'

Just before the town, Isaac turned to a track that led

through a valley lined with aspen trees. This led on to green meadows and increasingly hilly countryside. In the distance, they could see mountains.

Isaac yelled down, 'Catskills.' Then on another rise, he yelled, 'Bronx,' to name the river away to their right.

Passing through another canopy of aspen they turned the corner to find open grazing land, enclosed with white fences.

'Almost there,' Isaac shouted down.

As they turned around a hillock a large low-level ranch stood before them with a wide driveway of gravel. Burnt into a large circular cut from a tree trunk was the name, K RANCH. Behind they could see a series of log cabins. As Isaac reined in, the door opened, and Mr Peabody came out. Anna didn't wait for Isaac to lower the step she leapt out of the coach and threw herself into his arms. 'Oh, Mr Peabody, yer our saviour again, we don't know how ter thank yer.'

Mr Peabody held her tightly and put out his hand for Brendan, who took it. After a brief shake, he took both around the waist and turned them to the door. 'You must both be hungry and tired. I've a meal standing by, but I must warn you that however tired you are we have a lot to do this evening.'

CHAPTER 32

Inside, Anna was delighted by the simple elegance of the large lounge. In places, the rough timber had been left exposed and a variety of richly coloured blankets were hung, very much like tapestries. The end walls had been plastered and painted a pale cream, and on these were several paintings depicting country scenes.

For Brendan, his first interest was the huge stone-built fireplace and the built-in seats either side. The floor was part timber and part large flat tablets of stone. Two large settees were angled before the fireplace with several armchairs. Along the far wall sat occasional chairs. Above, the roof timbers were covered with a kind of rush matting and a series of lamps were suspended on chains that could be raised or lowered. In a little study that ran off, Anna was fascinated by a collection of Indian weapons, bows, arrows, and spears, also headdresses and brightly dyed tunics.

'It's wonderful, Mr Peabody. I've never seen anything so grand, er, so beautiful.'

'Ah, it's been featured in the *London Illustrated News*,' Mr Peabody said proudly. 'But I see Brendan only has eyes for the stonework.'

Brendan replied, 'Whoever did it was a craftsman.'

It was then that an almost invisible door opened, the wood pattern merging with the panelling. A black lady entered, smiled and said, 'Mr Peabody, shall I serve dinner now?'

'Five minutes, my dear, but first let me introduce Anna and Brendan O'Neil to you.' She came forward and shook hands before disappearing back through the door. Mr Peabody explained. 'Precious and Isaac, whom you have already met, are both friends and employees.' He paused before adding, 'I don't like the word servants because Precious was born to a slave. No-one knows her original name. A friend of mine found her abandoned and called her Precious and the name has stood. It's rather nice, I think. They will be joining us for dinner.' He moved to a sash on the wall and gave it a tug.

Isaac announced dinner was served. Moving from the lounge they entered through the disguised door to find a long room, wooden panelled with a long table in place. Only a small triangular corner piece with a vase of wildflowers broke the line, apart from a large map of New York State, cased in glass, set into the wall.

'Pot roast, an American meal in your honour. It's one of my favourites so I hope you'll enjoy it.' Precious served the roast, and as Anna said later, she had never seen so many different vegetables on one plate in all her life.

'I'm sorry I do not drink wine, I prefer nature's brew, water, but it has a lemon flavour.' Mr Peabody poured himself a drink and passed the jug to Anna who filled her glass. Brendan did the same and took a quick sip; it was delightfully cold. He wanted to discuss cold stores, but Mr Peabody wanted to hear about everything that had happened to them since he had waved them goodbye on the New York side of the river.

Brendan left it to Anna to outline their stay in Scranton and their flight to The Parade, believing that the Pinkerton man was acting for the police against them.

Mr Peabody gave an exasperated tap to the table, 'It's so unfortunate, if my name had been mentioned on first contact, then you could have avoided your mining.' He added, 'I suppose in a strange country it's difficult to assess these matters. Oh well, here you are safe and sound.'

Anna, wishing to change the conversation, turned her attention to their meal. 'Precious, it's the best meal I've had in me whole life, it'll last me many a day.' This pleased Precious and Isaac, and for a moment the conversation lightened. Even more so when Anna asked the question that Brendan wanted to ask but had decided to await a better moment.

'Mr Peabody, I have about me the curiosity of a cat.' Anna waved her arms to encompass the room. 'I have ter say yer not the poorest man I've ever met.' Brendan froze, but the others laughed. Again, he asked himself how Anna had the knack of not offending people when he most certainly would.

Mr Peabody made a sawing action and said, 'Timber! The nation may need coal but there's always a need for timber. You passed my sawmills on your way here, and of course, as I told you my second passion is railways, they're the future to open this vast country. And I should also explain that this is my country home. I spend most weekends here but during the week I have an apartment in Manhattan; it's too far to travel every day. And I also have a cottage retreat in the Lackawanna Valley, near Scranton.' His face clouded. 'K stands for Kathleen, but she never lived to see my success.'

Brendan asked about their stay in the city and how long the trial could take, but before an answer came, Precious brought in a selection of chopped fruits with cream.

After dinner, in the lounge with coffees in place, Mr Peabody outlined what had happened in Anna and Brendan's absence. 'It seems that the Paddy who robbed you is part of a gang who turn their hand to anything that will fund their enterprises, and one quick way is to rob new arrivals such as yourselves. He has several aliases: Sean, Robert, Regan, and others. Until this past year, he has been at the lower end of the crime scene, but we now suspect him of murder. His fellow gang member, the one you helped to dispatch, was a mean killer, easily identified because of his pockmarked face. His real name is Lewis Godden, known to many as Lew, but he also has a second identity, George Salter. He was born here, began his life as a runner for a crime syndicate, moved on to robbery and we now know he robbed and killed a French businessman whom he befriended. The day you came across him, along with part of Paddy's gang, they were stealing blue bricks stacked for a new wharf. There's a shortage at present with so much building going on. They could have made a small fortune, your intervention and my presence sent them scattering. I reported it all to the police department after I left you. Looking back, I should have put you into my care, but not knowing the full facts I advised you to move on to Scranton. I thought it best to get you out of immediate harm's way, and I could always find you in Scranton. However, the description you gave me of Paddy, and his close association with your so-called knifeman, identified them both in the murder of a watchman on the seafront. The gang cleared the warehouse of expensive fabrics. We have a witness, but he's been hidden away: he's the watchman's fourteen-year-old son. He came with a can of tea for his father, just as the gang arrived. He hid behind bales and saw his father pulled down and stabbed, and behind the knife, we have a perfect description of your Paddy.'

Brendan listened carefully; it was hard to believe that the amiable man they had met could be so vicious. 'Mr Peabody, what d'yer want from us? And what, if yer don't mind me asking, is yer part in this?'

Mr Peabody sat back and said, 'I am a magistrate, but I deal with what we call the minor cases, youths who need a firm hand to stop them from becoming the Paddies of this world. I know the judiciary, and of course, I am constantly in touch with the police. Chief Attorney Abraham Grant is well known to me and, with your testimony and identification possibly we can put Paddy away; he's already been arraigned so he can't slip away. Attorney Prosecutor Liam Lewinski will be here shortly, he will tell you all you need to know. It will be a late-night for him and an early start tomorrow. Indeed, an early start for us all. Liam will set down your testament and it must be ready for the court; we don't want any delays. Liam is optimistic. However, Paddy has managed to get the best defence attorney one can find, a man called

Meyer who is expert at turning prosecutions on their head. Of course, it's his job, and without a doubt, he will pull every trick in the book.'

Brendan listened and decided to say nothing, but the thought came, *I wished we'd moved on. This is some sort of game; why is it all so complicated? I identify Paddy and he goes down – simple!*

Anna for her part listened without really taking in what Mr Peabody was saying. She looked at the large clock in the corner; it was almost 10.30 pm. Tiredness was making the room spin. 'D'yer need me? I'm on me knees.'

Mr Peabody nodded. 'You are a witness. I know you only lost your coat, but it might be important.' Anna smiled and shook herself awake, the thought flashed, *only me coat, if only they knew.* Again, she thought of her ring and yet again decided it had gone forever; she would never tell Bren. She put these thoughts to one side on hearing voices in the entrance hall, and she knew that the lawyer had arrived.

Mr Peabody stood up. 'I'll say goodnight and leave you with Liam. Like you, I need to be up very early tomorrow.' He smiled and added, 'And age is not on my side.'

Liam Lewinski was a thin angular man who looked taller than he was. His droop moustache set in a long face gave him a sad look, while his tight suit gave the impression it was borrowed and not a good fit. His manner was brisk and after a few pleasantries, he prepared his pen, sat Brendan and Anna down in the dining room at the long table, and asked them to recall every detail of the robbery.

Brendan gave his account followed by Anna, and Lewinski carefully wrote down. Occasionally he asked questions as to how the men were dressed and had they noted any facial marks or other identifying irregularities. Brendan vividly described the knifeman's face and then decided to tell Lewinski about his fight with him on the shoreline. Without looking up Lewinsky continued writing and said, 'I've got a witness to the incident and I'm satisfied it was an accident. Let's move on.'

Anna, now fully awake asked, 'What about the fella who stole me coat, I saw him clearly, but no-one has mentioned him.'

Lewinski paused before replying. 'We think his name is Noel Hughes. He may have slipped away, possibly back to England, or Canada. Forget him, the man you call Paddy was born Michael Cutler. He arrived here as a three-year-old from Ireland, one of eight children, and from the age of ten he has been active in crime. He began as a pickpocket but quickly moved on to robbery, and generally anything that would bring in a buck. He's well known this side of Queens, and we've had him in on several charges but, he's clever, witnesses fail to turn up or change their minds; you can guess why, and he walks. With your help, we can hold him until my boss Chief Attorney Abraham Grant can bring new evidence against him for murder.' Lewinski paused. 'More than likely he'll hang, and few will miss him.'

Anna shuddered; this was the second time within days that the word hanging had settled on their shoulders. The thought of being responsible for someone's execution didn't sit easily.

Brendan, as if reading her thoughts squeezed her hand and said, 'Love, he'd have killed me without a second glance.'

Lewinski nodded agreement. 'Back to business. I have a short night and a long day ahead of me.' He read back their accounts and was even more delighted that, for some reason at the time, Brendan hadn't put the receipt of his transaction with Western Union in his money belt, instead, he had shoved it in a trouser pocket meaning to transfer it later. 'Proof, proof, proof,' enthused Lewinski. 'This is what I need,' and he placed it in his case.

Brendan asked, 'So, we go ter court te'morra and we give evidence against this Cutler? How long will it take?'

'It depends on the justices, but Judge Renshaw will not want it to go beyond two days. He knows that any delay can cause problems.'

'What kind of problems?' a worried Anna asked.

Lewinski closed his case. 'Don't worry, you'll have people around you every second.'

It was almost midnight when Isaac came in and told them he would show them to their accommodation. He led them behind the main building to a line of cabins, chose the first two and lit the oil lamps. Lewinski seemed to know the system well and bade them goodnight.

In their well-furnished cabin, Anna and Brendan thanked Isaac, who told them, 'Rise an' shine at six-thirty, folks. I'll place hot water outside your door.'

After another gruelling day both were quickly into bed. 'Six-thirty,' groaned Anna. 'I could sleep fer a week.'

Brendan tried to be cheerful. 'It's a new day te'morra.'

'God! What a wise man I've married.' Brendan didn't tell Anna how worried he was.

CHAPTER 33

The knock on the door came too soon for Anna. She heard Isaac's voice, and his warning not to be late. Brendan was instantly out of bed and Anna, yet again, marvelled at how quickly he could respond to the merest sound – instantly alert. He was like a cat and could move as lightly on his feet as any boxer as he had already proved. She dismissed the thought and waited for her half of the hot water. Dressed, Anna looked at herself in the mirror, then at Bren. 'My God, look at us, Bren, and just look at yer bowler, we must buy yer a new one.'

Brendan shrugged, gave his bowler a dust off, but found part of it unravelling around the rim. 'Well, we'll have ter do; we need our savings fer lodgings, but I promise yer the first chance I get, yer'll have a new outfit.' He advanced, kissed her and pulled her bonnet under her chin. 'Yer look lovely, wife; who'll look at me?' Anna pushed him away and shook her head in mock annoyance.

'Scrambled eggs, bread, and coffee.' Precious' voice brought them to the door, she gave them a big smile. 'Good morning, O'Neils, eat up, Mr Peabody wants a word with you before he leaves, and I suggest you wrap up warm because there's a cold wind blowin' in from the river.'

Anna, wearing her cape coat, and Brendan in his best finery, worn at his wedding in Dublin, his only change a new waistcoat (chosen by Anna) walked around to the main house to find Mr Peabody's coach and horses outside the entrance. He came out, greeted them warmly and told them he was going to the city. He paused as if not quite sure as to what to say, then he gestured to Isaac who helped him into the coach. Brendan realised that he seemed far from well. Mr Peabody took several deep breaths before leaning out of the window to tell them, 'I'll be in the courtroom at some time during today or tomorrow, but not in any official capacity. In a few minutes, a trap will take you to the station in Yonkers, where you will be met and escorted to the courtroom; they'll look after you.'

Anna and Brendan froze: it was Brendan who quietly asked, 'Mr Peabody, there's somethin' goin' on here that I'm not sure of, are we in any sort of danger?'

Mr Peabody pulled a face and said, 'Brendan, it's called precautions, you just never know, but I don't believe in being wise after the event, and with your lovely lady here I'm being wise before anything can happen.' He tapped the roof with his silver cane and gave a gloved-handed wave as his coach moved away.

Isaac led them behind the house just as a horse-drawn trap came around the corner. Up front was a young man wearing an old coachman's coat with a large cape that had seen better days. He wore a Stetson pulled down tightly around his chin.

'Hello there, I'm Sean. I believe yer from the ole country.'

Brendan recognised his brogue right away. 'At a guess yer from north Belfast?'

'Near enough; Newtownards and yer'll be from the south, I'm told Donegal, but get up will yer, we need ter get ter the station and we can talk there. Mr Peabody will have me guts fer garters if yer miss yer train.'

Anna was delighted by the trap that reminded her of jaunting carts back home. And the heavy blankets were most useful, especially for Brendan, whose topcoat had been discarded at Harper's Drift as too unfit for further use.

Sean never stopped talking, but both were surprised to hear that Yonkers was a popular place for the Irish and for the rich. 'I bet yer'll hear more Irish voices than any,' he told them.

Their route was a surprise: they drove around to the back of the cabins where Sean opened a large gate that led into a lane. Then they crossed an open field on a well-worn path until they reached a busy road and joined morning traffic into the town of Yonkers. In places, the road had been gravelled, in some places cobbled, and one section was planks of wood. The light trap bounced its way along merrily and Sean kept up a good pace.

The tall spire of the church came nearer, and as they entered the outskirts of Yonkers Anna was delighted with the new houses going up. 'My God, Bren, yer'd need a few pennies ter live here.' He nodded agreement.

As they moved into the town centre they were impressed by the very fine buildings, many of which were under construction. Brendan observed, 'In me book, it says Yonkers is a village – some village – there's plenty of money around here.'

Sean, hearing this, told them, 'Yer make yer money in the city, and yer live out here. Since the railheads arrived yer don't have ter live over the store.'

The street opened out onto a large square. Sean shouted back, 'Getty.' Even at the early hour, Getty Square was alive with the bustle of horse traffic, mainly deliveries, and people hurrying in all directions. The grand buildings, the street lighting, the jostle of people reminded Brendan of Scranton but, without the fog of industry, while Anna wondered what had brought them to live in Yonkers.

Brendan just smiled. He loved to see Anna at her vibrant best. In his way, he saw the same things and was just as excited, but his joy was directed inwardly.

'What yer laughing at?'

'You. I'm thinking that if I was of the same temperament as yerself, well, life would be very, erm – difficult!'

Anna tossed her head, gave a long 'hmmmm' and said, 'Boyo, at times I think yer brighter than yer look.'

'We're here, folks.' Sean slowed his horse to a walk.

Brendan had hardly noticed that they had passed through the square, and along with other carriages they were now outside a T-section of marked out platforms with rail tracks both sides. The middle supports held a simple roof that gave cover from both rain and sun. An engine was slowly moving into the side nearest.

Many coaches, carts and carriages were arriving and leaving, and Sean had to make two detours before he found a place to rein in. Luckily, one carriage pulled out and he was able to secure the place much to the annoyance of several waiting coachmen who had waited longer. In reply, Sean stretched his hat above his head and then let it snap down around his ears. As he helped Anna down, he told them he was twenty-two and had arrived in America when he was fifteen, with his parents.

'And what does yer da do?' asked Brendan.

'He got killed in an accident at work; timber fell on him, but Mr Peabody has been great ter me and me ma.'

Sean led them to a centre kiosk attached to a column that sold newspapers. 'This is the place, wait here and don't move away. Nice meetin' yer both, I'll be on me way.' Again, his hat stretched and snapped back, and he disappeared into the crowd.

The newness and the bustle of stations excited Anna, she loved to see the engines, the smoke and feel the atmosphere of people on the move. After village farm life it was exciting, but she knew that Brendan yearned for the open countryside. She shuddered at the thought of him day after day returning home covered in anthracite dust. No more! They would find a new life once this day was over: somewhere along the Lackawanna River, but not too far from Scranton. Ah, the best of both worlds, she told herself.

'Mr and Mrs O'Neil?' The voice made them jump.

Anna turned and exclaimed, 'Jesus!' and stepped back. The man in the checked frock coat was the Pinkerton man who had tracked them to Scranton.

'Sorry to startle you, ma'am. We're your escort.' He turned to Brendan and held out a hand, but for once Brendan's anger exploded and he refused the hand.

'I'd like ter know what the hell's goin' on here. Everyone seems ter know 'cept us.' Taking Brendan's lead, Anna cried.

'Fer Christ's sake, yer frightened us ter death in Scranton and look at me man here, down a coal mine because of yer. Why didn't yer explain yerself? If yer were a Pinker—' Anna was cut off.

'Ma'am, will you please lower your voice and do not use that word again.'

Brendan was about to react when something told him to wait, particularly as he could see another man moving in. 'Today we are your escort. The gentleman you see standing there, keeping a wary eye open for us, we'll call Luke, and you can call me John.' He lowered his voice. 'We are Pinkerton agents, working for the state. I didn't contact you in the restaurant in Scranton because while I was observing you, I suddenly realised I was being watched. Was the interest in me, or you? I could have been putting you in the path of some rogue from New York. I thought it unlikely, but I couldn't take the risk. So, I decided to sort out our friend first, and it turned out that he was the brother of a felon I helped to put away last year; the local sheriff took care of him. I tried to get in touch with you first thing in the morning, but you'd scarpered. That woman at reception told me you'd left very early and didn't know where you'd gone. I couldn't spend any more time on your case, and I may as well tell you that my time was paid for by Mr Nathanial Peabody.'

Brendan held out his hand and said, 'Right's on yer side, Mr John, and we thank yer, but what happens now?' Relaxing, John shook hands and accepted the warm smile of forgiveness from Anna.

'I'll be honest with you we don't know what influence Cutler has outside his patch – that is territories in New York. For myself, I think he's a rat scurrying around somewhere near the bottom, but we don't take chances. My friend there is my eyes, he will always be within reach but please ignore him and do not give any sign you recognise him. We are both armed, and if I shout "down", you hit the ground as quickly as possible, even if there's horseshit – right?

Anna smiled brightly. 'Ah, Mr John, we may be country bumpkins, but no problem; it was just like this in Donegal.'

John looked at Brendan, who smiled, shook his head and shrugged. John laughed, and replied, 'And why is it, Mrs O'Neil, that I do not believe you?'

They were about to move when the noise above made Anna and Brendan react in astonishment. Above the buildings, they had wondered at the long, trestle type structure that crossed a bridge close to them and snaked away into the distance. What was it for? This became clear when a cloud of steam announced a steam engine clattering over the bridge pulling several cars. Seeing their surprise John told them it was the overhead railhead. He added, 'It's safe enough but reliable it ain't. We're taking the horse-tram down to Harlem.'

John led them to the end of the marked-out platform, to a waiting tram. Luke walked a yard away covering Anna. In the cool morning air, the single horse snorted, blowing steam that drifted gently away. Anna, who would normally have delighted in their horse-drawn trip didn't have chance to pause as Luke quickly ushered her into a seat. John acknowledged the driver, had a quick word and they moved off. He told them, 'We have this car to ourselves until Harlem; it's a bit safer.' Luke sat opposite to Anna and fixed his gaze on the people outside.

Brendan was amazed at the pulling power of the single horse using rails, and John told him that it was almost as quick as steam. 'At least this one will be because it won't stop for passengers until we hit Harlem.'

Anna studied Luke, he was medium height with a square face, small darting eyes and he wore a heavy moustache that hid his mouth. He gave her regard a brief smile before moving to the opposite window where he remained looking out. A shroud of worry wrapped itself around Anna, all she could think of was that they had been robbed on their first day in New York, and now there was some risk on their return. She tried to push it aside and looked out of the window.

As they approached Harlem she was amazed at the poverty. Tenement buildings close together, washing strung from building to building, cart filled roads, children playing in the streets. She wanted to talk to Bren, but he was busy talking to John, discussing life in America.

At Harlem, they left the horse-tram, and as they hurried to the station, easily picked out by the noise and cloud of steam, Anna was surprised by how many dark-skinned people there were. At the docks, she had seen such a mix of people, as Brendan had said, from every corner of the world. She had also read accounts of the conflict between the north and the south and she knew there was still an undercurrent of division that often resulted in violence. Moreover, she had heard so many nicknames used in the street to describe just about every race that she was sure that this wasn't kind – and the Irish did not escape. She was a peasant, Bren, a dumb cluck. Peasant indeed! When she could read and write as well as the next person. She wondered how and when you qualified to become an American – if ever!

Putting such thoughts aside she held onto her bonnet in the crush of people trying to get onto the train to the city centre. John and Luke ushered them into the crowded car; all the seats were taken. That is until John and Luke had a quiet word with three suited young men who immediately gave up their seats. Brendan was both embarrassed and surprised at the power held by the Pinkerton men. He knew that he should be supporting Anna, but this was his chance to quiz John and Luke about their day in court, and he plied them with questions.

Anna tried to listen in, but her thoughts turned to home. *How was da getting on – and Etta? Has he received the letter I sent? I'd better not tell him that we're being guarded by Pinkerton agents, and we're back in New York as witnesses at the trial of the villain who attacked Bren on our first day.* Yvonne? *I must write ter her and Nadia; oh, an' ter Bridget; they'll want ter know how we're getting on.*

Nervously she tried to put all this to one side to

concentrate on the sprawl of buildings and factories as they neared lower Manhattan. She found herself looking down onto balconies, where soulless people looked up and passed by like paintings in a picture gallery. She had seen faces like this before on her journey across Ireland. People locked into circumstances that were best to be ignored, just get on with the job in hand and don't think too much about it. One child waved and Anna waved back. She had seen poverty in Dublin, but this was just as bad. Never had she seen so many people crammed into such a small area, yet within a short distance, rich mansions appeared. Her thoughts turned again to their first day when they had been violently robbed by Cutler and his gang. No, she didn't want him hanged; too awful. But she rather liked the idea used by the English to transport felons to hard labour in a penal colony.

The train slowed, and John announced, 'This is it, Grand Central Depot.' He waited until the car cleared, then at a signal from Luke they descended to the platform which was almost level with the door. Brendan stopped, looked up and said, 'My God, what's this?'

Anna bumped into him. Pushing her bonnet back, she looked up and gasped. John laughed. 'Some roof heh?' They stood in wonder; it was the biggest glass roof they had ever seen, held by metal frames that stretched away over their heads until lost in a cloud of trapped steam.

'We have to keep moving.' John was nervous and Luke moved in behind.

Brendan wanted to stand and gawp, but the crowd edged them towards the exit, while Anna couldn't believe so many trains could be in the same place; there seemed to be several platforms.

As they entered the large entrance hall Brendan could only admire the architecture. It was hard to believe it was a station. Two towers at either end, at least three storeys high, built of brick and stone, that supported a large arch leading to outside. He wanted to ask questions, but John was pushing ahead, while Luke was behind Anna, urging her on.

John moved to the shelter of the right-hand column. 'We'll pause here a while and let the crowd disperse. I feel safer with fewer people about and I'm waiting for a coach to take us to the courthouse.'

Luke, after a survey out front, gestured for them to move. Brendan could see a coach with a large chestnut horse pulling up behind a horse-drawn mail coach to his right.

'DOWN!'

Brendan threw himself on top of Anna. He could hear screams and voices yelling.

Anna's bonnet was again pushed right over her face and she was struggling to free her hands. Passing through Brendan's mind was something he had heard – *if yer hear the shot it's missed.*

'It's okay, okay; not meant for us.' John's urgent voice and hands helped Brendan to his feet.

Free at last Anna's face came into view as she pushed her bonnet back on her head. She lay there, gave a wide-eyed stare at Brendan, and said, 'Mr O'Neil, there's a time and place for everything, and this I would call a very public place.' Brendan just sat back and laughed. This was the same cheeky face he had opened his door to those months ago in Mollybeg.

John crouched down, chuckling away, both at Anna but more with relief that the disaster wasn't theirs. Luke came running, called the coach forward to shelter the group, and told them, 'The stupid bastard over there has shot his brother-in-law – some silly family dispute!'

John ushered Anna into the coach, stood back, nudged Brendan on the arm and quietly said, 'Brendan, that's one hell of a lady you've got there.' Brendan nodded.

CHAPTER 34

'We're heading for Lower Manhattan; it'll take half an hour so relax. I think we've had enough excitement for one day.' John tried to be genial, but Brendan could feel the tension.

Luke reached through the coach door window to shake hands. 'Nice meeting you folks. I'm in court five myself tomorrow, so I won't be seeing you again – good luck!'

John added, 'I'll say goodbye when we reach the courthouse, my job's done, but a new team will move in later today. You might think this is all about your safety, but it's also about ours. Around the courthouse there's always those making a note of comings and goings, particularly us Pinkerton men. Not all see us as a source for good. Luke and I are a team, we work well together but we try to keep our identities secret. You thought I was a danger, but I face danger every day; I've lost one buddy already.' He shrugged, 'It comes with the job.'

Brendan said, 'Mr John, we both thank yer most kindly.'

John leaned forward. 'Now, I can tell you all you need to know, at least for today. If it's fine buildings you're interested in wait until you see the courthouse called The Tweed. It's one of the finest buildings in New York, and it's got a history to match. William M 'Boss' Tweed used to control everything around here. He was a millionaire, and no wonder because it's estimated he embezzled over seventy-five million dollars. In fact, he owned this city and when you talk about corruption, he's king.' John laughed. 'Ironically he was tried in his own courthouse in '73 and sent down. However, give him his due, he gave New York a jewel, all marble, like a Roman palace, and it's vast with over thirty courtrooms.'

Anna gasped, 'Thirty! Just fer New York. If yer don't

mind me saying, Mister John, yer seem ter have more than yer fair share of felons. I don't think Ireland has that many fer the whole country.'

John shrugged, 'Remember, Mrs O'Neil, that this brave country has brought in millions of people from around the world. It would be nice if we could do a bit of choosing.' John relaxed back into his seat.

Looking out of the coach window Brendan remembered the route; he had sat beside Paddy and noted some of the buildings. Uneasily he told Anna, 'We're near ter the docks.' He sat back; the thought came: *have we done the right thing coming back to where it all started? Should we have moved on ter Philadelphia?* It was then any such dark thoughts were swept away. As the coach turned into Chambers Street Brendan could see the courthouse, it was as magnificent as John had described, it was like a Roman palace, with large marble columns and imposing steps leading from the road.

'We're moving around the side, there are several entrances, and Lewinski will be waiting.' John looked at his watch. 'Just made it.'

Quickly they were ushered into a side passage. Anna could not believe the grandeur, the floor was a mosaic of coloured tiles that ran away into the distance, she had never seen anything like it. Brendan thought only of the labour, and of how many craftsmen had been involved. However, John quickly led them down a corridor, then up an ornate stone staircase to the second floor, to a line of rooms that served the many lawyers and their clients.

Brendan, for the moment, had forgotten their purpose. 'Christ, Anna, I've never seen anything like this. I hope we gerra time ter look around.'

There wasn't time; from an open-door Lewinski called out, 'Ah, there you are.' Inside the wood-panelled room, filled by a long table with a centre console that housed several bound folders, Lewinski ushered them to sit down and introduced the other two men in the room.

'This is my research team, my Uncle Robert Lewinski –

who set me on my present path – and if there's anything to ferret out he's your man. And this is Abraham McCauley, who's studying law at university and he's with us for the year.'

Brendan moved forward and shook hands with the elderly man with a mop of silver hair that made him look possibly younger than his years and nodded a greeting to McCauley who was busy scribbling away in his notebook; both men made a bow to Anna while Lewinski escorted her to a chair. 'Please, sit down, we'll have coffee and I'll run through our day.'

Brendan listened intently as Lewinski outlined the day ahead. Cutler had been in detention for ten days, and the main charge against him would be his robbery of Brendan. A knife had been used to threaten him whereas Anna's coat had been dragged off without undue violence. Anna sat calmly, the thought ever present, *ah, if only they knew, but it's me secret that I'll take ter me grave.*

'I must warn you that Cutler will pull every trick he can, aided by his defence team. I've crossed swords many times with Ruben Meyer; he's good, he specialises in getting people off. However, it's the game we play, and no doubt you will feel very frustrated during the day, but remember our case is strong, we have the truth whereas Cutler must lie. If we can nail him on this charge, then it gives us a chance to bring in the murder charge. I stress again we need time to bring in another witness to make sure he gets his just deserts. My friends, Meyer will cross-examine you, and he will try every ruse to discredit your story. Keep calm, answer as honestly as you can, and remember I will be using all the tricks in my book.' Lewinski looked intently at Brendan. 'You are my main witness, Mr O'Neil. Don't get angry; angry words are often foolish words.' Brendan took the meaning; Lewinski had read his irritation. Brendan hated these word games played by highly qualified people, whom he said, seemed to have little concern for the truth. For him it was quite simple: he would identify Cutler as his assailant, and that would be it.

Everyone in New York, well – nearly everyone – knew he was an evil bastard, so what was the problem?

Liam Lewinski looked at his watch. 'Almost time, we're in court fifteen, Judge Renshaw will preside. He can, if he wishes, bring in a fellow judge to support him as I'm sure he will.'

All this time John had stood just inside the doorway with his arms folded. He moved forward, shook hands with Brendan and said, 'Mr O'Neil, I wish you well for the future.' Turning to Anna, he gave a small bow and said, 'Mrs O'Neil, I'm sure this country will welcome your spirit.' He chuckled and tipped his bowler. 'Good day to you all.'

Anna felt very nervous, she looked into the courtroom through the open doors as people came and went; its sheer splendour was overpowering. It was almost like a theatre, with seating around three sides of the room. To her left, she could see the defence team preparing their notes. She guessed that the very sharp-featured man was Ruben Meyer. He was clean-shaven, his dark hair was swept back, and he wore a beautifully tailored grey suit. In truth, Anna thought him to be a handsome man. His assistant was the opposite, an older man, bald, with a face that when drawn back sculpted three chins, while his suit seemed shabby and ill-fitting. To his left sat a young man, obviously a student.

Opposite to the defence, Liam Lewinski and his uncle sat at a table, while McCauley sat behind. Anna noted that Abraham McCauley seemed no older than herself, without his cap he displayed a shock of reddish hair; he was very intense and writing away furiously.

Brendan and Anna, as witnesses, were escorted to a small room adjoining the main courtroom. Their escort, a black lady, wearing a dark red gown, told them, 'Ma name's Margaret and I'm here to look after your every need. I'm what you call an usher. I'll call you when you're needed, so, folks, sit down and relax.'

Brendan looked around, there was only one door leading to the corridor, irritated, he asked, 'And how will we know what's goin' on if we canna see a thing, or listen in?'

Margaret smiled. 'I can tell it's your first time in court. You are here as witnesses and it's important your evidence isn't coloured by what you hear in there.' Again, she pointed at the court. 'But, and I shouldn't tell you this, there's a small crack in the panelling and when I'm not looking, well, I can't see everything now, can I?'

Anna peeped through and could see the high platform and the judges' seats. Behind them, unfurled and draped at an angle across the dark wood panelling was the flag of the United States. She moved to give Bren a peep, and he described the courtroom filling with clerks and recorders. Anna, back in place, watched as two judges entered from a door to the rear.

Brendan looked at his watch; ten o'clock. He gently moved Anna to one side. He couldn't hear what was being said but he saw a clerk stand up and speak. He guessed it was the charges laid against Cutler. At this point, Cutler, head down, was led in between two policemen and he took his place in the dock; he turned and looked up as he sat down.

'Jesus!' Brendan swung around, his eyes wild, he could hardly speak. Anna pushed him aside. The Paddy she knew was now dressed in a smart blue suit, and he wore a cravat. He was almost unrecognisable from the man who had befriended and then attacked them. He wore a white heavy moustache and black heavy-rimmed spectacles that gave him the look of a successful businessman. Brendan's anger exploded. 'He's in bloody disguise.' Anna turned to Margaret. 'We need ter gerra message ter Lewinski.'

Margaret considered for a moment, then went to the door and called a steward from the corridor. A young man, wearing an armband denoting his position, runner, listened carefully as Brendan told him to ask Robert Lewinski to come to the witness room and that it was urgent.

A minute later Robert entered and listened while Brendan excitedly told him about Cutler's appearance. For some reason Robert seemed amused, he put both hands up and said, 'Calm down, my friends, do you think Paddy's going to turn up dressed in his robber gear? Of course, he's going to do his best to throw us and the court off; wouldn't you do the same?'

Brendan and Anna realised the sense in Robert's claims and quietly sat down.

Robert chuckled, went up to the crack in the panelling, had a peep through, turned to Margaret and said, 'One of these days we'll have that fixed.' He turned again to Anna and Brendan, 'Don't worry, Liam knows what he's doing.'

Lewinski rose and outlined the events of the 27th May 1889, how the accused, Michael Cutler, alias Paddy, had robbed Brendan on his first day in America with an accomplice, now deceased, called Lewis Godden, alias George Salter. He said that the knife in question, held to the throat of Brendan O'Neil, was that of the defendant Michael Cutler.

It was at this point that Brendan was called to the stand. He was sworn in, and then Lewinski told him to tell the court what happened on the evening of the 27th of May. Anna could see that Brendan was nervous and agitated. She moved her gaze to Cutler who was just in sight, sat in an enclosure next to his defence team, and watched as he smiled in an incredulous way and kept shaking his head in disbelief.

Slowly Meyer got to his feet. 'There is still a doubt that the man who robbed you, Mr O'Neil, is the man who stands accused before you. Are you sure that Michael Cutler is the man because I will be bringing witnesses who will tell this court that on the evening of 27th May Mr Cutler was dining with friends?'

Brendan responded. 'When someone lies on top of yer with a knife ter your throat it's not easy ter forget.'

Ruben Meyer persisted, 'But Mr O'Neil, I put it to you that Mr Cutler will fit the description of many a man in New York. Well?'

'Are yer making me out ter be a liar? I'd know that rogue anywhere.'

Lewinski shook his head and conferred with his team; Brendan stood down.

Anna, her eye glued to the crack, could see how angry Brendan was. She knew that the Bren who had downed Watts, so cold and calm, was out of his depth in a courtroom. He could deal with what he called "real situations" but this was, as he had said, 'A silly game played by people with more money than sense.' Brendan came in, threw himself down beside her. 'Jesus! Yer ought ter hear 'im, he was as Irish as Paddy's pig when we met him, and now yer'd think he was a rich banker.' Brendan shook his head. 'He'll get off.' Once again Anna saw the tormented Brendan who had sat feeding the fire at the vagrants' camp. He could not sit down and moved around the small room muttering, 'I wish ter hell I could hear what's goin' on.'

Margaret looked up and said, 'If yer put your ear instead of your eye, you might pick up something.' She returned to her book. Brendan made a funnel with his hand over the crack and pressed his ear firmly against it. His eyes lit up, he gestured to Anna to keep quiet and mouthed that Cutler was on the stand.

Lewinski suggested to Cutler that he had changed his appearance to try and mislead the court, but Cutler said he had worn a moustache for the past two years, while his glasses was a recent need because his long-range vision was impaired. At this point, Lewinsky consulted with Robert who disappeared out of court. All this time the defence sat making notes and smiling as if it was all just a question of false identity, and a conclusion was near.

'Cutler's bloody enjoying himself.' Brendan turned to Anna. 'We've spent all morning talking about whether Paddy is Cutler; even the judges are fed up.'

Anna took over listening duties. 'Robert's back with something; two new witnesses; shush!'

'I have here two statements from witnesses willing to testify that—' Lewinski didn't finish.

Instantly Ruben Meyer was on his feet to object. The judge called both attorneys before him. He then announced that as it was midday, he was adjourning the session for an hour and a half.

Robert opened the witness room door and Anna and Brendan returned to Liam's chamber. He told them a runner would bring in sandwiches and hot drinks but there was much to do; he then further explained, 'I have two sworn testimonies from a warder and a cook at the Denton Detention Centre where Cutler has been detained these past ten days. At no time did he wear spectacles, that is, until a few days ago. However, he will claim, as he already has, that his need is recent. But a moustache can't be grown in a day, and the cook, until his recent job at the centre, is ready to swear that when he worked at Bar 8, as a waiter, only weeks ago, Cutler, whom he knows well because he served him on several occasions, was clean-shaven. So, Cutler's change in appearance is recent and we all know why. Ruben will pursue the false identity route. I only hope our two witnesses turn up.' Liam Lewinski further explained that any new evidence or call on witnesses had to be given to the defence.

Brendan was astounded. 'Why fer Christ's sake – yer telling me that if yer have an advantage, yer have ter share it with the enemy?'

Lewinski laughed. 'I often have dinner with Ruben, he's a good laugh, tells some very funny stories.' Lewinski chuckled away. 'Brendan, I keep telling you it's a game but a very serious one, there are rules but generally the truth will out. Meyer will fight for Cutler, but he won't lose a minute's sleep if he goes down.

When the court resumed Lewinski called Cutler to the witness stand, and this time Cutler blustered that he often wore a moustache but couldn't be expected to remember such times, but he could call on friends to vindicate his story. Meyer refused to allow the matter of identification to be dropped and how it could have been a man of similar appearance. At this point, the judge interrupted and asked for both defence and prosecution to move on.

Anna, listening in, recalled in her mind's eye how she had sat behind Paddy in the cart as they left the docks at Castle Gardens. On the small seat, all she could see of him was the back of his head and his red neck, and she remembered he had a brown mole behind his left ear.

'Margaret! We need the steward; it's urgent!'

Robert appeared, looking less pleased than before. He listened intently, gave a little whistle, and returned to the courtroom. Brendan, no longer sure of what was going on held Anna's hand, more for his own comfort than hers, while Anna took a deep breath and waited. The call came and she made her way to the stand and swore the oath.

Lewinski, who had been awaiting the arrival of his new witnesses, but not sure they would arrive, as both had expressed their unwillingness, decided to give Anna her head. An attractive female could sway a few minds, and he asked her to say in her own words why she could identify Michael Cutler as the man who had attacked Brendan O'Neil.

Anna pushed her bonnet back on her head, looked around the courtroom, and to the amusement of all began her story using a pattern of words that echoed those used by the lawyers, and an exaggerated English accent.

'On the 27th May, a man who called himself Paddy befriended us and offered us a lift in his cart from Castle Gardens to the Western Union building. We were extremely fatigued after our voyage from Ireland, and we put our trust in whom we thought was a fellow Irishman. Foolishly, we confided our intention to withdraw money from the Weston Union. That man – I now identify as Michael Cutler – led us to believe he was taking us to his sister's where she would give us lodgings for the night.' As she said this Anna flung out her arms embracing the whole court and dramatically declared, 'And you all know what happened,' she pointed at

Cutler, 'he robbed my husband of our life savings. My husband worked for two years to raise the money to give us a start in this wonderful country.' Meyer went to interrupt but Anna ignored him. 'How do I know he is the assailant? My husband Brendan O'Neil sat up front in the cart, driven by the man I now identify as Michael Cutler. I sat on a small wooden seat behind and I was able to study him. I noted his thick red neck; but more importantly, I could see that he had a large brown mole behind his left ear. Will the court please note that at no time during my time in this court have I been in a position to see other than a front view of Mr Cutler, and today is the first time since that dreadful day that I again see the man who called himself Paddy. I am confident that if you look behind Mr Cutler's left ear you will see the mole I have described, and it will leave no doubt that he was the villain who robbed my dear husband.'

There was silence, then a ripple of laughter ran around the courtroom, and even a few handclaps that were quickly silenced by Judge Latimer. Lewinski and his uncle sat back in admiration, while Abraham McCauley wrote furiously. Meyer leapt to his feet and told the court that many men had such marks and that he himself had a birthmark on part of his body he would not care to mention; this enforced humour missed its mark. Moving on he was about to call his first witness when Judge Renshaw called time. He explained that it was past four o'clock and he hoped that a new day would see a conclusion to the case, which he said was moving far too slowly.

Back in Lewinski's chamber, Brendan expressed his frustration but was ignored as the team gathered around Anna.

Robert couldn't stop laughing. 'I've never seen Ruben in such a state.' He turned to Anna and asked, 'Have you been on the stage? What a performance.'

McCauley looked up from his notebook and added, 'Two great performances. Cutler knows his lines.'

Lewinski tempered the jovial atmosphere. 'Tomorrow is

the big day. We've done well, but let's see what Ruben has
for us tomorrow.'

CHAPTER 35

Lewinski and his team left immediately to see another client. Liam warned Brendan and Anna not to leave the building until contact had been made. Therefore, it came as a surprise when a man of gentle appearance and voice quietly asked, 'Mr and Mrs O'Neil?' Brendan's immediate thought was that he must be a friend of Mr Peabody. He appeared too elderly to be an agent.

'I'm Mathew, I'm here to escort you to your lodgings for the night… my colleague—'

Brendan interrupted, 'Yer goin' ter tell us he's called Mark!'

Mathew smiled, drew back in mock astonishment. 'My word, Mr O'Neil, I do think we could find you a place in our organisation.'

Brendan said, 'Mathew, I'll be straight with yer, I'm a simple man who likes the simple life, but yer buildings here in New York well, what can I say, they're impressive, and before I leave here I must see the facade of this magnificent building.'

Mathew gave his gentle smile. 'Absolutely no problem, I will be near, and when you are ready – I will not walk with you – make your way to the main street, Broadway. Turn right and continue until you reach a restaurant called Milano. Go in and you will see a staircase, take the stairs to the first landing, and you will be met.'

The terrace was crowded, and it was hard to move. Clients, lawyers, families and interested onlookers filled every corner, while the road was packed with waiting carriages.

Brendan took Anna by the hand and they crossed the road to admire the grand facade.

'My God, Anna, how does any man put that down on

paper, and how d'yer find people who can... what's the word?'

'Interpret it?'

'Build it! Just look at the columns, yer canna afford ter be an inch out.' He again took Anna's hand and began the walk towards Broadway. 'Anna, yer one clever girl, but one of these days...' Brendan laughed; his thoughts returned to her evidence in the courtroom.

Anna walked in silence telling herself: *yer a show-off, Anna O'Neil, why d'yer do it?* This thought was quickly replaced when, suddenly, she felt unsteady. Possibly it was after the drama in the courthouse. She inhaled deeply, took Brendan's arm and told him, 'It's truly a wonderful building, we'll see it again te'morra. I'm out on me feet, all I want is a good sleep.'

A young man stood outside the restaurant. He took no notice of them as they passed through the open doorway, but he followed them in. As they approached the staircase a voice told them, 'I'm Mark; see you tomorrow.'

On the landing, a little fat lady came out of the far door. She introduced herself as Carlotta. She was Italian, with black hair swept back in a severe style. She wore a red dress that reached the floor that somehow made her look smaller than she was. Her English was good, and her pleasant nature amused the O'Neils.

'Oh! You Irish; do you know what we call you? The potato eaters, but you'll find none here. For dinner, you can have spaghetti, spaghetti, and more spaghetti.'

Brendan replied, 'It'll be another experience fer us, we've never had spaghetti in our lives.' Then more seriously he asked, 'What is this place? Is it a hotel?'

Carlotta touched her nose. 'Ah! There are some questions you don't ask. What can I say? You'll be safer here than in a hotel, we have our eyes open all the time.' She laughed and added, 'And we're a lot cheaper; you won't be getting a bill tomorrow morning.' She touched her nose again and showed them into a bedroom that overlooked a small yard and tenement buildings that filled the sky. 'At seven make your way to the restaurant, the far corner by the alcove.' Carlotta swished away.

The room was simple with a large bed against the one wall, a wardrobe in the corner and a dresser with a washbasin along the opposite wall. The room was gas lit with instructions not to touch the mantle. However, Ann's interest was more on the bed.

'Bren, I'll have ter lie down, me head's spinning.' Brendan had never known Anna to complain of illness, not even during their difficult times on the road to Queenstown, but he was sure it was the stress and worry of the trial, not to mention some very long days. He looked at his watch – time for a nap before dinner. He joined Anna on the bed; she was already asleep.

The loud knock and Carlotta's voice brought Brendan awake. It was five minutes past seven.

'Anna, Anna, we're late fer dinner. Come on, wake yerself.'

After five minutes of combing, a quick cold wash, and a few adjustments, the O'Neils were ready. In the dining room, there were few diners. Carlotta was waiting at a table, she flourished a large menu. 'Look through and I'll be back in a minute.'

Brendan was amazed at the choice but couldn't really understand it. Carlotta was soon back with her notebook and told them, 'We start with antipasto, which for you means before the meal.'

At this Anna said, 'Carlotta, I'm sorry but I'm not at me best, so can yer suggest somethin' light fer me.'

'Ah, I think for you a Tuscan bread salad, and Mr O'Neil, would you like our vegetables with olivado?' Brendan nodded but wasn't sure what olivado was.

Carlotta told them that the first course was called primo, she suggested soup which Brendan agreed to, although he had never had pork soup before. Anna shook her head; the thought of soup was too much. For the main course, called secondo, Brendan chose the meatballs with a white wine sauce, while Carlotta suggested for Anna grilled chicken. Both found it strange to have their meal served as individual courses, and when Carlotta told them that the final course was called contorno and they could have patate al forno — baked potato – they burst into laughter.

Carlotta waved her arms. 'You see, you Irish eat, all the time potatoes and we Italians, spaghetti? You see, it one big lie.'

Both enjoyed the baked potatoes with plenty of butter added. Anna felt better, but she refused the coffee while Brendan, who had never received such a small cup, enjoyed the strong black coffee.

As they were about to leave Carlotta introduced the cook, her brother, Umberto. He came from the kitchen and they thanked him for their meal and told him how good it was.

'Here, everyone calls me Bert. I still remember Milan, and I miss it.'

Carlotta laughed and said, 'You miss Milan? There are more Italians here in New York than Milan.' Then she sniffed and added, 'Oh I forgot about the Irish.' Her laughter carried up the stairs as Brendan, a little concerned that Anna wasn't her usual bright self, took her back to their room; very quickly she was asleep.

Brendan sat at the window watching an approaching storm. When it came his mind went back to the one at The Parade. The rain lashed down for an hour and the temperature dropped. When lightning lit up their room he closed the curtains, thought about an early night but felt wide awake. Near to ten o'clock he heard singing and an accordion. He looked at Anna, she was still fast asleep. Quietly he left the room, locked it and put the key in his pocket. As he descended the stairs, he was aware that a man was behind him.

In the restaurant, Carlotta pointed to the curtain at the far end of the dining room. He pulled it back to find a room full of people of all ages. The elderly sat along the bench seating, while the younger set had tables pulled together; wine and cheese seemed to be the thing.

At the bar, Brendan asked for a root beer. The barman pulled a face, and in a heavy accent said, 'We 'ave wine, wine, and more wine.'

Brendan responded, 'Wine and me head don't go together,' which confused the barman, who shrugged.

'I give you lemonada.'

Brendan found a corner and sat back to enjoy the accordionist, who was playing traditional Italian songs that most seemed to know. However, it was the elderly who did all the singing while the young ones did all the drinking. Then, to Brendan's surprise, the accordionist played 'The Rose of Tralee', sung in a mixture of English and Italian. It was at this point that Brendan decided to return to Anna. As he moved up the stairs the same man he had seen earlier followed him to the landing, where he nodded 'goodnight' and sat down in a small annexe and pulled a curtain across.

Brendan unlocked the door. Anna was sprawled across the bed fast asleep. Still wide awake, he lay down beside her, his mind full of their day. *They were being guarded day and night. Why? Was Cutler really such a danger ter them? Te'morra, as Liam had said, was the big day; with Cutler down would they be able ter put everything behind them and move on?*

Anna stirred.

'Come on me, luv, time fer real bed, let's get undressed.'

Anna struggled awake and said, 'D'yer know, Bren, I've had a wonderful dream. Me da was playing the accordion and I was singing me 'Rose of Tralee'.'

CHAPTER 36

Brendan was quickly out of bed. 'Anna! It's time ter move. Come on, this is our day, let's grab it by the throat.' Anna looked at Brendan, the man she remembered outlining his plan to get them to the other side was back, full of enthusiasm. She felt better and quickly washed and dressed.

In the restaurant, two men in earnest conversation looked up, then resumed speaking more quietly. The other man, who sat alone, was dressed in a naval uniform that looked very foreign to Brendan. Anna acknowledged all with a cheery good morning that received polite nods and a mumble from one of the men.

They sat at the same table as before, and Carlotta was quickly out with a large jug of coffee, this time made with milk. She returned with a basket of bread, still warm from the oven, a pot of jam and butter. 'All mine, everyone likes my bread. It's cold this morning, you must wrap up; you have good coats?' Anna smiled a yes, while Brendan decided that he would double up on his shirts, he had meant to buy a good topcoat but somehow, he had never got around to it.

Brendan enjoyed the bread, different from the bread of home, crisper, but with the butter and jam, it was a change from doughnuts. He looked at Anna. 'Eat up, we've gorra big day ahead.' Anna struggled through one piece, shook her head and left Brendan to clear her plate.

She drank the milky coffee but, still feeling a little unsteady when she stood up and not wishing to alarm Brendan, she said, 'I've been eating te'much; me clothes are groaning.' Brendan wasn't too concerned, he loved his breakfast, while Anna was always, as he said, "a picker".

Back on the landing, Carlotta followed them into their room. 'I hope you enjoyed your breakfast, now it's time for you to pay,' she chuckled, 'all you have to do is to sign this form and I get my money.' Brendan's first thought was that Mr Peabody had made the arrangement but recognised an official government document. He signed, and they thanked Carlotta for her kindness.

Brendan had checked the timing of their walk to the courthouse; it would take twenty minutes. Outside Milano's, they found a very wet scene: umbrellas, capes, and all sorts of improvisations were to be seen; one worker passed with a cardboard box over his head. However, within minutes the rain settled to a patter, the sky cleared, a large blue patch to the south appeared, while a weak sun, breaking through, heralded a pleasant but cool day. The air was fresher but the smell of liquid horse manure, running in the roadway, brought many handkerchiefs to noses.

As the rain eased the two made their way to Chambers Street, and it was here that Brendan picked out Mark walking on the other side of the road, then, as they approached the Tweed, he could see Mathew.

At the court steps Brendan lost sight of them, the jostle of people, moving in several directions led him to ignore the architecture and concentrate on getting Anna up the steps without her skirts fouled by the swirl of water still running strongly from the terrace. Inside, Brendan took Anna to one side and looked around to find Mathew and Mark standing quite close. Mathew gave a gentle nod of greeting and led the way to the same chamber as the previous day. Lewinski greeted them with a warm smile, while McCauley nodded a welcome.

'Uncle Robert is out; you won't find a better bloodhound. He's over the Bronx, doing a little sniffing, and I hope he'll get back before Meyer parades his witnesses. I must warn you I have a list of them, three in all, and ready to swear an oath that Cutler was with them in the Bronx on the evening of the twenty-seventh.' Lewinski smiled and shrugged, Brendan couldn't believe it.

'D'yer mean these judges might let the bastard off?'

Lewinski said, 'Look, after yesterday, and Anna's testimony, I think we're a length clear. Ruben only has one line he can follow, mistaken identity. His intention is to create doubt so the judges can't convict. He will argue that it is your word against his.'

Anna was shocked. 'But surely everyone knows that Cutler has been a felon all his life, doesn't that count?'

Lewinski pointed in the direction of the court. 'In the background, yes, but we have to prove it in there, time to go – let's nail him.'

The judges took their places and Meyer again outlined to the court that while he had every sympathy with the O'Neils, that on their first day in America they had been robbed, surely the speed and trauma of the assault, and in a dark alleyway, would make it impossible for anyone to make a true identification.

Anna, her turn to listen, murmured to herself, 'And who'll believe that?' The shock came as Meyer prowled the courtroom floor and named her.

'Mrs O'Neil rightly identified that the defendant has a mole behind his left ear. The question is as to whether the person who gave them the lift from Castle Garden to the Western Union is the same person who attacked Mr O'Neil. Mrs O'Neil entertained us all yesterday with her dramatic account, but can Mr O'Neil swear that the attacker had a mole behind his left ear? I ask again, could it not be that the attacker was of a similar build to Mr Cutler, and a mistake has been made? And, you may recall that the assailant, according to Mr O'Neil, had a strong Irish accent and called himself Paddy. Has Mr Cutler a strong Irish accent? I think not and he is called by all, Michael. I am now going to bring to the stand, my first witness.'

Anna could hear what was being said, Meyer had a strong dramatic voice and it was only when he moved to the far side of the courtroom that his words were lost. She knew the truth, but how many would believe the woman in the dock? Moving from ear to eye she peeped out at the woman who had taken the stand. She looked like any woman you passed in the street. Brendan took over; the woman spoke clearly and quietly. On the 27th May she had held a party to celebrate her birthday, but because she was alone – her husband away working on a whaling ship – her good friends the Cutlers and her sister came to celebrate her birthday and she had made a meal for them.

Lewinski moved in front of Mrs Elaine Rutter, looking at his notes before speaking. He asked quietly, 'What date is your birthday?'

The woman hesitated, 'May sixteen.'

Lewinski responded, 'I usually celebrate my birthday on the day, why do you suddenly come up with the date of May twenty-seven? It strikes me as very convenient.'

Her place was taken by her sister, a Mrs Mavis Herrington, a woman much taller and more smartly dressed, who told the same story, adding that because she had been to stay at Buffalo her sister had held back her birthday celebration until her return; and she was delighted to meet up again with Mr and Mrs Cutler. Brendan's spirits fell by the minute. Anna relayed the information, it was all so damned convincing, if he had been one of the curious public, he would surely believe these women.

At midday, Judge Renshaw called an adjournment, and as a policeman moved in to secure Cutler, he smiled and waved to a few of his supporters away to the left of the courtroom.

Lewinski seemed unconcerned by events. Brendan decided not to speak out, while Anna sat quietly, again feeling a little faint. She drank a coffee to pick herself up, and for the first time a suspicion came that possibly it wasn't just the stress of the trial causing her problem; she tried to eat a sandwich but gave up.

The door opened, Robert came in with a large smile on his face, threw down some notes on the table, and said, 'What sad faces; things not gone well?' Liam explained all that had happened and asked if Robert had found out anything to their advantage. 'Herrington in Buffalo, was she? Her husband away whaling? I have it here that her husband's in prison for embezzlement. In fact, she visited him at Levington prison. I need to cross-check the dates,' he continued, 'but listen to this, the good wife Moira Cutler is here to testify that she was with her husband in the Bronx with the two sisters. Fine! But I know that Cutler is shacked up part of the week with a Polish girl whose name I can't pronounce, I wonder if our Moira knows this?'

For the first time McCauley, who seemed forever to be writing, looked up and shook his head. Lewinski whistled and said, 'Mr McCauley, now you've found your tongue, what do you make of this?'

McCauley replied, 'I wouldn't go down that path, erm; it could be rather awkward. We have to prove his witnesses are lying.' McCauley paused and looked around. 'And there's another reason which I don't like to tell you, but I do know that Judge Latimer is married, and he has a mistress.' No-one spoke, McCauley added, 'I know because the mistress in question is my aunt!'

Lewinski slapped the table and said, 'None of this leaves this room – right? Moira Cutler is the answer. If we sneak in a few facts the loyal wife may lose some of her loyalty. It's time to go.'

Back in the courtroom Meyer called Mrs Moira Cutler to the stand. Brendan, curious to see the wife of Paddy, his assailant, was about to take a peep when Margaret gave a cry, he turned to see Anna staggering back about to fall. He caught her just in time and lowered her onto the seat. Margaret quickly moved to her other side, and while Brendan held Anna, she went to get a glass of water and returned with a colleague to help. Anna drank, took several deep breaths, smiled, and said, 'Thank yer both, but I'm fine now, it's very warm in here.'

The second lady, called Etta, suggested that Anna left the witness room, there was a medical room where she could lie down, but Anna was insistent she was much better. Brendan knew his place was with Anna, yet his eye was drawn to the peephole.

'Are yer feelin' better, me darlin? I just need ter have a peep.'

Anna took another deep breath and waved him away. She took a sip of water and released Margaret's arm from around her. As she went to stand, she saw Brendan flatten himself against the panelling. He turned, his mouth open, he could hardly get the words out. 'She's... she's... the bitch is wearing yer coat.'

Anna, adrenaline rushing through her body, pushed Margaret and Etta aside and squinted through the peephole. 'It's me coat, me lovely coat, the one I had stolen, just look at the top button; I sewed that on meself – I'd know it anywhere.' Margaret and Etta stood by; they had no idea what was going on.

Brendan took over. 'Margaret, fetch the steward and get Robert Lewinski here, tell him it's important.'

Robert, irritated at yet another witness room call when he wanted to be in the courtroom entered, 'What the hell's going on?'

'Cutler is wearing Anna's coat, the one she had stolen.'

Robert looked at Brendan in astonishment. 'Are you sure? I mean it could be...' Anna grabbed him by the arm.

'It's mine, a girl knows her own coat. I travelled with it all the way from Mollybeg. Tell Liam.'

Robert looked at the excited faces, took a deep breath and said, 'If you're right this will put the cat among the pigeons.'

Etta caught up in a drama she didn't understand decided to stay to help her colleague, while Margaret, equally intrigued, decided she would like to be in at the end.

The door opened and Lewinski entered. 'I've asked for a brief recess, now clear me on this, Anna, you are one hundred per cent sure the coat Moira Cutler is wearing is yours?'

Anna looked at him, and simply said, 'Put me on the

stand, I can prove it.'

Lewinski smiled. 'Now we have to tell Meyer, this will please him.' Lewinski moved to Anna. 'I'm told you are not well, and you don't look well… it could take some time.'

Anna took another deep breath. 'I'm well enough, Mr Lewinski, I never expected ter see me coat again and I want it back.'

'Right! This is what we call the final curtain call – let's go.' Liam and Robert returned to the courtroom.

Through the peephole Brendan could see Meyer talking to Cutler, his angry reaction brought home the other side of his nature. From this Brendan laughed inwardly, the clod had taken the coat from Noel Hughes and given it to his wife but hadn't explained where he'd got it from. Now today, of all days, an unusually cold day, she had decided to wear Anna's coat; his spirits soared.

Moira Cutler was a surprise to Brendan: she was well-spoken, had a confident look about her, and it was hard to believe she was in any way attached to the vicious man she was married to. Lewinski kept Mrs Cutler on the stand and remarked on her fine coat and asked where she had got it from. After a quick glance at her husband who was shaking his head, Mrs Cutler said she couldn't name the store because it was a present from her husband, but she had had it at least three years. At this Meyer intervened, and the judges allowed it.

'Yesterday we spent time talking about Mr Cutler's moustache and glasses, and now it seems we are to spend today talking about Mrs Cutler's coat, a coat of quality but one to be seen in many of our great stores.'

Lewinski addressed the court. He pointed at Mrs Cutler's coat. 'That coat was stolen on the 27th of May by Noel Hughes, an accomplice in the robbery of Brendan O'Neil. He is a known associate of Michael Cutler, and on the evening of the 27th May along with Lewis Godden, Hughes attacked Mrs O'Neil and stole her coat. Mrs O'Neil has identified the distinctive top button which she sewed on using her own fair hands. Proof of ownership is the key to what happened on that terrible evening. Is it not remarkable that Mrs Cutler now owns the coat, so well described by Mrs O'Neil in her police statement? Coincidence? I think not. That coat connects Michael Cutler to the robbery, not only of Brendan O'Neil but also of his wife Anna O'Neil.'

Anna, at the peephole, could not believe that anyone could be so convincing. Moira Cutler wasn't thrown by the questions and immediately put forward a plausible story, quickly recognising that the button had a history. 'I was getting out of a carriage when I slipped, and my top button was lost. I couldn't match it, so I bought, in the market, this squarer button, with a harp in the middle.' Anna thought, *clever bitch; she can smell danger.*

Lewinski sarcastically dismissed Mrs Cutler declaring, 'Now we will get to the truth,' and Anna heard the call for her to take the stand. She turned to Brendan.

'Well, me love, yer've won two fights, now it's me turn.' With Etta on one side and Margaret on the other, they escorted the still unsteady Anna to the stand. This left a confused Brendan alone in the witness room, the thought came, *how can she prove the coat is hers?* He looked out through the open doorway, and with no-one to stop him he decided his place was in the courtroom with Anna. He took a chair behind Liam and Robert, while Margaret, with an excuse to be in the main courtroom joined him. She gave him a quick shrug and a smile, while Etta moved to a seat by the door.

Brendan was worried: the bright, inventive, even flamboyant young woman who had been so effective only twenty-four hours before had disappeared. Here was a vulnerable young woman who suddenly looked very young as she stood before the court.

'Tell us in your own words, Mrs O'Neil, why you are certain that the coat that Mrs Cutler is wearing, is the one you were wearing when you were robbed on the evening of the 27th May.' Lewinski stood back.

'Me Grandma Harriet gave me the coat fer me journey

ter this country. It had the top button missing, and I couldna find a match, so I took a large square button from an old shawl, an Irish shawl, and that's why it has the emblem of a harp. I widened the buttonhole ter make it fit and make it a feature.'

'Objection!' Meyer addressed the court. 'Both are very plausible stories, but I ask again, are we to spend all day talking about a button on a coat? Mrs Cutler has given a very good explanation, and I must say that Mrs O'Neil's story is very inventive and, of course, based in Ireland. We can argue all day about who is the true owner of the coat, but where will this get us? How can it be proved one way or the other?' Meyer moved in front of Anna, stood back and pointed at her. 'Mrs O'Neil, why should we believe your story any more than that of Mrs Cutler?'

'I am telling the truth. She's a liar.'

Lewinski shut his eyes and thought, *where do we go now?* The answer came immediately. He heard Anna address the judges. 'Sirs, I have more ter tell and I can prove that the coat is mine.'

Judges Renshaw and Latimer conferred; the latter said, 'Mrs O'Neil, yesterday we listened to your testimony regarding the assault and robbery of your husband, and it was, to say the least, a colourful account. Now you claim that you can prove, without a shadow of a doubt, that the coat Mrs Cutler is wearing is yours. I must tell you that your button account is inconclusive.'

Anna replied, 'Sir, I need ter examine the coat.' Meyer objected but Lewinski, sensing the tide was about to change, called for Mrs Cutler to hand over the coat. He argued that if indeed Mrs O'Neil could prove beyond all doubt that the coat was hers, then Mr and Mrs Cutler would have a lot of explaining to do. He stressed yet again that the coat had been stolen on the 27th of May, as stated to the police.

The judges conferred again, and Judge Renshaw commanded that Mrs Cutler should hand the coat over. She objected but was overruled and a clerk took the coat to a table hastily placed below the judges' high seats, where it was laid out for inspection.

Judge Renshaw called the two attorneys to him and gave his decision that Mrs O'Neil could inspect the coat under his watchful eye, and that of Judge Latimer. Lewinski now took his cue from Anna; he had no idea what she could prove. He turned to see Brendan behind him. He gestured, and with a raised eyebrow asked if Brendan knew; he shook his head.

Lewinski stood to one side of the table and Meyer the other as Anna inspected the coat. She knew exactly where to look but carefully moved over the coat, until finally, her fingers reached the hem. No-one in the courtroom could see the increased pressure she applied to the part where she knew her ring was hidden. Throughout their journey, she had constantly squeezed that hem to ensure her ring was safe. Anna's heart was thumping, she had never expected to see her coat again but here it was. The reassuring little lump told her that her ring was still hidden away. Calmly she told the judges, 'This is me coat.'

Immediately Lewinski asked her to return to the stand and continue her story.

Brendan could see that Anna was in an emotional state. He could always tell because she had a habit of throwing her head back and breathing deeply. 'I've told yer about the button, but I haven't – as yet – had chance ter tell yer about the ring.' Brendan looked up. What ring? Lewinski was equally baffled.

'Me Grandma Harriet gave it ter me. 'Tis a fine ring set with diamonds, and she was given it as a gift from a rich lady in England. Me grandma was a nanny and when a fire broke out in the great house where she worked, she saved the four children she was lookin' after from disaster. The lady never fergot me grandma, and when she left ter live in India with her husband, who worked for the government, she gave me grandma the ring along with a letter. I think yer call it the provenance, but she couldna find it ter give ter me. She swore me ter secrecy, and its value was only ter be used when I – we – were down ter our last farthing. I knew that ter wear the ring would attract every rogue in Ireland – I fergot about America.'

A ripple of laughter ran around the courtroom.

'I thought of suspending the ring around me neck on a chain but was that safe? I further knew that wearing the ring in America might raise questions as ter how an Irish turnip, such as meself, could have come ter own such a ring. I didn't want ter be arrested, so I undid the hem of me coat and wrapped me ring in linen and hid it in between the padding.'

At this point, tears slipped down Anna's face. She tried to control herself but memories of Mollybeg and Grandma Harriet fastened into her mind. She looked at Brendan and mouthed, 'Sorry, me love.'

A hush settled over the courtroom. Lewinski quietly addressed the judges. 'The answer is quite simple, the hem must be opened, and we will see.' He moved to Anna. 'Mrs O'Neil, to ensure that we are not accused of sleight of hand, will you please describe this ring.'

Anna took another deep breath. 'It has three clusters of gold holding the diamonds, and one of the clusters, the middle one, has a petal that is bent back and needs repairing.'

Meyer sat slumped in his chair, arms folded, a heavy frown on his face, while Cutler, for once, looked less sure of events and sat with his glasses in his hand, his head lowered.

Brendan wanted to go to Anna. She sat, pale and unsteady, quietly sobbing, her hands clasped in her lap.

Judge Renshaw told the court that there was a seamstress in the building, and she should be sent for. He then advised that Mrs O'Neil should be escorted back to her seat. Margaret went to meet her and guided her to Brendan. The two sat either side holding Anna's hands; for once Margaret's book was forgotten, this was the best drama she had ever witnessed.

While they awaited the seamstress, Brendan looked around the courtroom and the gleam of a silver cane caught his eye as it was raised. Mr Peabody looked across the courtroom and nodded.

The door opened and a seamstress, wearing a purple gown, entered and Lewinski pointed out the seam to be opened. The courtroom went very quiet. The lady took a small hook from her pocket and set to work. Brendan anxiously looked on. *Christ, what if the ring isn't there!*

The seamstress, her back to the court, stopped her work and handed something to Judge Renshaw, who held it up for all to see. Between his forefinger and thumb, he held a small linen wrap. He opened it and took out a ring. He slipped it onto his forefinger and slowly moved it from right to left before the court. The sunlight from the large window on the east side caught its sparkle, applause swept around the courtroom. Lewinski went to speak but found his voice faltering. Even Judge Renshaw had to find his voice twice before declaring, 'This ring is exactly as described by Mrs O'Neil, a petal – if that is the correct term – the middle one, IS bent backward.' He again consulted with his colleague and said, 'In all my years as a judge I have listened to conflicting evidence, where, at times, it has been difficult to ascertain the truth. However, in this case, there can be no doubt, Mrs Anna O'Neil is, and was, the original owner of this coat, and indeed this ring.'

Anna tried to stop sobbing but couldn't. Brendan put his arm around her. Judge Latimer suggested that she leave the courtroom, her role as a witness was over, and with usher Margaret on one arm, Brendan led her back to Lewinski's chamber.

CHAPTER 37

It was quiet in the chamber. Anna didn't dare look at Brendan: *what must he be thinking, ter find out about me diamond ring in an American court of law; this wasn't how it was meant ter be.*

'I'm sorry, Bren, but I made a promise ter me grandma, and I thought how marvellous it would be when I could tell yer we had all the money we needed. I never thought I would lose me coat.'

'So, Mrs O'Neil, yer a rich lady, a catch fer any man. I'm wondering if yer'll have time fer me now.' Anna folded her arms.

'Well, Mr O'Neil, I haven't had a chance, as yet, ter evaluate me wealth but I'm thinking, I'll most likely keep yer on. I might buy a coal mine and put yer ter work.' It was hopeless, Brendan collapsed laughing. Anna looked up through her tears. 'Hold me, Bren.' He gathered her in his arms, nothing was said; there was no need for words.

The noise in the corridor moved them apart. The door opened and Liam Lewinski came in, followed by his Uncle Robert and student McCauley; they were laughing. 'Poor Ruben, his summing up, poor fellow, how do you explain that away? I'm glad I wasn't in his shoes.' Liam turned to Brendan. 'We've got what we wanted; he's guilty as charged and Renshaw has delayed sentence. My boss, Abraham Grant, will jump for joy; the new evidence will see him charged with the murder of the warehouseman.'

Anna, now a little more composed, sat smiling. Liam Lewinski knelt before her, took both her hands and said, 'My dear young lady, when you said you could prove without a shadow of a doubt that the coat was yours, I took a chance, I thought you must have some secret mark, even a name hidden somewhere – but a ring! This story will hit the newspapers. The artist from the *New York Gazette* turned up and I've seen some of his drawings, and you, Mrs O'Neil, will be in all the newspapers.'

Brendan was alarmed. 'Fer God's sake we've been hiding away fer months not knowing who the hell is after us – this is the last thing we need.' Robert laughed.

'My friend, it's all over, Cutler is down and finished. He won't even be able to plea bargain. Any interest in you disappeared an hour ago. Cutler has his little band of cut-throats, but by now they'll be selling their talents elsewhere.'

McCauley, for once not scribbling away, felt obliged to feed into the conversation, added, 'Who's going to listen to Cutler now? He's a dead man walking.'

'Nicely put, Mr McCauley.' Lewinski patted him on the shoulder. 'What a good story you've got to take back to university.'

Anna's thoughts were elsewhere. 'Mr Lewinski, me coat an' ring. When can I gerra them back?' Lewinski explained that both items could be claimed from the administration office.

He looked at his watch. 'It'll be tomorrow, but not before ten.' He signed a release form and gave it to Brendan.

The door opened. Mr Peabody stood in the doorway, behind him Isaac. He smiled broadly and moved around the room shaking hands, congratulating Lewinski and his team. He halted in front of Anna, leaned on his silver cane, bowed and said, 'My dear Mrs Anna O'Neil, your husband keeps telling me that he doesn't know what he would do without you.' He gestured around the room and added, 'What would WE all do without you?' Anna moved to him.

'Oh, dear, dear Mr Peabody, we owe everything ter yer.' He held her tight.

The door opened again; Brendan froze – it was Meyer. Lewinski greeted him like a long-lost brother. Anna didn't know what to think, even Mr Peabody seemed to know him and like him.

Meyer moved to Anna. 'Ma'am, I salute you; there are

times when losing brings me great pleasure, and today is such a day.' He turned to Brendan and laughed at the doubtful look on his face. He didn't shake hands, instead, he put his hand on Brendan's shoulder and said, 'Mr O'Neil, who would have thought that a ring in a coat would bring such a result.'

Brendan, still confused at the geniality, sat beside Anna listening while Meyer and Lewinski discussed family matters and arranged to meet for dinner. Meyer left with a cheery goodbye.

Liam Lewinski and his team collected their cases and said goodbye. At the door Liam told them, 'Stay as long as you like, a new client calls.' He shook hands, and added, 'It'll be a long time before I forget this day – if ever.' His team left.

Mr Peabody leaned on his cane. 'My dear young friends, it's too late to get back to the ranch, and I have to stay in town, so I've booked you into a hotel, it's new and it has a good reputation. Tomorrow, Isaac will pick you up about midday.'

Brendan could see he was far from well. Anna, equally concerned, moved and took his hand. 'Mr Peabody, I know nothin' about rings, but I do know that if I try ter sell it I will most likely be arrested or robbed again. Can yer help us?' Anna was sure Brendan would approve. 'And we owe yer money, and we must pay yer back, an' when we gerra the money, we can settle what we owe yer.'

Mr Peabody nodded and told them he had good friends in the trade. He asked, 'Do you want it valued, or delivered in dollars?'

Brendan answered, 'Dollars and yer'll need this release form fer Anna's ring and coat.'

Mr Peabody took it and told them, 'The ring will take a few days, but your coat will be with Isaac when he collects you tomorrow at midday.' Mr Peabody led the way, helped by Isaac.

When his coach stopped outside the Manhattan Hotel he couldn't understand the O'Neils' merriment. Anna pointed across the wasteland in front of the hotel, where a pall of smoke told them the vagrants' camp was still there.

'Mr Peabody, that's where we spent our first night in America.'

Mr Peabody pulled a face. 'I think you'll find this place a step up, I'm told it is one of the finest in town. I'm staying with friends, so I'll see you both tomorrow; enjoy your evening.' Mr Peabody raised his silver cane and gave a little bow, Isaac touched his cap, and they watched until his coach moved away.

Inside, the O'Neils had never seen such luxury. Anna nudged Brendan. 'There's carpet everywhere 'cept the ceiling.'

A boy in uniform led them to their second-floor room. He hovered about until Brendan realised he wanted what was called a tip. He gave him ten cents; the boy thanked them and disappeared.

It was the biggest bed they had ever seen; Anna bounced up and down. 'Now I know why the rich spend so much time in bed.'

A knock on the door revealed a Mr Bockhoefer, who told them he was the assistant manager. 'Anything you want just ask; the dining room opens at 7 pm.' He paused, slightly embarrassed. 'We do have a laundry if you wish to use the bathrobes. I can have your clothes washed and pressed and if you wish you can have dinner in your room.'

Brendan, without changing expression, thanked Mr Bockhoefer, who bowed and left. He turned to find Anna holding her nose, squealing with laughter. A knock on the door told them a large basket was outside. Furtively it was brought in, and all their clothes went in and Brendan put it outside again. Anna was embarrassed at the thought that other people would be seeing, what she called, her more intimate garments. Brendan just laughed and told her that the hotel didn't want two dirty Irish peasants wandering around the place. He lay back in the soft bedside chair and looked at Anna sprawled on the bed. She looked better, the colour had returned to her cheeks, and her agitation had subsided. For the thousandth time, he counted his good fortune that Anna Ferguson had come to his door that day in Ireland. How could a self-educated girl, from a village such as Mollybeg, have such a turn of words? He had sat amazed in the courtroom, as did Lewinski and his team, at her command of English and her delivery. When they were leaving the courtroom, he had heard a man say, 'Some turnip.'

They chose meals from the menu and placed it outside in a holder on the door. An hour later, a knock on the door announced it had arrived. Two young men laid out their meal, the one produced a bottle of champagne, compliments of Mr Peabody, with a note: *Dear Anna and Brendan, this is a new beginning and time to celebrate. Nathanial.*

'I've never had champagne in me whole life, Bren, this is turning into a dream.' Anna wiped away a tear. 'Christ, if I don't stop, I'll run out of water.'

Brendan shrugged. 'Well, when yer a man of the world and yer've worked in England...' He didn't finish, a light cuff around his head stopped him.

Their chicken with potatoes and vegetables was superb but more wonderful for Anna was the ice cream dessert with fruit. Brendan admitted he had had ice cream in England at the house of George Moffat.

As the evening wore on, they lay on the bed enjoying the stillness, and for the first time, Brendan felt his whole-body relaxing. He tried to run over events in his mind, but they slipped away; only the future was now worth contemplating. For her part Anna snuggled into Brendan, she thought back to his farm, when she had invited herself in, and told him that she was the girl for him. Her final thought before falling asleep was, *well, me girl, yer gorra that right.*

CHAPTER 38

A call, 'laundry' told them their clothes were ready. Outside the door Brendan found their garments hanging on a covered frame with their smaller ones neatly stacked in a wicker box. Dressed, Brendan looked at Anna, then at the crease in his trousers, and remarked that he had never had one before. Anna was delighted at her appearance; now they could go to breakfast with confidence.

In the restaurant, they were amazed at the display of food and chose fruit, hard-boiled eggs with fresh bread, and of course coffee. And it was while they were eating that an unusually quiet Anna said, 'Bren, d'yer know what I'm thinkin?'

Brendan nodded. 'The people around the fire, I expect they're still there.'

Anna also nodded. 'When we had nothing, they shared what they had.'

Late morning Mr Peabody's coach arrived, with Isaac at the reins. Anna took out her coat; it had been cleaned and the hem repaired.

'Isaac, can yer wait awhile, we've gorra somethin' we must do.'

Isaac shrugged. 'No problem, will half an hour be enough?' Brendan nodded, and they crossed the waste ground towards the plume of smoke.

'I love me coat, Bren, but I canna wear it now, not after that vixen's been in it.' Brendan didn't answer, he wasn't given to superstition but, for him, the coat belonged to the past, indeed if he could have his way everything they possessed would be thrown away. Today was a new day, the trial was over, their fears ended, it was time to look forward not back.

As they approached the group around the fire, a few of the vagrants stood up. Brendan picked out blanket-man who recognised them immediately; he didn't say anything but grunted a welcome. Anna looked around the group, the woman with the child had left, so too the Englishman who had been most helpful; new strange faces looked at them.

'Some months back yer gave us yer help when we were down. I would like ter help yer all but I canna, but I can help one of yer.' Anna looked around the group. A young woman quickly stood up.

'God! It's nice to hear your voice. I'm from Derby in England.'

Anna looked her up and down, she was about the same size. 'Yer'll need a warmer coat on yer back soon. Try this on cos it's yours.'

Brendan listened as Joyce Harper told them that she had been in America for a year. She had come over with her husband, but he had had a fall and broken his leg in three places, and they had lost their lodgings. Brendan asked where her husband was, and Joyce told them that the company had been very good; he was in the infirmary.

'I visit him every day. He'll be fine, but it'll take some time before he can walk – or work again. They look after him but what about me? I can't find work and I've nowhere to go. I need every cent I can get, but how do I get it?' She paused. 'A woman on her own...' she didn't finish.

Anna stood back. 'It's a wee bit long but it fits yer fine.' She held Joyce by both shoulders to whisper, 'Yer'll find a note in the pocket telling any busybody that a Mr Peabody, magistrate, has given yer the coat and yer'll also find a quarter, but keep it ter yerself.' Joyce embraced them both. They said goodbye to the curious faces assembled around the fire and in silence they walked back, both heavy with their own thoughts.

For Brendan, his mind went back to the Russian ship and its captain who had been very generous to them, while for

Anna, dark thoughts flooded her mind. She could see Brendan, her gentle man, angrily stoking the fire and mouthing vengeance at Paddy and his crew; she shuddered at the thought. She squeezed his hand and looked into his face; she hadn't seen him so happy since their first lovemaking and their marriage in Dublin.

Back with Isaac, they set out for Yonkers, it would be a long journey, the horses would have to be rested. Isaac explained on the way that Mr Peabody had a court session, and later a meeting with shareholders, and they were to make themselves at home and relax until he got back; it could be the next day.

Precious was there to welcome them and they returned to their cabin.

When the dinner call came the two found the long table crowded with workers from around the ranch, seven in all. They were all curious to know about the O'Neils, but Isaac steered the conversation away from their day in court.

Brendan, for his part, was intrigued that only two of his fellow diners had been born in America, Benny and Jack. A young man of twenty, Hamilton, named after the town of his birth, told them he had been a jockey, but he had grown too tall and heavy; he now looked after the horses and helped with the estate maintenance. David, also from Scotland, had arrived in America at the age of five but had lost his parents in a tenement fire. A woman, heavily built, with a mass of black hair, listened but said little. Later, she told them that she was from Mexico. She was a cleaner and part-time cook when Precious needed help on social occasions.

Meanwhile, Anna was absorbed in talking to an elderly man called Benny, who oversaw the horses. He told of how, as a cowman, he had driven longhorn cattle two thousand miles across the prairie as well as wild mustangs to market. Anna could not believe it. 'Two-two thousand miles?'

Benny's son Jack, who looked just as old as his father, added how ten of them had driven a herd of a thousand cattle to Denver. This prompted the other two young men, called Al and Grove, who were from the sawmill delivering timber and mending fences, to sit back in wonderment as Benny told them about life out on the prairie.

'There are no trees on the prairie: all the water is underground, and you have to pump it to the surface to feed man and beast. My first house was a soddy. As there's no wood you cut the turf into bricks and build with that.'

Anna was mystified. 'But what about when it rains? It must rain at times.'

Benny, enjoying his story, told them, 'Well, the rain helps to join all the bricks together. In the summer it's cool and in winter it keeps the heat in.'

Isaac asked, 'But what about the roof? You need timber.'

Benny nodded. 'Yeah, we had to wait three months for the timber to arrive, thank God it was the summer.' Fascinated, Brendan told them about similar cottages in Ireland.

Jack laughed and told them, 'I think it was the Irish who came up with the idea.'

Later, as they walked back to their cabin, Brendan remarked, 'Anna, I knew this country was big but a thousand miles of grassland without a tree in sight. It takes some believing and how the hell d'yer drive cattle a thousand miles without reducing them ter skin and bone?'

In bed, Anna suddenly sat up and smiled at Brendan, who was still in his chair by the small table. 'D'yer know, Bren, the courtroom seems a dream away. Here we are thinkin' about this country, and fer the first time I'm beginning ter think we're part of it.'

Brendan chuckled. 'Anna, not only are yer part of it, yer famous. Yer say it's just a dream but will yer look at this.' He handed her a page torn from the *New York Gazette*. There was a drawing, indeed a very good likeness, of Anna pointing dramatically across the courtroom. The caption read: THE IRISH TURNIP AND HER SECRET RING!

Anna put her hands over her face; she didn't read on.

CHAPTER 39

After a good night's rest, Brendan, feeling he had to give something back, helped to clean out the stables. Later, with Al and Grove, they mended the coach house roof replacing broken tiles. Anna, aware of how much Mr Peabody must have spent on them since their first meeting, feeling very much the same, helped Precious in the kitchen and set about cleaning any item that showed the slightest mark; much to Precious' amusement.

In the early afternoon, they walked around the ranch. Anna spent time with the horses, while Benny told her about breaking in mustangs and skirmishes with Indians when he was eighteen. Brendan was equally interested but wanted to know about big horses, the type to pull a plough. At this Benny lost interest. He shrugged, 'I'm a cattleman.'

In the late afternoon, Mr Peabody returned, and he told them, 'Tomorrow we are going to the Lackawanna Valley, six miles from Scranton. I'll explain more when we are there, but we'll need an early start. Oh! By the way, Brendan, I've your satchels here, bring all your possessions.' From this Anna and Brendan assumed they would be staying the night in Scranton, possibly they could see Yvonne and give her all the news. Anna wanted to ask about her ring but decided not to; it would be very rude.

Over dinner, the subject of the trial was discussed, and the part Anna had played. Mr Peabody was amused at how fate had also played its part. 'If it had been a warm day and Mrs Cutler hadn't worn your coat, who knows your ring could have been lost forever, and Cutler may have walked.' Brendan decided to remain quiet: for him, the word of decent people should be enough for a conviction.

They passed a quiet evening. Mr Peabody retired early while Precious and Isaac had visitors from Yonkers.

The next morning, they joined Mr Peabody in his coach and Isaac delivered them to the ferry. Mr Peabody was his usual attentive self, but Anna sensed that there was something "in the air". She couldn't discuss this with Bren, who was listening to Mr Peabody outlining the many changes taking place, and what the future held. The train journey to Scranton was all too familiar to the O'Neils, while Mr Peabody dozed the time away.

In the town, they moved to a restaurant for a late dinner. Brendan, embarrassed that he hadn't the funds to meet the bill, was waved away by Mr Peabody, who insisted they were his guests.

At a large livery, a man called Elmer brought out an open carriage and two horses. Mr Peabody took over the reins, but Brendan insisted he would drive the team, and with Anna beside him Mr Peabody was happy to relax on the rear seat. It was a glorious afternoon as they left the smoke of Scranton behind. Brendan was thrilled again to see the Lackawanna River and its fertile banks. He drove on savouring every second, enthusing and imagining what a life they could have given the chance to live there.

'Take the next track on your right.' Mr Peabody moved to the front seat to give directions. The track was gravelled, and it widened as it descended towards the river, before turning left along a partly paved road that followed the river. Ahead, Brendan could see a large cottage and in front a turning circle. There was a small garden with a stone wall and built into it, Brendan read, River Bend. It was the type of cottage, part wood and stone that he had designed in his mind's eye. He noted that a balcony had been added to the far side and he guessed it led from a bedroom.

Brendan reined in the team. Mr Peabody sat for a minute looking upriver then he slowly got out and walked to a tree, a type of willow, then turned to look downriver lost in thought.

Brendan sat admiring the view; the river turned away under a copse of trees and disappeared around another bend ahead. The water sparkled, sunlight dancing on the ebb and flow of scurries of water finding their way past the ochre yellow, and the pink-grey stones in the shallows. Beyond lay a meadow and in the distance, he could just make out the trail that Tom and his team used. He shuddered at the thought of Harper's Drift and The Parade.

Mr Peabody tapped the tree. 'Kathleen planted this all those years ago.' He looked so sad that Anna moved in and took his arm; nothing more was said for several seconds. 'Magnificent isn't it? I've caught many a good trout on this stretch.' From his pocket, Mr Peabody took out a large key and moved to the door. Turning, he smiled and said, 'My dear young friends, mister sounds so formal, my name is Nathanial.' He opened the door, stood aside and welcomed them in. The furniture was of good quality but quite simple, arranged around a stone-built fireplace that had a large hearth with a built-in griddle. Offset, there was a scullery. Nathanial led them from room to room saying little. There was an office downstairs with a door that opened to the stables. Upstairs were three bedrooms, the larger one with a balcony that overlooked the river. He moved to the rail and looked out, again lost in thought. Anna went to move to him, but Brendan held her back.

Nathanial said, 'This was our first home, this is where it all began.' Anna had known instinctively that River Bend was part of Nathanial's early life. She also knew that Nathanial saw in her his wife Kathleen, or perhaps, as Brendan had said, the daughter he had never had.

Nathanial turned to them. 'I should have had it modernised years ago, but...' he paused, then added, 'it's full of memories; come on, there's more to see.' Outside he showed them the stables, big enough for four horses. Moving on along a field track they passed a meadow and Nathanial pointed out that it gave enough hay in springtime to cover winter. Brendan's mind was on fire as he listened to

Nathanial explaining what could be achieved on his eight acres of land. The fertile soil was perfect for vegetables and could be watered during the hot months of summer by a mule-operated water pump. He told them, 'I was going to invest in a steam pump but most of my work is now in the city, or at the ranch.'

Brendan's thoughts were somewhat different. *What I could do with all this,* hammered in his brain. Possibly Anna's ring would buy them a bit of land further along the river. BUT! Was it as valuable as Anna had said?

At length, Nathanial reached a path that ran from the house towards the upper road. Ahead there was a grove of trees and the path led to this. Anna was walking behind Nathanial as they entered the grove; suddenly she stopped, halting Brendan in his tracks. Nathanial gestured for them to join him. A grave outlined with pebbles from the river and a headstone made from a large slab of riverbed stone caught a ray of sunlight in the small glade. Nathanial moved to the headstone and slowly knelt. Brendan could see the name outlined in black.

Kathleen Sarah Peabody, born 1819, died 23rd June 1841. Underneath was inscribed, *Joshua Nathanial, died 23rd June 1841.*

Anna's hand flew to her face, Nathanial had lost both his wife and son giving birth. She didn't know what to do or say. Nathanial slowly straightened, looked at them and said, 'There are no words...' Brendan stepped forward, held out his hand and the two men shook hands. 'Thank you, Brendan.' Anna turned away tears stinging her eyes, at that moment she realised that there was a bond between men that often words didn't – couldn't – express.

Nathanial smiled. 'A sad moment but it's a glorious day.' He waved his hands at the sky. 'The sun comes out, a cloud darkens, the sun returns, just like life. My young friends, you have brought joy into my life; let's go back to the house.'

From a store, Brendan brought out a table and chairs and arranged them on the delightful terrace overlooking the river. Nathanial told Brendan to go down to the jetty, by the rowing boat, where he would find a large sealed flagon in a stone-lined gully and bring it to the table. Nathanial undid the seal and took out two bottles of Precious' homemade chilled lemonade. He chuckled, 'Never ignore nature – make use of it.' Glasses filled, they sat enjoying the sheer peace of the riverside.

Nathanial Peabody looked at his watch. 'It's five o'clock. Now to business, you are most likely waiting for me to tell you about your ring. Well, I have good news, your ring is very valuable and should build you a home.' He paused. 'However, life is about choices and I am giving you a choice – so listen carefully. I can arrange for its value to be placed in a bank, in your name, or it can go into my bank. If it goes into my bank, River Bend and everything I have shown you is yours.' Anna and Brendan sat stunned. Nathanial continued, 'Soon I will be joining Kathleen. I don't want tears; I have little time left. The choice is yours, but you would make an old man happy at the thought of you living here.' He looked at his watch again. 'I have friends to visit in Scranton, and I will be spending the night with them. I've arranged with Elmer to ride out and drive me back. Well, I repeat the choice is yours, but I do hope to leave here a happy old man.'

Brendan looked at Anna, neither of them asked about the ring's value. Anna took a long breath. 'Yer mean, Nathanial, that from this very minute we can live here?'

Mr Peabody smiled and said, 'You've got all your possessions in the carriage, some vegetables in the garden, there's a shotgun in the cupboard and plenty of game about.' He leaned towards Brendan. 'You can get milk from Elias, just over the hill there, further up the road grand houses are being built, wells need building, cold stores, and of course walls and chimneys. Brendan, this area is on the move, and you have the skills needed. My fervent hope is that this wonderful stretch of river will not suffer the ravages of the industry you see close to Scranton.' Nathanial pulled a document from his case. 'The moment you sign these deeds all this is yours, and they will be lodged with my lawyers, Simon and Gill, in Scranton. And to realise the full value of your ring I have ten dollars to give you, which should tide you over until you get settled.' He placed a small bag on the table.

Brendan knew it was nonsense, was the ring so valuable? Indeed, were the stones even diamonds? He had no idea, but Nathanial wanted them to have River Bend.

Nathanial spread the deeds on the table and asked, 'Well?'

Anna, who had sat mute, breathing deeply, her head back, found her voice. 'Dear Nathanial, we'll only sign on one condition, that this will always be yer home, and yer'll visit us whenever yer can.'

Nathanial nodded agreement and held out a pen taken from a small writing case. 'If you care to read the deeds you will find that I will retain one small part of your domain, I will be joining Kathleen in the grove.' He turned to Brendan. 'I need your signature, sir.' Without a word, Brendan took the pen and signed. 'Brendan, one day soon we must go fishing together.' Nathanial took back the pen. Brendan smiled agreement but knew in his heart that the day would never come.

The sound of a horse and the response from the carriage horses told them Elmer had arrived. Anna and Brendan walked slowly back with Nathanial to his carriage, neither could speak. Elmer unloaded their belongings and took them into the cottage. Anna embraced Nathanial without a word said, while Brendan shook his hand with both hands. Nathanial Peabody climbed into his carriage and Brendan tied Elmer's horse to the frame.

'The deeds will be lodged tomorrow morning. Goodbye, my dear young friends, I shall return home a very happy man.' The O'Neils watched until the carriage was almost out of sight; the late sun caught the head of a silver cane as it was raised.

Anna took Brendan's hand and they walked to their

cottage, their new home. Inside, Brendan stood with his back to her, his shoulders heaved, Anna heard a stifled sob; she had never seen a man cry. She moved to the terrace and sat down.

Later, Brendan sat down beside her; again, she took his hand. 'Bren, I have another secret but this time I'm not going ter keep it ter meself; yer going ter be a da.'

EPILOGUE

On the 16th of June 1890, Nathanial Brian O'Neil was born and never was there a prouder da than Brendan, nor was there a more loving ma than Anna; their lives were complete, that is for the moment. Nathanial had rich dark brown hair like his mother. He was tall and strong for his age and at twelve months he was making his first tentative steps.

On his first birthday Tom and Alma came with a present, a large model of a prairie schooner, with two detachable horses made from cowhide that Nathanial loved. He quickly found out how to release the one horse, and this he moved around the room, bumping along on his bottom, making suitable horse sounds. Alma remarked that his build was from Brendan and his colour from Anna. For Anna, he was like his da, and nothing could be better.

On one visit, over dinner, Tom told them that Harper's Drift was now a busy railhead, and the new line ran right through The Parade; soon it would reach Scranton. The cabins had been taken over by railhead workers. As for the colonel, the mine was closed, and he had invested in the railhead and was moving to a village near Philadelphia. Proudly, Tom told them that their Barnwell Coach Service was both popular and profitable. And, as he had predicted, passengers needed transport to get to the trains.

For Brendan, his dream of combining farming with stonemasonry was working out very well. The top road, as Nathanial Peabody had said, brought in clients who needed a local builder, particularly one skilled in stone. The abundant supply from the river and an adjacent quarry and its rich, warm coloured stone were much favoured by rich folk. More worrying for Brendan was the demand for wells, at least for a time, until he was reassured by Anna.

'Boyo, it's easy; yer start from the top and work down.'
He managed to overcome his concern!

Most profitable was their small market garden. The soil
was perfect for potatoes, carrots and a variety of greens that
sold well to a market in Scranton as well as at the door to the
passer-by, and those who lived locally. The two pasture fields
he rented out to a large livery adjoining their land and they
shared the hay. Within the year Brendan's business was
booming and showing a small profit. In October he
completed his yearly return, took Anna in his arms and told
her, 'Anna we're on our way.'

Anna wrote regularly to Nathanial Peabody, a full diary of
their lives, and of course every detail about little Nathanial.
Promises were made that Mr Peabody would visit soon, but
somehow, with Brendan so involved in his work, the months
passed.

As the area grew so did the postal service and a daily
service reached River Bend. Anna was thrilled when she
heard from Da and Etta Oakley; both were well. Sadly,
Grandma Harriet had had a fall and was confined to bed. He
also added that Anna's ma had moved to England to join a
Temperance Society. Later, her brother Richard wrote to say
that he had married and moved to Cork. Brendan had less
good news. His sister Mary had lost her husband to
consumption, thankfully Andrew was fine. His two brothers
were still working the fishing boats at Galway but hoped,
soon, to own their own boat. Yvonne became an even better
friend and visits to Scranton always saw an hour spent at
Chester Street. Anna wrote to Bridget but never heard from
her again. Nadia's store now served the railhead at the halt,
called The Parade, and her profits had soared, and a cold
bunker had been built for fresh meat.

Their first winter was cold but very dry, with several feet
of snow in the new year. Travel was difficult until Brendan
was introduced to a horse-drawn sleigh, which he borrowed
from his new friends at the livery. Anna found this to be

wonderfully romantic.

River Bend was snug in winter, but the heat of summer caused them problems. As Brendan said, 'I can always get warm when I'm cold but it's harder ter get cool when yer hot.' To some extent, this was solved by the river. After a day in the field or in Scranton, the river was a joy. Also, a copse of trees just within their boundary made a welcome shelter during the hottest days.

It was towards the end of October that a very concerned Anna told Brendan, 'I haven't heard from Nathanial fer two months; he must be ill, we must go and see him.'

Brendan, engaged in the middle of an extension to a large part stone and timber-framed house, agreed but asked, 'But can we leave it till the end of the month?' However, a letter from Mr Albert Staunton, a business friend of Mr Peabody confirmed that he was too ill to write, and he urged them to come as soon as they could.

'Bren, bugger yer work; we must go NOW!'

Brendan visited the owner of the house he was working on and explained to Mr Randell how he would be obliged if he could suspend work for a few days. Mrs Randell joined him, and she was visibly upset when Brendan told them he needed time to visit Nathanial Peabody. 'You must go, poor Nathanial, what a lovely man. I knew his wife Kathleen. I was only a girl, but I remember her and him well. Oh, what a shame.'

'We'll go te'morra.' Anna brushed tears away. Brendan felt guilty, Anna had urged him many times to find the time, but his work seemingly filled every working hour.

It was a cold but clear October day when Albert Staunton picked them up at the ferry landing. Little Nathanial, at sixteen months, loved the train and ferry, but he needed watching every second.

On their way to the ranch, in an aside to Brendan, Albert told him that Cutler had been found guilty of the murder of the night watchman and he was to be executed; he felt Brendan should know. This news shocked Brendan, he recalled the smiling face of Paddy when he had befriended them at the dock gate. He still found it hard to see Paddy as the same man who had so violently robbed him. He decided not to tell Anna; at least for the time being.

Isaac and Precious were delighted to see them, and this time they were shown to a large bedroom in the house where Precious had also made up a bed for Nathanial. Later, they dined with Precious, Isaac and Albert Staunton. Albert told them that Nathanial had his meals in his room, and a nurse attended to his needs. It was too late to see him; the morning would be best. After dinner, he bade them goodbye.

The next morning the nurse, called Ursula, told them Nathanial wanted to see them. He lay back on large pillows, his long silver hair cascading over the red pillow; both were shocked by the pallor of his face. Brendan pulled up chairs, sat close and placed his large hand over Nathanial's. 'How are yer, dear friend?'

Nathanial picked up right away. He chuckled and said, 'I hope your pump is working better than mine.' Anna moved to the other side and held his other hand.

Nathanial turned to her. 'And where's my little Nathanial?' Anna went to the door and asked Ursula to bring him in. Anna sat on the side of the bed holding Nathanial on her lap, the little boy reached out a hand to the old man. He took it and his eyes welled. 'When I received your letter that you had been safely delivered of this lovely child I was delighted, but, when I read you had named him after me... well, I cannot recall a happier, prouder moment in my life. I wanted so much to come to his christening but...' Anna gently squeezed his hand.

'Dear Nathanial, don't yer know? Yer with us every minute of every day, we're family and yer his adopted granddad.' Nathanial sunk back, a smile on his face which lessened as his breathing became heavier. Nurse Ursula moved in.

'I think he needs to rest now.'

At midday, Brendan and his family were driven back to

the ferry by Isaac. It was near to nine o'clock when Brendan opened the door to River Bend.

Ten days later came the news that Nathanial Peabody had died.

On the 29th of October, Anna and Brendan waited by his freshly dug grave. His funeral had been held the previous day at St Patrick's in New York, attended by over five hundred people. Then a special train had delivered his body to Scranton for an overnight vigil at St Michael's. Mourners from Scranton, and even some from New York, made their way to River Bend. On the road above the grove the Peabody black coach, pulled by his black horses wearing black plumes on their heads, stopped. As far as the eye could see coaches, carriages, and mourners crowded into the small space, while many looked down from the road above.

Albert Staunton gave the eulogy, followed by Father Vaughan who gave the final blessing as the coffin was lowered into the grave. Brendan and Elmer filled the grave, and the many tributes were laid in place; too many for the small area. The coffin bearers, six in all, arranged the tributes row upon row until they reached the top of the embankment. The funeral party retired to Scranton, but the O'Neils didn't join them. In the house, Alice was looking after little Nathanial.

As silence settled on the grove, Brendan watched as Anna made her own small personal tribute. She carefully arranged a heart of stones taken from the riverbed. Both stood in tears; no words were said.

Later, they sat by the fireside saying little, each with their own thoughts.

As night settled under a moonlit sky, Brendan went alone to the grove and moved the wreaths to one side and replaced the border river-stones so that the two graves became one. As he did so, moonlight entered the grove and illuminated the graves. Brendan, though not a spiritual man, felt the need to say a prayer.

On his return to the house, Brendan found Anna on the

terrace, wrapped in a blanket. He moved behind her and encircled her with his arms; neither spoke. It was a cold but beautiful autumn evening, time again to reflect on their day. Both loved to watch the moonlight play across the water and listen to the sounds of the night.

Brendan said, 'Looking back ter Mollybeg and all that has happened, at times I ask meself is it real, did it really happen?'

Anna sighed. 'Well it's all in the past, memories, good and bad; now we must look ter the future.'

A week after the internment Anna and Brendan received a letter telling them to go to Simon and Gill, Mr Peabody's solicitors. Mr Gill greeted them. He told them that the will of Nathanial Peabody had been settled, and all he had to do was to return an item to Anna O'Neil of River Bend. Anna took the little box – both knew what they would find. Anna opened it. Her ring sparkled; the damaged petal had been repaired.

The End

ACKNOWLEDGEMENTS

My grateful thanks go to my editor, Helen Baggott, for her patient help in guiding me through the various stages to finally see my story in print.

For my research, what would we do without Wikipedia?

Printed in Great Britain
by Amazon